AN UNCOMPROMISING POSITION

Hester felt the mesmerizing power of Trent's gaze, and then his hand stroking her cheek terderly. But when in the next moment, his lips covered hers, she knew she was in the hands of a master, and she was not sure her legs would continue to hold her up.

When he did stop, releasing her very slowly, Hester drew a deep breath, and with more calm than she knew she possessed, she said "You do that very well. And I can't say that I didn't enjoy it. But it won't do. Please don't do it again, or I shall have to take measures."

If she had dashed a cup of cold water in his face, Trent could not have been more astonished. He whirled on his heel and left the room. In a moment, she heard the slamming of the front door and she relaxed. Her strength had won over her weakness. This time, at least. . . .

SIGNET REGENCY ROMANCE
Coming in December 1996

Martha Kirkland
The Honorable Thief

April Kihlstrom
The Widowed Bride

A Rake's Reform

by

Anne Barbour

A SIGNET BOOK

SIGNET
Published by the Penguin Group
Penguin Books USA Inc., 375 Hudson Street,
New York, New York 10014, U.S.A.
Penguin Books Ltd, 27 Wrights Lane,
London W8 5TZ, England
Penguin Books Australia Ltd, Ringwood,
Victoria, Australia
Penguin Books Canada Ltd, 10 Alcorn Avenue,
Toronto, Ontario, Canada M4V 3B2
Penguin Books (N.Z.) Ltd, 182–190 Wairau Road,
Auckland 10, New Zealand

Penguin Books Ltd, Registered Offices:
Harmondsworth, Middlesex, England

First published by Signet, an imprint of Dutton Signet,
a division of Penguin Books USA Inc.

First Printing, November 1996
10 9 8 7 6 5 4 3 2

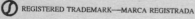

Chapter One

A night of intermittent rain showers had served to freshen the morning that burst on London one summer day in the year of our Lord, 1817. Dawn spread her banners across an amethyst sky as the sun rose to touch first the city's church spires with golden fire, then the humbler dwellings of mortals. At last a single beam of radiance stole through the curtains of an elegant Mayfair town house to bathe the admirable figure of Charles Trent, fifth Earl of Bythorne, Viscount Spring, Baron Trent of Grantham, of Creed and Whitlow—who sat on the edge of his bed with his head in his hands.

He was getting too old for this sort of thing, by God. He had arrived home only minutes before. When he had gone to Vivienne's dinner party the night before, he had only a few hours of dalliance in mind, but the beautiful widow had been desirous of much more. Lord, her demands—on his time, his energy, and his purse—were growing untenable.

Perhaps it was time to end that particular liaison. The Earl of Tenby's sadly neglected wife had been sending out some interesting lures lately.

Thorne sighed. On the other hand, the young countess, though undoubtedly a diamond of the first water, was also young and very silly. Perhaps he should reestablish his connection with Maria Stafford. She was a bit on the hard side, and selfish as she could hold together, but in her favor—besides a complaisant husband—she was thirty-ish—near to his own age, in fact, and an excellent conversationalist and a comfortable companion.

Good God, he thought in dismay, Had it come to this?

Was he actually weighing his potential mistresses on a comfort scale? Had the thrill of the chase and the sensuous delights of victory given way to the desire for—for what? Friendship? He snorted. He had enough friends.

Thorne bent his thoughts once more to the delectable Countess of Tenby, she of the ripe, thrusting bosom and swinging hips. He thought of the little pink tongue that slid out to moisten full, pink lips and felt a gratifying tightening of his loins. Comfortable, hell. He still knew what he wanted from a woman, and it wasn't conversation.

With this conviction turning reassuringly in his brain, he prepared to sink into the softness of his bed, only to be deterred by a scratching at his door, followed almost immediately by the entrance of a soberly clad gentleman whose anxious demeanor seemed at odds with features that seemed almost cherubic in their insouciance. In a hand that fairly shook with agitation, he carried what appeared to be a note.

"My lord?" whispered this apparition.

"What is it, Williams?" asked Thorne wearily.

"It's Miss Chloe, my lord. Her maid just brought this to me."

He waved the paper before him as though it had suddenly caught fire, and advanced into the room. Hastily, he thrust the note at his employer.

"Now what?" Thorne distastefully eyed the wrinkled missive, noting the blotches and the tearstains with which it was liberally embellished.

"'*My lord,*'" he read aloud. "'*I can no longer bear your unfeeling interference in my life.*'" Thorne cast his eyes heavenward. "Good Lord, more histrionics," he muttered. "'*Now, you have committed the cruelest transgression of all. I tell you again, my lord, I will not be shackled at your whim to a man I do not even know. Your complete disregard for my feelings, as well as your contempt for everything I hold sacred has driven me to flee your tyranny.*'" The earl glanced at his valet with foreboding. "My God, don't tell me . . ." He trailed off, his eyes once more on the note. "'*I have, therefore, left your dubious protection to seek sanctuary with One Who Will Understand. Do not at-*

tempt to pursue me, for my mind is made up. You won't find me, anyway,'" read the last sentence, somewhat smugly. *"'Yours truly, Chloe Venable.'"*

Rising, Thorne swore long and fluently. "The little twit! I might have known she'd try something like this. How long has she been gone?"

"I could not say, my lord. Pinkham seems to feel that she departed the house late last night after all of us—er, that is," he added with a sidelong glance at his master, "most of us—were asleep, for the young lady's bed has not been slept in."

Thorne sighed heavily. "Well, there's nothing for it. I'll have to go after her. Does Chloe's maid—what's her name—Pinkham?—have any idea where she might have scarpered to?"

"No, my lord. She has any number of friends here in London, but surely the parents of these young ladies would not act as accomplices. And, of course, she has no close relatives."

The earl, removing his lace-trimmed cravat, nodded grimly. "The devil take it, Williams, the chit has brought me nothing but grief since her arrival here. It's only been a few months, but it seems like a lifetime."

"Indeed, my lord," replied the valet, divesting the earl of his rumpled evening clothes so that he might garb himself in more appropriate day wear. "Being saddled with a ward of—of so nubile an age has proved an onerous responsibility."

Williams offered a discreet sigh.

"I suppose you'd better roust Aunt Lavinia," said Thorne, winding a fresh cravat about his neck. "She will no doubt expire from the vapors when she hears the news, but perhaps she will have some clue as to where Chloe has loped off to."

The valet bowed himself from the room and Thorne repaired to Chloe's bedchamber, where he began flinging open drawers and cupboard doors. All to no avail. She had left nothing behind to tell him of her whereabouts. A search of the little rosewood desk that stood near her bed was more fruitful, however. Thrust in a far corner of the uppermost drawer was a faintly drawn, hurriedly sketched map. Perusing it carefully, Thorne exclaimed in disgust. Why, it depicted the area around his country seat, Bythorne Park near Guildford, not twenty miles from here. Chloe must have drawn the map last month, when they had spent a week there. Thorne peered more closely at the names of nearby villages laboriously marked on the paper. The road wound past them all, coming to an end near the top of the map at a village called—what was it—Overby? Oddsbeck? He tossed the paper aside impatiently and for several moments stood in the center of the room running his fingers through soft, dark hair that already looked as though it had been churned by a baker's whisk. He moved to the fireplace, but realized after a moment's stirring of the ashes that everything that had been placed there in the recent past had been thoroughly burned. Except : . . A single charred piece of paper fluttered in the draft created by the flue.

Ah, good, he could read the date—only a week previous. And it had been written to Chloe. The rest of the missive, unfortunately had been almost wholly consumed by the fire.

"'—how very pleased I was—'" he muttered, searching for readable fragments. "'—heartened by your—please do come—understand your—' Wait a minute. 'Please do come'?" His gaze swept to the bottom of the letter, but the signature was unreadable. Underneath, however, the writer had scribbled, "Rosemere Cottage," and the name of a village, which was also virtually indecipherable. The first letter, he was almost sure, was "o"—or "d"—or possibly "c," and then an "m," perhaps or a "w" or a "v." Overcross! The name fairly leaped into his mind.

"Overcross." He tasted the name on his lips. Where had he heard it before? Turning, he scooped up the map from where he had tossed it on the floor. Yes, he was sure the name at the top of the map was Overcross, as well, but where had he heard it before? The village was not a great distance from the Park, but far enough so that it was unfamiliar to him. Yet—he was sure he had heard of it, and not too long ago.

He paced the floor, the map clutched in one hand, the let-

ter in the other. His desperate ruminations were cut short a
moment later as the bedchamber door opened to admit a
short, plump woman whose feathery gray hair escaped in
tufts from a cap tied sadly askew.

"Bythorne! What has happened? Williams told me—"
Her gaze swept about the room. "Oh, merciful heavens. It's
true! She has flown! Oh, the ungrateful little wretch! I believe I'm going to have a spasm! Beddoes, my vinaigrette!"

Holding a hand to her pillowy breast, she sank down on
the bed, gesturing wildly to the maid who had hurried into
the room behind her. Thorne crossed the room to seat himself beside her.

"Aunt Lavinia, you must not excite yourself so. I will find
her. There, there," he said soothingly, patting his aunt's
hand as she continued to bemoan her charge's perfidy. Lady
Lavinia St. John, his mother's sister and a spinster of some
fifty years, had acted as his chatelaine ever since the death
of his parents, some years previously. She was a master of
domestic arrangements and had kept Bythorne Park running
smoothly for years. When he had requested that she come to
live with him in London to act as chaperon for his newly acquired ward, she had acceded without demur. Unfortunately,
she was not a disciplinarian, and young Chloe had run virtually roughshod over all her well-intentioned precepts. Poor
Aunt Lavinia, mused Thorne fleetingly. She did not merit
this sort of chaos in her declining years. He augmented the
hand-patting with a few more "there, there's."

When, at last, the lady's bosom began to heave less spas-
modically, he asked, "Do you have any idea where Chloe
might have gone?"

At her woeful shake of the head, he continued. "Does the
name Overcross mean anything to you? I believe it's a village some distance to the north of Bythorne Park."

"Overcross? Overcross." She repeated the word several
times, until at last enlightenment spread across her comfortable features. "Yes. Chloe traveled there last spring when
we visited the Park. There is some woman living there
whom she—just a moment."

She rose and moved to a shelf of books hung above the

desk. Removing a volume, she returned to the bed. "Yes," she continued, reading from the cover. "It was this female—this Hester Blayne."

She handed the book to Thorne, who read aloud. " '*Women's Rights: An Apologia.*' Good God!" He dropped the book as though it had bitten him.

"You are familiar with the name?" asked his aunt.

"Of course. Good God," he said again. "Hester Blayne is one of the most vocal of that incomprehensible breed, English feminists."

"Yes." Lady Lavinia nodded bemusedly. "Besides this book, Miss Blayne has written several others, all espousing the betterment of women—and two or three novels, as well, on the same theme. Chloe is a great admirer of Miss Blayne's. She has attended several of her lectures here in Town, and in April, while we were at the Park, it was all I could do to prevent her from haring up to see the female at her home—which apparently is in Overcross."

"I remember now." Thorne clenched his fingers. "Chloe nattered on at me for days to allow her to visit the Blayne woman—although I didn't pay much attention to her name at the time." He rose from his seat on the bed. "It's obvious that's where she's gone, but—good Lord, how did she get there?"

"Well," snapped his aunt, "I wouldn't put it past the little wretch to simply hire a hackney to take her to White Horse Cellars, where all the coaches depart for Surrey. Oh dear, Bythorne, she did not take her maid, so she must have set out on her own. Oh, merciful heavens, what if something has happened to her—a young girl traveling by herself . . . At the very least, she will be ruined."

"Not if I can help it," replied Thorne grimly. "If I set off now, I shall be in Overcross by this afternoon, and I shall have her back home before anyone is the wiser."

Thus, it was only a very short time later that vehicles and passersby on the Portsmouth Road were treated to the sight of the Earl of Bythorne's famous red-and-black racing curricle flashing southward from London.

*   *   *

It was some hours later in the same day that England's premier feminist, Miss Hester Blayne, knelt in the front garden of her cottage just outside the village of Overcross. She presented a rather unprepossessing figure, for she was of less than average height and slender of form. Tendrils of brown hair escaping from under a neat linen cap drifted about absurdly youthful features, for her upturned nose and rounded chin belied her eight-and-twenty years. At the moment, she presented an even more nondescript appearance than usual. Garbed in sturdy boots and a serviceable muslin gown, she was engaged in a vigorous program of weed removal from her front garden.

She had been hard at this task for most of the afternoon and she felt almost drugged by the sun and the sweet early-summer scents of the afternoon. She lifted her head at a sound from the cottage.

"Hester!" An elderly woman stood at the doorway, peering nearsightedly into the blazing warmth.

"Here, Larkie. Come see what I've accomplished."

"Good heavens, child. You've been out here for hours. Why didn't you let the new servant girl attend to this? You said you planned to work all day on your book."

Hester stood and stretched muscles pleasantly tired from her exertions.

"Perkins has been busy all day in the kitchen with Cook, I think, and I simply had to get out into this glorious day. I'm well ahead of my deadline for once, so I decided to play truant."

The older woman smiled fondly. "Well, you'd best come in. The vicar's wife will probably be dropping by sometime soon. She said she would stop on her way back from the village with the embroidery floss she promised she'd pick up for me."

"I'll stop in a minute, Larkie. I just want to finish this border."

Miss Larkin made no response, but smiled and returned to the cottage.

Hester experienced a wave of contentment as she bent

once more to her task. Her life, she thought with pardonable satisfaction, had never progressed so smoothly. The leap from her early days as an underpaid governess with a burning hunger to redress the outrageous treatment of women in England to her present position as the foremost proponent of feminism in the country had been made in giant strides. Such was her success as a writer and speaker that she was at last financially independent of her family.

Her mouth twisted as she recalled the words her brother had spoken to her not a month earlier.

"Really, Hezzie, I wash my hands of you. If you persist in making us all a laughingstock, I have no choice but to cut the connection. You can't know what it's like to have people point at you, saying, 'There goes Sir Barnaby Blayne. Pleasant fellow, but his sister is demented.'"

She had replied wearily, "Barney, do what you must. I haven't accepted a penny from you in ten years, nor do I plan to avail myself of your dubious largesse at any time in the future. If you are so concerned about what people are saying, why don't you just leave me alone?"

Indignation had sparked in her brother's pale gray eyes as he spoke. "Because—well, dammit, Hezzie, you're still m'sister. I don't like to see you making a public quiz of yourself—even if you don't seem to mind it."

Hester had been forced to laugh. "No, I don't mind at all. You will be surprised to learn, Barney, that there are a number of people in this country who applaud my work."

"Nobody who counts for anything," replied Barney promptly, thus destroying the brief moment of amity that had flickered between then. Since that moment, she had seen nothing of him, or his wife, the officious Belinda, nor her own two sisters, both of whom were firmly planted beneath Sir Barnaby's thumb.

Well, so be it, thought Hester. She was happy here in her snug cottage, with her books and her friends, of whom she numbered some of the foremost intellectuals of the day. And there was Larkie. God bless the day she had accrued enough money to rescue her former nurse from her dismal flat in one of London's seamier neighborhoods.

Hester smiled, but almost immediately afterward her lips turned downward. There was one minor cloud on her horizon. Well, perhaps not so minor. Her bequest from an indulgent aunt and the money she earned from her writings and lectures paid for most of the necessities of her life but there were other expenses that were a constant worry. The cottage mortgage, for example. The payments were not heavy, but every month she found that in order to meet them, other problems were ignored. The roof had been extensively patched and now it had become evident that a new one was needed. The chimney was in desperate need of cleaning—and Larkie needed new spectacles.

She sighed. Perhaps she should have embarked on another novel instead of a work of pure philosophy. The novels, of which she had published three, had proved unexpectedly successful, and while yet another tome on the plight of women in England would garner a substantial readership, it would not be nearly so profitable. It was not too late to abandon this work, entitled *Women as an Underclass,* in favor of another novel, but Hester felt compelled to produce something more serious at this point.

Hester leaned back on her heels, brushing the earth from her stained fingers. She remained so for a moment, her thoughts still on her financial difficulties. She had promised her publisher to finish *Women as an Underclass* in record time so that she could start on another novel, one that was to be much more Gothic in nature and would, he assured her, make them both a staggering amount of money. As a rule, she abhorred the Gothic genre, but—

"You, there! Girl! Run inside and fetch your mistress!"

In her abstraction, Hester had not heard the rattle of horse and carriage, but she jumped at the peremptory insistence of the masculine voice. Good God, was he speaking to her?

"I said, you there! I wish to speak to the mistress of the house."

Fire building in her eyes, Hester turned to behold a very large, extremely angry man bearing down on her.

Chapter Two

The stranger, having descended from an exceedingly dashing sporting vehicle, pushed through the gate, banging it against the post. As Hester rose to face the intruder, she became aware that she had been mistaken in one of her assumptions. Though he was tall, the man was not extraordinarily large. It was his barely controlled fury that made it seem as though he were looming over her. Actually, if it were not for his expression of disdainful wrath, he would have been considered handsome. He was dressed in the height of fashion, from the top of his curly-brimmed beaver to the soles of his blindingly polished Hessian boots. His hair, dark as midnight, waved lightly over his collar and his brows were slashes of jet over eyes that were also of a pure, flinty black. At the moment, they fairly glittered in the slanting rays of the afternoon sun.

The stranger paused to stand directly before Hester. "Did you not hear me?" he demanded. "I am in a hurry, girl. I wish to speak to your mistress."

Taking a deep breath, Hester spoke pleasantly. "Well, I am in no hurry at all. In addition, I am not a girl, sir, and I am mistress here. Now, what can I do for you?"

The gentleman took a step back. "You?" He snorted. "That is impossible. I am looking for Miss Hester Blayne."

"Present," said Hester.

The gentleman's expression grew insultingly incredulous. "Hester Blayne, the, er, the feminist?"

"One and the same," replied Hester, still in a voice of controlled calm that would have boded ill for anyone who knew her well.

"If that is the case"—the words fairly crackled with disdain—"I demand that you produce my ward at once."

At this, Hester drew herself up to her full, if somewhat inadequate, height.

"My good man, I do not know who you are, and I have no wish to remedy that circumstance. I will merely ask you to stop raving in incomprehensible periods and remove yourself from my front garden."

So saying, she turned her back and began to walk toward the cottage. Thorne stared after her in astonishment. Affront was evident in every line of the woman's body, and, he noted detachedly, a fine little body it was, too. He shook himself irritably and strode after her. He grasped her arm, but released it hurriedly as she whirled on him, fist upraised.

"It's no good your taking that attitude," he barked. "I know Chloe is here, and I demand to see her."

"Now look here," said Hester, and Thorne noted that the brown eyes that had seemed so large and soft a few moments ago had turned to miniature volcanos, spitting fire and brimstone. "You may stand there and demand till your eyes bubble, but I will tell you again, I have no idea what you are talking about. I do not know any Chloe and I do not know you, a situation I devoutly hope will prevail. Now, if you do not leave, I shall be forced to send for the constable."

Once more she turned away from him, and Thorne, loath to repeat his mistake, did not touch her, but stopped her by the simple expedient of placing himself in front of her.

"It is I who may be forced to call the constable, Miss Blayne. I am the Earl of Bythorne, and I have every reason to believe that you are giving refuge to my ward, Miss Chloe Venable."

The lady did not seem impressed with either his title or his statement. For a long moment, she simply stared at him. At length, she drew a deep breath.

"Though I feel that at this point it is unwarranted—my lord—I shall do you the courtesy of assuming you are not mad, but simply misinformed. I decline, however, to stand here brangling with you before the world. Will you come inside, please?"

Without waiting for an answer, she moved past him to open the cottage door. Again without waiting to see if he followed, she entered the little house.

Growling silently, Thorne trooped in behind her, then glanced, with some surprise, about the room in which he found himself. Though small, it was comfortable and furnished with an unusual degree of elegance. Her family must be fairly well-to-do, he surmised, or perhaps she was under the protection of a gentleman of means.

Gesturing to a chair, she rang a small bell placed on a sideboard and seated herself on a small settee opposite the seat taken by the earl.

"Now then," she began with some asperity, "what are you blithering about?"

Grasping his temper with both hands, Thorne said harshly, "I am not blithering, Miss Blayne. My ward, Miss Chloe Venable, has run away from home, and it appears that she ran to you. Now, if you would have the goodness—"

"I do not know anyone named Chloe Venable, my lord. And, even if I did, what makes you think she has come here?"

Thorne gritted his teeth and pulled Chloe's note from his pocket. He read it aloud.

Hester heard him in silence. "Well, I can certainly understand why she would not wish to remain in the same house with you, but do you actually believe," she continued in astonishment, "that *I* am the 'Someone Who Will Understand'?"

Thorne then drew forth the charred letter he had found in Chloe's hearth. "I believe this leaves little doubt as to your relationship," he snarled. "It seems quite clear that you have encouraged her in her willfulness. This is your handwriting?"

He stood to wave the paper before her nose, and she snatched it from his hand to peruse it.

"Yes," she said slowly. "It appears to be, but, I have never—"

"Do you see," continued Thorne acidly, "where it says, 'please do come'? If that is not encouragement, I should very much like to know what is."

"Oh, don't be stupid," retorted Miss Blayne, and Thorne felt himself swell with indignation.

"I tell you, I have no recollection of ever having met your ward. Apparently, I did write to her, but I write to hundreds of people, particularly young girls, in response to letters written to me. Now, do be quiet and let me think."

Thorne stiffened. No female in his adult life had ever spoken to him thus. "Confound it—" he began, but Miss Blayne merely lifted her hand. To his own astonishment, he subsided into his chair. He watched her, disgruntled.

"I rather think," she said at last, "that I do remember Miss Venable. As I recall, she wrote to me sometime last spring. She told me my book had changed her life." She broke into a wide smile, and Thorne caught his breath at the sheer magic of it. Her cheeks pinkened, her eyes sparkled, and her face was transformed instantly from that of a rather plain spinster to that of a woodland sprite.

"No writer can resist those words, my lord. She wrote that she was visiting in the area and very much wished to see me, but was being prevented from doing so by her family. In my response, I thanked her for her kind words and added something polite to the effect that I should be pleased to see her should she ever be in the neighborhood." She paused, frowning. "Where is that girl?" Rising, she went to the sideboard and rang the bell once more. She turned again to the earl. "And that, I'm afraid, is all I can tell you about your ward, my lord. I'm sorry she has run away, but I cannot help you."

Thorne slumped in his chair, deflated. He had been so sure he would find Chloe in the clutches of the female rabble-rouser that he could only stare at her blankly, unmoving. She cleared her throat.

"I said, my lord, that I cannot help you."

Thorne started.

"Yes," he said petulantly. "That's all very well. I shall take your word for it that she is not here, but I cannot help but feel it is all your fault that she has put me in this uncomfortable situation."

Miss Blayne gasped. "Well, of all the—" She drew herself up. "It concerns me not in the slightest *what* you feel, you arrogant—" She clenched her jaw, then moved to the door and wrenched it open. "I think it is high time you—"

She was halted by the hurried entrance of a young woman dressed in servant's garb.

"Oh, I am so sorry," said the girl breathlessly. "I did not hear the bell at first, and—"

"Chloe!" bellowed Thorne. The maid whirled about, white-faced, and catching sight of the earl, uttered a sound of choked horror.

"Uncle Thorne!" she gasped.

It was a good fifteen minutes before the chaos of the ensuing scene subsided.

"All right," said Thorne at last, sinking once more into the chair from which he had leaped a few moments before. "I will accept, Miss Blayne, that you had no knowledge that your new serving maid was my recalcitrant ward—although one would think that it would behoove a female living alone to at least question the background of a young girl who appears suddenly on one's doorstep asking for work."

"I told you, my lord," snapped Miss Blayne, "it was my companion who hired her. I have scarcely laid eyes on her since she arrived this morning."

Remedying this omission, Hester turned to survey the young girl. She was a pretty little thing, all flying golden curls and blue eyes that were presently filled with apprehension. With a pang of guilt, Hester absorbed the fact that Miss Venable could not have presented to a prospective employer the impression that here was a competent maid-of-all-work. Those slender fingers had obviously never completed a task more onerous then embroidering a fine stitch and her roses-and-cream complexion bespoke a pampered existence. How could Larkie have hired her so un-questioningly?

As she spoke the name in her mind, the lady herself appeared.

"Gracious!" she cried, wiping her hands on her apron. "I just came back into the house from the kitchen garden. Whatever is all the uproar, Hester?" She stopped short at the sight of the earl, still seated on the edge of his chair. "Oh! I did not know you were entertaining guests, my dear."

Hester smiled tightly. "Entertaining is not perhaps the *mot juste,* Larkie. This gentleman—"

But Miss Larkin's mind had leaped to what appeared to be a critical flaw in the scene before her. She smiled nervously. "Perkins, why have you not brought tea?" She then stared, aghast, as the serving maid burst into tears.

Another fairly lengthy interval passed before Miss Larkin was put in possession of the facts.

"Merciful Heavens!" she gasped at last. "Why, the little minx lied to me! She said she was the daughter of a family fallen on hard times, just moved into a neighboring village."

"I'm so sorry, Miss Blayne." The girl sobbed. "I was afraid if I just walked up to the front door and told you who I was, you would simply have returned me to my guardian." She flung a bitter glance at the earl. "I thought that if I could obtain a position here, I could—well, make myself indispensable—and become your friend, and—" At that point, Chloe was once more overcome by her emotions, and broke out anew in a noisy flood of tears.

Thorne was beginning to feel as though in the space of an hour he had stepped from his neat, ordered world into a universe inhabited by lunatics. He roused himself from the numb disbelief into which he had sunk. Rising, he moved to his ward, grasped her arm, and pulled her down to a settee beside him.

"Now, see here, my girl," he barked, shaking her slightly. "This will not do. It's all very well to apologize to Miss Blayne, but what about me? What about Aunt

Lavinia? Did you give any thought to us? No, of course you did not. You simply wove your ludicrous plot and carried it out regardless of the consequences. Now, go upstairs and gather your belongings and we will—"

He stopped, suddenly aware that his acerbic discourse was not having the desired effect. Beside him, Chloe had stiffened alarmingly, and across the room, Miss Blayne and her companion were staring at him with undisguised hostility.

"Do you see how I am beset?" cried Chloe to Miss Blayne. "Oh, please, ma'am, may I not stay with you?"

The feminist transferred a startled gaze to Chloe.

"My dear, I find myself in utmost sympathy with your predicament, for"—she turned to glare once again at Thorne—"for, in my opinion, your guardian is one of the most odious men I have ever met. However," she continued in the face of Thorne's burgeoning protest, "if he is, in truth, your legal guardian—"

"What do you mean, 'in truth'?" The words burst from Thorne in a torrent. "Of course, I am her guardian! Or," he finished sarcastically, "are you accusing me of plotting to kidnap the little twit? I should imagine that line of thought would greatly appeal to a female scribbler of absurd notions."

For a moment Thorne thought Miss Blayne would fly up from her chair and strike him. Her cheeks reddened and her slender fingers curled into fists. In the next moment, however, taking a deep breath, she relaxed.

"No, I believe you are truly responsible for Miss Venable, unfortunately for her." She turned her gaze once again. "My dear," she said to the still-sobbing girl. "All I can tell you is to hold fast to your ideals. You will not be in this man's thrall forever. In the meantime, if he is actually being cruel to you, you must tell me, and we shall call in the authorities. I am not without some influence in these matters, and I will help you."

Under Thorne's appalled gaze, she crossed the room to sit beside Chloe, taking the girl's hand in hers and staring earnestly into her face.

Evidently, this suggestion was too much even for Chloe's exaggerated sensibilities, for she jumped a little.

"Oh, no," she said, blushing. "He does not beat me—or anything like that."

For a fleeting instant, Thorne beheld an odd expression in Miss Blayne's eyes—one almost of satisfaction. Could she have been leading Chloe on to an admission that her situation was not as desperate as she had led her hostess to believe?

"But," continued Chloe in a rush, "he is forcing me to marry a man I cannot love!"

"What?" gasped Miss Blayne and her companion in unison, and Chloe shot her guardian a triumphant glance.

"Of course," snarled Thorne. "In order to secure her vast fortune, I have promised this innocent young bud to an elderly reprobate. The man is two-and-eighty years old, toothless and spavined. He drinks heavily and has already driven three wives to their graves, but he is immensely wealthy and has promised a handsome settlement on the day he weds my ward, thus saving me from debtors' prison. I gamble, you know. I can only regret that I do not possess a mustache that I could twirl for your edification."

On the settee, Hester's lips twitched. "Very well, my lord, we will concede that you are not a villain from one of those wretched novels put out by the Minerva Press."

"Oh, no," interposed Chloe. "That is, Mr. Wery, the man Uncle Thorne chose for me is *not* old or wicked, or any of those other ridiculous things he said. I suppose, in fact, he's a very nice man. The point is, I do not love him, and cannot envision spending the rest of my life with him."

"Love!" snorted the earl.

Hester raised her brows.

"You do not approve of love, my lord?" she asked innocently.

"I simply do not believe it it. At least, not the fairy-tale version that my ward seems to dream about. I believe that marriage should be based on a sensible agreement between two people and their families."

Chloe simply looked at Hester, lifted her eyes heavenward, and shrugged her shoulders.

"I see," Hester said. Gracious, what a perfectly ghastly fellow he was. "And is that how you chose your wife?"

"I?" asked Thorne, startled. "I am not married—nor do I plan to fall prey to parson's mousetrap in the foreseeable future."

Chloe dimpled. "That's not what Aunt Augusta says," she remarked with a twinkle.

"Aunt Augusta is a scheming busybody," he retorted, then looked about in some embarrassment. "However, that is neither here nor there. Come now, missy. You have imposed for long enough on Miss Blayne's good nature. Get your things together and let us be on our way."

Chloe's features crumpled. "But I do not wish to return home. I want to stay here," she wailed. "Why cannot I remain—just for a little while?" She whirled toward Hester. "I shan't be any trouble. In fact, I shall be happy to act as your maidservant. I have so much to learn from you."

Hester's impulse was to add her voice to Chloe's distressful plea, for she understood perfectly the desires that were at work in the girl. Lord knew she had ached to be away from her family when she was that age. One look at the earl's forbidding features, however, brought her to her sense of duty.

"As I said, my dear, that cannot be. However, I promise to answer any letters you might send, and when you are a little older—"

The earl strode forward and took his ward's hand. "That will be enough, Chloe. We are leaving—now. You may send for your things."

"No!" cried Chloe dramatically. "Never!" So saying, she wrenched out of her guardian's grasp and ran from the cottage.

Surprise held Thorne immobile for a moment, but after a startled oath, he bolted in pursuit. Hester hurried after them, trailed by Larkie. Before she reached the open door of the house, however, a sharp sound caught her ears, followed by the sound of a body crashing to earth. Next, a loud "Oof!" reached her, embellished by a stream of curses.

She dashed out of the door to be greeted by the sight of the Earl of Bythorne stretched supine on the brick pathway that led from the front door. Entangled in his feet were the trowel, spade, and gardening fork Hester had dropped upon the earl's arrival.

Chapter Three

Sometime later, Thorne was ensconced on the little settee in the front room of Hester Blayne's cottage. His left boot had been removed and his foot was swathed in a cold cloth.

"Nonsense," he said for the third or fourth time. "I do not need a doctor. I have merely turned my ankle. Now, if you would be good enough to return my boot—"

"Young man," interposed Miss Larkin austerely, "the doctor has already been sent for. You may not have your boot, for your ankle is swollen to twice its normal size. You have clearly suffered a very bad sprain, and there will be no traveling to London for you today."

Her tone put Thorne so forcibly in mind of his old nurse that he was momentarily silenced. He sent a supplicating glance to Miss Blayne, but received no succor there.

"Indeed, my lord," she said, "I do apologize again for my carelessness in leaving my gardening tools in the path, and it would be compounding my offense to send you off in such a state. Tomorrow, the swelling will probably have gone down a little, and—"

"Tomorrow!" roared the earl. "I cannot possibly stay the night here." Good God, he thought wildly, he had plans for this evening. He was expected at Desirée's place. Her name was something of a misnomer, since she was coming up on fifty and weighed close to thirteen stone, but her girls were attractive and clean. He could not possibly undergo a night in a houseful of good women. In the morning, he would no doubt find himself covered with a lace doily and polished with beeswax.

"On the contrary," retorted Miss Larkin. "You will spend the night here, and after that we shall see what we shall see."

Incensed, Thorne twisted around to stare at her. "My good woman, I am perfectly capable of looking after myself, and I tell you, I do not choose to stay here!"

Swinging his legs over the edge of the settee, he attempted to stand, only to fall back in an ignominious heap.

Damn! he thought despairingly. It needed but this to set the seal on one of the most wretched days he could remember. If he had brought Williams with him, he could probably have managed, but the only servant on hand was his tiger, a diminutive lad who was far too slight to be of any support going to and from the curricle. He scowled at Chloe, who had returned to the house after becoming aware of her guardian's mishap. She stood now a little away from the commotion centered on the settee, her blue eyes filled with penitent tears.

"I'm sorry, too, Uncle Thorne. I did not mean that you should pursue me."

"Tchah!" was Thorne's only response to this ingenious speech.

The doctor, when he arrived an hour or so later, confirmed Miss Larkin's diagnosis.

"I think," he said judiciously after a careful examination of the offending appendage, "that if cold compresses are applied throughout the rest of the day, the swelling might diminish enough for you to depart tomorrow. I shall send along a crutch for you, and with your young servant's help, you should be able to get home without too great a discomfort."

With this, Thorne had to be content. The doctor helped him upstairs to Miss Blayne's guest bedroom, a surprisingly commodious chamber that contained a comfortable bed and was otherwise handsomely furnished.

The doctor assisted him in disrobing, and after he was settled in the bed, garbed in an ill-fitting nightshirt proffered without explanation by Miss Larkin, Thorne sank back into the pillows with a deep sigh.

Downstairs, Hester turned to her companion and uttered a sigh nearly as profound as that of her guest. "Larkie, what can you have been thinking of to invite that man to stay here? He was right, you know. He could have made his way home with the help of his tiger and Miss Venable."

"Hester, I am shocked." Miss Larkin's spectacles bobbed with the violence of her feelings. "You would have me violate the most basic rule of hospitality—turning an injured man out of our home, merely because he presents a slight inconvenience?"

"Slight inconvenience! Larkie, we are not accustomed to entertaining gentlemen. In addition, the earl is one of the most unpleasant of the species I've yet encountered. Lord only knows what his demands will be while he's here."

"It will only be for one night, my dear," Miss Larkin reproved gently, "and for that I suppose we must be thankful." She hesitated. "Lord Bythorne's reputation is—is not what one would wish in a guest of this house."

Hester lifted her brows. Larkie had a sister in London who had worked as housekeeper for the Viscount Manning for some years, and was looked on by Larkie as a font of information and gossip. Thus, Miss Larkin considered herself an expert on the foibles of the *ton*. She pursed her lips. "Not to put too fine a point on it, Hester, the man is the most notorious rake in the country. They say he has conducted illicit affairs with half the married women in London, and has actually fought duels over them. Why, only last year it was said that he had a meeting with Lord Archer—" She caught herself. "Well, that's neither here nor there. At the moment, he is not a threat to your virtue, at least, nor is he in a position to be demanding anything."

Hester fell silent, recalling the moment she had ushered the Earl of Bythorne into her home. His presence had seemed to fill the room, exuding an arrogance bred of centuries of privilege and an overpowering maleness that created an odd flutter of panic in the pit of her stomach. She shook herself. What nonsense. She had been dealing with male bombast all her life and she was no green girl to be cowed by the overweening pride of one peer—no matter if he was a registered rake. She sighed.

"You're right, Larkie. He's no better nor worse than any other man, I suppose, and he is a guest. I shall go and see what I can do to make him comfortable."

Her resolution, however, suffered an immediate setback when she reached the bedchamber given over to his lordship. Her soft knock brought a gruff response from within, and she entered to behold the earl propped up on a mound of pillows, glaring at her. Again, she experienced a stir of unease deep within her. Even lying in bed in relative helplessness in a cotton nightshirt, his fashionably styled hair rumpled and a shadow of pain on his features, he reminded her forcibly of a predatory animal—a large, temporarily discommoded creature from the heart of a primeval forest.

Once more, she shook herself free of her fancy.

"Is there anything more we can do for you, my lord? I know you cannot be wholly comfortable right now, but perhaps—would you like something to read?"

The earl grimaced. *"An Apologia for Women's Rights,* perhaps?"

Hester laughed, and Thorne was struck anew by the extraordinary combination of spinsterish severity and womanly softness displayed by this female who fancied herself a person of letters.

"If you like, I would be happy to provide you with a copy of that notable work, but I can also offer you selections by Scott, Miss Jane Austen, Jonathan Swift, Addison—or perhaps you would prefer poetry. Coleridge? Keats? Blake?"

"An eclectic group, to be sure," replied the earl smoothly. "On the other hand," he continued, "perhaps it would behoove me to become acquainted with the prose that has so stirred my ward." He grinned. "Bring on the *Apologia.*"

Smiling, Hester left the room to return a few moments later with a small book. Placing it in his hands, she withdrew again from the room, informing him that the dinner hour would soon be upon them, and that a tray would be brought to him. With a soft rustle of skirts, she was gone, leaving, he thought, a faint scent of violets behind.

He glanced at the book. It was not intimidating, being slender and tastefully bound. Opening it at random, he waggled down into his pillows and began to read.

"Women are not inherently inferior to men in the matter of basic intelligence."

Thorne lifted a slash of eyebrow. Oh, indeed, he thought in some amusement. And pigs have wings. On the other hand, he conceded, after a moment's reflection, many of the women he knew were not unintelligent—although certainly none of them were capable of truly profound meditation. Women as a sex tended to clutter their minds with such a tangle of extraneous trivialities that there seemed little room for coherent thought. No, he mused judiciously, Miss Blayne, in claiming that female intelligence was on a par with that of their male counterparts, was sadly off the mark. He continued.

"Unfortunately, the female mind is constricted from birth. Like the feet of Chinese women, it is not allowed to fulfill its normal potential. Only certain narrow pursuits are allowed us. We must limit our mental resources to finding a suitable mate, bearing and raising his children, and providing for his comfort. Included in this category are fashion (we must attract the beast), food (the beast must be fed), domestic arrangements (we must keep the beast comfortable), and morality, all defined in the narrowest sense (we must keep ourselves and our daughters chaste in order to meet the beast's admittedly one-sided view of proper behavior)."

Whew! thought the earl, both brows lifting into his hairline.

"Girl children are not allowed education in matters of import, as are young men. Thus, our nation deprives itself of a great resource, the not inconsiderable brain power of half its citizens."

Education for women? thought Thorne incredulously. What the devil for? Did Miss Blayne really believe that the nation required women who could speak Greek or discuss the philosophy of Descartes? Good God, they'd soon be getting above themselves. Next thing one knew they'd be wanting to vote—and who would wish to marry any of 'em? Not that he wished to marry any of 'em anyway, of course. Women were nice little creatures, but marriage seemed like such an encumbrance.

He smiled muzzily. His thoughts were getting muddled—no doubt as a result of the laudanum the doctor had given him. He settled more comfortably into his nest of pillows and quilts and closed his eyes. His formidable Aunt Augusta intruded into his thoughts. Mm. With a proper education she could no doubt qualify as prime minister. He chuckled. Or, how about Miss Blayne? Her writing displayed passion enough for a true statesman—stateswoman? Was that passion, he wondered, confined to her writing? Certainly her austere exterior did not indicate fires banked beneath. Not, of course, that he was interested in Miss Blayne's interior, austere or otherwise.

Contentedly, he breathed in the lavender scent of fresh linen and listened to the breeze that whispered through starched white curtains. The book slipped from his fingers and his breathing deepened as he sank into a dreamless slumber.

Downstairs, the plain Miss Blayne sat in her parlor with Miss Larkin and Miss Chloe Venable. Chloe still wore her servant's gown and looked somewhat incongruous sipping tea from Hester's finest Spode.

"I am so sorry," she said, the militant spark in her eyes belying her words. "I know I should not have deceived you, but I could not just fold my hands and wait for deliverance, after all. It was the best plan I could come up with. I would have revealed myself in—in the fullness of time."

Hester grinned to herself. If she were not mistaken, the girl's inadequacy as a servant would have been revealed the first time she was asked to peel a potato.

"You just do not know how wretched I have been!" continued Chloe, her voice throbbing dramatically. "I am watched constantly. My friends are chosen for me, and I am told how to speak, how to dress, how to comport myself, how to—" She paused. "Well, you see what I mean. But, the very worst part is John Wery."

"John Wery?" asked Hester and Miss Larkin in unison.

"The man my guardian has chosen for me," replied Chloe bitterly.

"He is distasteful to you?" asked Hester.

Chloe shuddered. "Oh, yes. He is so—so insipid. His hair is thin and brown and he talks of nothing but his estate in Hertfordshire and his animals and his crops. He does not share my passion for righting the wrongs of our country. Would you believe that he simply does not care that women have no rights? That we are merely chattel, subject to our husband's every whim? We have *nothing* in common! I have told Uncle Thorne that I refuse to be shackled to a man who would treat me so, but all he does is tell me to go away and stop sulking."

"How old is this John Wery?" Miss Larkin's spectacles glittered. "I suppose he is not really two-and-eighty as Lord Bythorne said."

"No," muttered Chloe through clenched teeth. "I think he is six-and-twenty. But he might as well be an old man for all the boring information he spouts on draining his marshes, or his everlasting sheep or—" She twisted suddenly to face Hester. "Oh, Miss Blayne, you are so independent. You do not know how it is to be obliged to bow to the wishes of an unfeeling tyrant. I cannot bear the idea of spending my life in thrall to such a man. Please help me."

Hester blinked. "My dear," she said at last in a gentle tone. "I do sympathize with your plight. And I do know what it is to live with men who strive to rule every facet of one's life. But, I am afraid that there is nothing I can do. I can offer advice, but that is all."

"Advice!" Chloe sprang to her feet. "It is not for advice that I crept from my home in the middle of the night. I had to bribe one of the footmen to procure a ticket for me to Guildford—for one must be listed on the waybill before being allowed to board the stage. I had to bribe him further to find a hackney for me, and I rode through town—with no one to attend me—to the White Horse Cellars in Picadilly. In Guildford, I had to pay a wagoner to take me to Overcross, and he kept looking at me in a way I did not like at all." Tears sprang to Chloe's eyes, clustering in a silky profusion of lashes. "It was a dreadful ordeal, but I kept my goal before me, for I was sure I would find succor with you. And now—" Golden curls were tossed in disdain as Chloe reached the climax of her peroration. "And now, you wish to offer me advice! Oh!" She sank down again in the settee. "It is all too much!"

Hester exchanged an amused glance with Miss Larkin before rising from her own chair to sit beside Chloe. "Miss Venable," she began, taking a slim hand in her own, "your guardian has complete authority over you. I cannot shield you from him. I will agree with you that he is a difficult person with whom to deal, but you must do so. Now, here is my advice. I do not, of course, insist that you take it, but at least consider my words.

"If a match between you and John Wery is truly repugnant, you must convince Lord Bythorne of this." She held up a hand as Chloe opened her mouth indignantly. "Expressing your unhappiness in long, loud melodramatic periods is not the way to convince him. I am sure that his lordship does not actively wish to persecute you, and if he thought he was acting contrary to your true interests, he would modify his goals for you. The earl is obviously not used to dealing with young persons of an, er, excitable temperament, and such a display only sets his back up."

Hester drew a long breath. From the expression in Miss Venable's eyes, it was rather doubtful that her words were having any effect, but she plowed on.

"You must see, Miss Venable, that—"

"Oh, do please call me Chloe," the girl interrupted.

"Very well—Chloe, you must see that by indulging in these mad starts—making wild speeches and running away—you achieve precisely the opposite effect than that which you desire. You are convincing him that you are just another flighty female, with more hair than wit."

"But, how can I sit demurely by, whispering, 'Yes, Uncle Thorne—no, Uncle Thorne,' when he does nothing but order me about?" Chloe fairly bounced in her chair with indignation.

"Have you no other relatives besides your uncle?" asked Hester, a sense of desperation creeping over her.

"Uncle?" Chloe's delicate brows rose in puzzlement. "Oh, he is not really my uncle. He was Papa's best friend—Papa saved his life at Waterloo, and according to an agreement they made, I was put in his care when Papa died a little over a year ago." Her mouth trembled. "Mama died giving birth to me—I have no brothers or sisters. Nor any aunts or uncles. Oh, I do miss Papa so!" Tears glistened in her eyes once more. "He was so kind—so understanding. *He* would not dream of pressing me into a loveless marriage!"

"Yes," replied Hester, her ready sympathy touched. "It must be dreadfully difficult for you. But, about John Wery. Have you told him that you do not wish to marry him?"

"Well, he has not asked me yet—precisely. But Uncle Thorne has been so obvious in his desire for us to marry—and Mr. Wery—well, I know he's working up to a proposal."

"Do you discourage him?"

"Do you mean do I refuse to see him—or spill tea in his lap when he comes to call?" asked Chloe in a serious tone. "No, I have not taken that tack. And, he never does anything that would require discouraging. He never tries to hold my hand, or tell me that I am pretty—or anything like that. He simply proses at me about sheep!"

Hester refrained from glancing at Larkie and she firmly suppressed the bubble of laughter that rose within her. "I see," she said simply. "Well, perhaps you could endeavor to give him a dislike of you. When he—proses about sheep, turn the conversation to books—or feminism, or something else that you feel would not interest him. That has certainly worked for me," she concluded with a smile.

"Well," said Chloe, "I might try it." She sighed gustily. "But even if it does, Uncle Thorne will just turn up another candidate for my hand. He knows every family in London, and if there's an unattached son or nephew lying about with a respectable portion to his name, he will hear of it."

"Have you no friends who share your views?" asked

Hester curiously. "Young people who might lend you moral support?"

"Pooh," Chloe snorted. "Every girl I know is simply panting to marry well. All they think about is balls and routs and Almack's. Except for Sarah, of course."

"Sarah?"

"Sarah Wendover. We went to school together and she is my best friend in the world. She shares my passion for justice for women—" Chloe lifted her hand in a theatrical gesture. "And she, too, is being persecuted by her family. Just last month her parents betrothed her to Lord Bascombe, who is three-and-thirty and rides to hounds every day that he can."

"Oh dear."

"Yes, she pleaded and cried, but to no avail. I encouraged her to run away, but she is somewhat poor-spirited. Her family lives near Bythorne Park, but I have not seen her since they left London last month—right after the betrothal. I have written to her frequently since then, and am hopeful she will take my advice."

"As I hope you will take mine," said Hester with a smile. She rose and smoothed her skirts. "Larkie, we must see about dinner."

"Oh!" Chloe jumped up. "Do let me help."

Miss Larkin stiffened. "But of course you will not. You are our guest, Miss—Chloe, and—"

"Oh no," replied Chloe with a laugh. She glanced down at her dark muslin gown. "I am your new servant. At least—if I had not hoaxed you, you would have a real servant now."

Miss Larkin opened her mouth to protest, but Hester spoke first. "Thank you, my dear, your assistance would be welcome."

Thus, when the Earl of Bythorne was wakened sometime later from his slumbers by a gentle scratch on his door, he roused himself to greet his ward. She carried a precariously balanced tray laden with dishes, and her face was flushed from her exertions.

"There!" she said, plumping the tray on his bed with a

triumphant air. "Here is a lovely dinner for you. And I helped!"

"You?" asked the earl, his lips curving in a smile of disbelief.

"Yes, indeed. Do look at the green beans. *I* prepared those."

"*Did* you?" His amused skepticism remained undiminished.

"I washed them, and strung them and sliced them up. Miss Larkin actually cooked them," she added magnanimously. "I helped baste the chicken, too. I must say, I never realized that cooking is such fun."

"Ah, perhaps we should put you to work in the kitchen when we return home." Thorne held his breath for a moment, awaiting his ward's reaction to what she might well view as a deliberately provocative speech.

Indeed, Chloe stiffened at his words and opened her lips as though to protest, but the next moment, as though thinking better of her attitude, she smiled.

"Well, perhaps I should not wish to go so far, but I think I would like to learn how to bake. Miss Blayne says every woman, no matter what her station in life, should know how to perform the most menial tasks in her household."

"Really?" returned the earl. "You surprise me."

"Of course," added Chloe, "she also thinks men should acquire the same skills."

"Now, that, somehow, does *not* surprise me."

She glanced uncertainly at him. "I shall leave you to your meal, Uncle. Enjoy it—especially the beans—and I shall return for your tray presently."

However, it was not Chloe, but their hostess, who entered his chamber an hour or so later.

"Ah," she said, approaching the bed, "I see you made a good repast."

"Indeed, I did," replied Thorne, proffering the tray. "I rarely have a chance to enjoy good country food, and this was excellent. My compliments to the chef—or am I addressing that personage."

Hester laughed. "It was rather a combined effort, my lord. Chloe—"

"Chloe produced the beans," finished Thorne. "*And* basted the chicken."

"To say nothing of preparing the salad vegetables. She was most eager to help."

"I daresay," replied Thorne dryly, "if *you* were to ask her, she would no doubt carry ashes from the hearth and scrub the floors."

"Mm, I think perhaps that would be pushing her desire for independence rather past the limits." She took the tray in her hands and turned to go, but Thorne put out his hand.

"No—please. Could you sit with me for a moment?" He assumed the most charming smile at his disposal.

Hester's returning smile was one of mild apprehension, but she set the tray down and perched on the edge of a small chair near the bed.

"Since you are awake, my lord," she said somewhat distractedly, "we should resume the cold compresses ordered by the doctor. Does the swelling seem to be going down?"

In reply, Thorne thrust his foot from beneath the covers for her inspection. She started at his sudden movement.

Good Lord, she thought irritably. Granted, the man is a little intimidating, but there's no need to jump like a startled rabbit at the sight of his bare foot. She bestowed a look of what she hoped was cool appraisal on the foot and its accompanying muscular calf resting almost in her lap. "Yes, it looks much better. After a good night's rest, I'm sure you'll be fit to travel in the morning."

"Much to your relief, I'm sure," murmured the earl.

"Oh, no—" replied Hester, flustered. "That is—"

"It cannot be comfortable for you—or for your companion—to house a strange man. I know my own aunt would be quite uneasy at the thought."

Hester detected a spark of unholy amusement in the depths of his dark eyes, and she stiffened.

"Not at all, my lord. There is nothing about you to make one uneasy, after all."

Thorne threw up his hand in a fencer's gesture. "*Touché,*

Miss Blayne." He drew his foot back under the coverlet and gazed at her for a moment. "Tell me, why have you chosen to live virtually alone in this remote village. Have you no family?"

"I have several brothers and sisters, my lord. My oldest brother is Sir Barnaby Blayne, and he resides in our family home near Shrewsbury. As for living by myself, I simply prefer it that way."

"And Sir Barnaby does not begrudge the extra expense of maintaining a separate household for one lone female?"

Hester stiffened even more rigidly. How dare this insufferable man ask her questions that were so blatantly rude? "My brother has nothing to say about this household. I maintain it at my own expense."

The earl's brows shot up. "Your own expense? You must have a most comfortable competence."

"I cannot see that this is any of your concern, my lord," Hester retorted. "But I received a small inheritance on the death of my father, some four years ago. With it I purchased this cottage. However, I provide for myself and Miss Larkin from my own earnings."

She almost laughed aloud at the earl's expression of blank surprise. "But, you're a female—a gently born female. What money could you possibly earn?"

"I realize," replied Hester sweetly, "that the concept of one of the so-called upper class earning his or her own way in the world must be utterly foreign to you, but, as you are aware, I write books. There is a very nice man in London who pays me to write books, and who pays me even more from the sale of those books. There are people, my lord, who pay to come and hear me speak. My earnings are not large, but, as you can see, Miss Larkin and I live in reasonable comfort—which even stretches to the hiring of a maidservant or two when one turns up on our doorstep."

The Earl of Bythorne flushed to the roots of his hair, and for a long moment did not speak. "I suppose I deserved that," he said at last. "It's just that—that—"

Hester took pity on him. "I know," she said, her voice kind. "The idea of a 'gently bred' female providing for herself without benefit of masculine protection is unsettling. I think you ought to get used to it, though, for in the not-too-distant future more and more women are going to wish to strike out on their own."

"At least," said Thorne with a smile, "if you have anything to say about it."

"Precisely, my lord. I take it," she continued, searching for a change of subject, "that you and your ward are once more on speaking terms."

Thorne grinned, and Hester was struck by the manner in which his harsh, rather jaded features lightened suddenly. "Yes, the little minx was all affability when she brought in my tray. I think it would be too much to hope that she regrets her precipitous action in fleeing to you, but at least she did not throw a tantrum when I mentioned returning home—together—tomorrow."

"She seems like a nice child," said Hester hesitantly.

"She is. Very nice. However, the operative word there is 'child.' She is flighty and totally undisciplined, and, frankly, I am at my wits' end with her."

"Have you ever tried really listening to her?"

Thorne laughed shortly. "My dear Miss Blayne, it seems to me that I do little else *but* listen to her, for she is always treating me to a tirade about one or another of her hobby-horses."

"Did it ever occur to you, my lord, that she is trying to talk to you about something in which she believes very passionately?"

Thorne's only answer was a derisive snort.

"Have you never believed passionately in anything?" asked Hester curiously.

Thorne laughed. "I believe that life's pleasures are transitory and should be enjoyed to the fullest while one is capable of doing so."

"A laudable goal, to be sure," Hester replied, unsmiling. "It is fortunate that there are those whose goals are bred from what you, I suppose, would call a social conscience."

"You, for example."

"I do try to raise the country's awareness of those who desperately need help." Hester found that her fingers clenching the arms of her chair had whitened, and she forced herself to relax.

"Poor, unfortunate wretches such as my ward, for example." Thorne, too, had lost his smile, and he eyed her with unconcealed hostility.

Hester, unintimidated, nodded. "Yes—and all the other women in this country who are treated, at best, like cherished pets and at worst, like beasts of the fields. And I try to speak for the children whose childhoods are wrenched from them in factories and chimneys—and, for those who are hanged for stealing bread to feed their starving families, and—"

Thorne, despite himself, found himself stirred by the passion in her words, but he raised a hand in a plaintive gesture. "You have made your point, Miss Blayne. I suppose one might say that gadflies such as yourself are fundamental to a progressive society, but they are a bit overpowering in one's bedchamber."

Hester rose with a snap of her skirts. Snatching up the tray again, she whirled and moved to the door, where she paused.

"In that case, I shall bid you good night, my lord. Miss Larkin will see to your needs for the rest of the evening, and I sincerely hope you will be recovered enough by morning to set out for the City."

She did not wait for a reply, but whisked herself from the room, and once outside, leaned against the door panel, exhausting her indignation in great, gulping breaths. Odious man! Lying at his ease, expecting to be waited on hand and foot—the very embodiment of all she detested in the male sex.

At any rate, she thought as her breathing slowed and a measure of equanimity returned, he would be gone in the morning, and she would never have to set eyes on the Earl of Bythorne again.

Chapter Four

Lord Bythorne and his wayward ward departed the next morning, and after the alarums and excursions pursuant to their intrusion into the routine of Rosemere Cottage, life returned to its usual sedate pace. Miss Larkin resumed the inventory of household linen in which she had been involved for some days, and a new serving maid was hired—one with the unquestioned ability to peel potatoes.

Hester returned to her manuscript in progress. She had, after a great deal of soul-searching, decided to shelve the philosophical work for the time being and bowing to the demands of her publisher and her purse, had begun a new novel. Even so, she admitted, she would be skating on extremely thin financial ice during the months between the present and the time the book would appear on the country's bookshelves.

Thus, she sat daily, penning a sprightly, if highly colored tale of a moral miss beset with the most immoral of villains whom she defeated handily with her own ingenuity and daring. The book featured a hero, but Hester was forced to admit he was rather pallid and not a little timid, possessing only a fraction of the fortitude displayed by her intrepid heroine. Her villain was proving to be much more interesting. Late one morning, she nibbled on the end of her pen, searching for just the right adjectives to describe Maximillian Fordyce, evil rake and despoiler of women.

She found her thoughts drifting, perhaps inevitably, to Lord Bythorne. This she put to the rarity of visitors in their quiet little corner of the realm. She chose not to delve into the reasons she persisted in running their conversations

over and over in her mind. She was loath to admit that she
found them unsettling and oddly exhilarating. Goodness,
she was not so starved for company that a day and a half
spent in the company of an arrogant peer could so discommode her—was she?

Agreed, the man possessed a certain degree of charm and
his face, while not precisely handsome, was certainly ar-
resting, but then what successful rake did not possess these
attributes?

As she worked at the desk that occupied one corner of
her bedchamber, her concentration was disrupted by the
sound of a vehicle clattering to a halt outside. She rose and
moved to the window to behold an all-too-familiar racing
curricle, black with red markings. She hurried downstairs,
something within her fluttering in trepidation, tinged with
an unexpected stir of anticipation. She opened the door to
confront the Earl of Bythorne, his fist upraised to rap
peremptorily on the panel.

"Is she here?"

His shoulders sagged at her expression of blank surprise.

"Oh dear," said Hester. "Has Miss Venable, er, gone
missing again?"

"Yes," replied the earl shortly.

"Oh dear," said Hester again. "Well, you'd better come
in."

With a dismaying sense of *déjà vu*, she turned and led
him into the little parlor. Gesturing him to a small settee,
she rang for tea and took a chair nearby.

"Did you and Chloe have another quarrel?" she asked
diffidently.

"You could say that. Sir George and Lady Wery, the parents of the young man I have selected for Chloe, invited
us—Chloe and my Aunt Lavinia and I—to a small dinner
party. All very proper and unexceptionable." He grinned,
and Hester was once more struck by the surprising warmth
that flooded his harsh features. "It is normally the sort of
function I would avoid at all costs, but I am prepared to undergo almost any sacrifice to get Chloe safely bundled into
the bonds of matrimony. Chloe, of course, would have none

of it. She ranted at some length when I told her of the invitation, even when I made it plain that she had no choice in the matter. The next morning, she was gone, this time without so much as a note."

"I suppose you inquired among her friends—again?" asked Hester, more out of courtesy than from any desire to involve herself once more with the earl and his tiresome ward.

"Yes. I made the rounds. Or, rather, Aunt Lavinia did. She's better at directing discreet questions than I. She achieved no better results, though. At least, this time Chloe took her maid with her."

Hester's face lightened. "Well, that's good news. Perhaps she's gone to visit a friend out of—"

She was interrupted by the appearance of the new serving girl bearing a tray containing a teapot and the usual appurtenances. Thorne jerked to attention at her entrance and bent such a hard stare on her that the girl nearly dropped her burden midstride.

"Thank you, Clara," said Hester, hurrying to take the tray from her. "Would you find Miss Larkin and tell her we have a visitor?" She smiled encouragingly at the maid, who was obviously unused to dealing with the gentry, particularly large, powerful members of that class who looked as though they might erupt all over the parlor at any moment.

"Yes, mum," she stammered, and hurried from the room as though pursued by demons.

Hester poured a cup of tea and gestured toward the milk and cream with lifted brows. Shaking his head, Thorne accepted the cup from her abstractedly.

"As I was about to say," continued Hester, "perhaps she is visiting someone in the country. I suppose you inquired at the various posting inns."

"Yes, but none of the ticket agents remembered a young girl accompanied by a maid." He shook his head in annoyance. "Those places are so chaotic, I doubt they'd recall an elephant traveling with a giraffe." He ran his fingers through dark hair already tousled into disorder. "I don't suppose you'd have any idea where she might be, do you?"

"I?" Hester found the earl's dark stare singularly unnerving and she shifted defensively. "I trust you do not think I have been conducting a clandestine correspondence with her."

"Of course not," replied Thorne hastily. Good God, the woman was as prickly as her absurd philosophy of female enslavement. "I just thought—that is, you seem to have established a certain rapport with her, and—"

"Possibly because I did not attempt to ride roughshod over her sensibilities," interposed Hester sharply.

The earl stiffened. "That's true, but, of course, you do not have to deal with Chloe's sensibilities on a daily basis."

Hester flushed. What on earth had possessed her to snap at the man in such a fashion?

"No. I merely meant—if you will pardon my saying so, my lord, you seem to have not the slightest notion of how to deal with a young girl's—er, aspirations."

"No, I do not. In fact, I find the whole subject of young girls a closed book."

"I suppose that is understandable," replied Hester placatingly, "but—ah, Larkie," she finished with some relief as that lady entered the room.

"Why, Lord Bythorne." Miss Larkin extended her hand as Thorne rose. "How very nice to see you again. Your foot is healed?"

"Good as new." Thorne extended the appendage in question and waggled it to prove its soundness.

"Lord Bythorne is looking for his ward—again," said Hester as all three settled once more about the tea table. In a few words she apprised her companion of Miss Venable's latest start.

"Oh, my gracious!" exclaimed Miss Larkin. "The little imp. Though perhaps, I should not—" she added, conscious-stricken.

"Never mind, Miss Larkin," replied Thorne with a bark of mirthless laughter. "That is one of the kinder descriptions that occurs to me."

"You know," said Hester, who had remained silent during this interchange, "Chloe mentioned a name to me while she was here. A dear friend, she said—one who entered into her feelings on the inadvisability of marrying Mr. Wery, is it not?"

"Yes. But who was she?"

Hester stared into space, searching her memory, which unfortunately remained uncommunicative.

"Oh dear, I'm afraid I'm drawing a blank."

Thorne drew in a quick breath of irritation.

"Damnation! That is—I do apologize, ladies, but perhaps, Miss Blayne, if you were to think a little harder . . ."

Hester assumed a reflective expression, but found herself unable to think beyond the desire that the earl would remove his intent gaze from her. After a few moments, she shook her head apologetically.

Thorne frowned. "Well, let's see. Chloe's acquaintanceship among girls of her age outside London is limited—at least, those she has met since coming to us from India. Living in the neighborhood of my estate are Susan Shaw, and Lady Charlotte Wellbeloved. I believe Chloe was also friends with Sarah Wendover, as well, and there was—"

"That's it!" cried Hester. "Sarah Wendover. Miss Venable said the girl was recently forced into becoming betrothed to a gentleman to whom she had formed a strong aversion. I wonder if—"

But Thorne had already leaped to his feet. "I don't know, but it's worth a try." He moved to Hester and grasped both of her hands in his. "Thank you, Miss Blayne, I am indeed indebted to you. And now, if you will excuse me, I had better be on my way."

He strode to the doorway, but halted with his hand on the latch, causing Hester, who had risen to see him out, to bump into him from behind. Turning, Thorne steadied her.

"Excuse me," he said awkwardly. "Something just occurred to me."

To Hester's surprise, Thorne returned to his seat and sat down. Having accomplished this, he seemed at a loss.

"Ah," he said at last, and Hester and Larkie gazed at him expectantly. "I was wondering. That is—last time—with Chloe—as I mentioned, you and she seemed to get along so swimmingly. You were able to convince her, with astonishingly little effort, to return home. I was wondering . . ."

Hester exchanged a quick glance with Larkie and stared warily at the earl.

"I was wondering," he finished in a rush, "if you would accompany me to Miss Wendover's home."

"I beg your pardon?" gasped Hester.

"Sarah Wendover lives near Bythorne Park, so she is no more than fifteen miles from here. You—and Miss Larkin, of course—could come with me and still be home by this evening. Please," he added, in the face of Hester's expression of blank disbelief. "If she has fled to Miss Wendover, it's going to be next to impossible for me to winkle her away, at least without tying her up like a Christmas goose and flinging her over my shoulder. But if you were to talk to her . . ."

He left his sentence unfinished, but bent on her the most charming smile at his disposal, one that he knew from experience was unvaryingly effective. On this occasion, however, he could sense that it had failed in its purpose.

"No," she said uncompromisingly.

"But—but why?"

"Lord Bythorne," returned Hester patiently, "I sympathize with your, er, difficulties with your ward, but you can hardly expect me to disrupt my life in order to come to your rescue. In fact, I find myself extremely reluctant to try to persuade her to acquiesce in what I can only consider your unreasonable desire that she return home to marry a man whom she holds in repugnance."

Thorne rose and advanced on her, experiencing an irrational urge to grasp Miss Hester Blayne by the shoulders and shake her until that tidy little bun on the top of her head tumbled down her back.

"Now, wait just a moment, Miss Blayne. First of all, as I thought I had explained, I am not the villainous uncle from some third-rate melodrama. Chloe is my ward and my responsibility. I consider finding an acceptable match for her the most important of those responsibilities. The husband I have chosen for her is a fine young man. I have investigated his family. The fact that Chloe has dug in her heels against the idea only goes to prove how woefully inadequate she is to determine her own future. Second, I did not ask you to disrupt your life, I merely asked you to spare me an afternoon from your busy schedule." He drew a deep breath and stepped away from her abruptly. "However, you may consider that request null and void. I regret having disturbed you. Thank you for telling me of Chloe's reference to Miss Wendover. And now, if you will excuse me . . ."

He turned on his heel and rigid with anger made once again for the front door.

"Wait." To her own amazement, Hester heard herself speak the word. She put out her hand. "I apologize, my lord. I'm afraid I have been conditioned to attributing the worst motive to any male plan for a female's well-being."

"Indeed, Hester," interposed Miss Larkin, tendrils of gray hair flying about her face. "Lord Bythorne's request is not unreasonable. You told me yourself just this morning that you are ahead of schedule on your book, and we have no social engagements pending—at least, not until Tuesday next when we have been invited to Squire Maltby's."

Hester smiled reluctantly at Thorne. "Very well. We shall be pleased to accompany you—if you still wish us to do so."

Thorne's grin of relief told her her apology had been accepted. "Absolutely," he said. "My curricle, unfortunately, will not accommodate all of us, so I'll have to hire a vehicle at—the White Stag, is it?" he asked, naming the posting inn on the outskirts of the village.

"Yes," replied Hester. "That would probably be best, since I'm afraid our only vehicle is a rather smallish gig."

Thorne nodded and hurried from the house with a marked air of relief, returning less than an hour later with a commodious coach and four with attendant postboy.

Scarcely more than another hour elapsed before they arrived at The Willows, home of Mr. Jonathan Wendover, Esquire. Present to greet them were the squire himself and his lady, as well as his oldest son Miles and oldest daughter Melissa. The little family seemed somewhat flustered at finding themselves unexpectedly invaded by the august presence of the Earl of Bythorne, but ushered him and his guests into their drawing room with alacrity.

"But we did not expect you so soon, my lord!" exclaimed Mrs. Wendover, whereupon the earl turned upon her with a suddenness that nearly overset the lady.

"So soon?" he echoed sharply. "Is Chloe here, then?"

"Well, of course—that is, she is not precisely here. She and Sarah took the pony cart into the village, but they should return momentarily. However, we had thought dear Chloe's visit would not be so brief. From what she said, we assumed she would be with us the greater part of what is left of the summer."

"Indeed," said Thorne, drawing a long breath. He turned to Larkie and Hester. "May I introduce my, er, cousin, Miss Blayne and her companion, Miss Larkin."

Hester glanced at him, startled. Well, yes, she concluded after a moment's reflection, it would look more than a little odd for the earl to be tooling about the country in the company of an unrelated spinster and her elderly companion. She put out a hand to Mrs. Wendover and the squire, professing herself delighted to make their acquaintance.

The little group settled down to tea and conversation, and it was only a few minutes later when a commotion in the entry hall and the sound of girlish voices indicated the arrival of the youngest daughter of the house and her guest. A few moments later, the young ladies burst into the drawing room, curls and ribbons flying.

"Mama!" cried Miss Wendover. "You will not believe what I found—"

She was interrupted by a strangled gasp from Chloe, who had followed her into the room. The color fled from the girl's cheeks, and her eyes grew wide with horror.

"Uncle Thorne!" she cried before crumpling to the floor in a faint.

Chapter Five

Not surprisingly, it was some time before order was restored to Squire Wendover's household. Chloe revived within a few moments of her dramatic collapse, but for many moments the air was rent with her piteous cries for deliverance from her horrid circumstances, to which Miss Wendover added her own supplication.

At last, the squire and his lady, having been assured by the earl that he placed no blame on them for the defection of his ward, ordered Sarah to her room to cool her heels and her heated sensibilities. They then paraded from the room with their remaining offspring, leaving Chloe to Lord Bythorne's tender mercies.

Chloe displayed no surprise on finding Hester in the earl's company. Instead, on finding herself under a threat of impending retribution, she flew across the room and flung herself on Hester's bosom.

"Oh, Miss Blayne!" she exclaimed tearfully. "Please do not let him take me."

"Now, see here, Chloe—" thundered the earl, whereupon Hester shot him a minatory glance. Her voice, when she spoke, however, was mild.

"Perhaps, my lord, if you and Larkie were to take a turn on the terrace and give Miss Venable a chance to recover herself . . ."

She frowned meaningfully, and after an instant's hesitation Thorne nodded shortly. Turning stiffly, he offered his arm to Miss Larkin and the two proceeded through the French doors that opened from the drawing room to a pleasantly landscaped terrace.

"Now then, Chloe." Hester led the weeping girl to a set-tee and lowering her gently, seated herself beside her. Fish-ing a handkerchief from her reticule, she applied it to Chloe's swollen eyes and smiled comfortingly. "Let us see what we can do to remedy your situation."

"There is nothing that can be done to remedy my situa-tion." Chloe sniffed, taking the handkerchief from Hester's fingers to continue the mopping-up process. "You have seen how he is. He is determined to inflict his will on mine."

"Well—yes—" Hester's lips curved upward. "He is somewhat, er, dictatorial, but you must realize, that like most men—particularly men in his position—he has been used to being obeyed without question for nearly all his life."

"Well," muttered Chloe, "he'd best get used to being *dis*-obeyed, because I have no intention—"

"I applaud your spirit, my dear," interposed Hester gen-tly, "but it is never wise to mount an insurrection from a position of weakness. Do you remember what we discussed on the occasion of our first meeting at my home?"

Chloe stared at her blankly.

"I think we agreed at that time that your best plan of at-tack at the moment was to show your guardian that you are quite grown up and capable of making your own decisions about your future."

Chloe's gaze fell to the handkerchief, now twisted in a damp knot. "Y-yes, I remember." She lifted her eyes. "I—I suppose you think that running away—again—was not a very good way of demonstrating my—my maturity."

"It does not matter what I think. It is your view of your actions that is important. And, of course, that of Lord Bythorne. Try, if you can, Chloe, to put yourself in your guardian's place." She lifted her hand as a protest formed visibly on Chloe's soft pink lips. "No, I have found this to be very useful in my own skirmishes with the male animal. I think we can agree that his lordship is not a genuinely bad man."

"N-no, I suppose not," admitted Chloe grudgingly.

"Therefore his transgressions spring merely from his misguided attempts to do what he thinks is right." Hester sighed gustily. "Such well-meaning ineptitude on the part of the male animal is the cause of many of our problems. So often what is right in their estimations is at direct odds with what is really the best for us. But I digress. Tell me, Chloe, just what do you think is best for you?"

Again, she was rewarded by a blank stare.

"That is, what are your goals?"

"Oh." Chloe fumbled with the handkerchief. "Why—I suppose—Oh, Miss—Hester—I want to be just like you!"

Now it was Hester's turn to gape. "I beg your pardon?" she asked vacantly.

"Yes," replied Chloe, this time with more assurance. "I wish to spread the spirit of feminism in writings and speeches. I think I should like very well to make speeches. I would be willing to suffer persecution for the cause, and I would never, ever let a man tell me what to do—and I would rather die than marry!" By now, Chloe had become quite flown with her own oratory and her cheeks flushed with passion. Hester placed a hand on her sleeve.

"That is all very well, and I wish you the best, if this is truly the course of action you wish to pursue, but—"

"If?" cried Chloe. "Why, there can be no doubt. You, and Mary Wollstonecraft before you, have pointed the way for the others of us who wish to throw off the shackles of female bondage, and I—"

"Yes," interposed Hester gently, "but have you ever actually written anything? I mean, have you tried yet to put your thoughts on paper? It is not as easy as you might think. And as for shackles—I have never spoken against marriage. In fact, as an institution, I am highly in favor of it."

"You are?" Chloe's eyes grew round.

"Yes, for I feel that the family unit is important in a child's development, and that unit should include both a mother *and* a father. I merely feel that women—and men—should be left to make their own choices in their mates. Certainly, they should listen to their parents' wishes, for our elders speak from a wealth of experience that we would be foolish to ignore, but the decision should be left ultimately to those who will be living with one another for the rest of their lives."

For once Chloe was silent, merely staring doubtfully at her idol. Hester laughed.

"Well. I have given you much to chew on. Perhaps you will wish to think over what I have said before deciding what you think is of value and what you may wish to throw out the window. But, if I might suggest . . ."

Chloe did not respond, but she lifted her expressive brows.

"Return to London with your guardian," continued Hester. "Attend the dinner party with good grace and be courteous to Mr. Wery and his parents. If nothing else, by doing so you will throw Lord Bythorne into utter confusion."

"But, what will all that accomplish?" asked Chloe in some indignation. "If I am nice to John Wery, will I not find myself at the altar that much sooner?"

"Mm, perhaps, but perhaps not. Just what is it that your guardian finds so desirable in Mr. Wery?"

"Well—he's steady and reliable and dependable and all those boring things, and he has his own estate, which produces a comfortable income."

"I see. Formidable attributes indeed. Does he not have any flaws? Does he gamble, or is he a womanizer?"

"No," replied Chloe bitterly. "He is a perfect pattern card of virtue. Do you wonder that I cannot abide him?"

Hester's lips twitched. "He sounds perfectly impossible. I wonder," she added thoughtfully after a moment, "if you should adjust your strategy."

Chloe glanced at her questioningly.

"I think we discussed the possibility before that instead of trying to convince Lord Bythorne to abandon his campaign to wed you to Mr. Wery, perhaps you should be endeavoring to convince Mr. Wery that you are not the bride for him."

Chloe's expression changed slowly to one of comprehension. "Mm, yes, I recall your advice, but so far I have done nothing to create an aversion to me."

Hester nodded. "I do not mean that you should plunge yourself into a scandal, of course," she said hastily, "but simply get to know him well—his preferences, his plans for the future, *et cetera,* and then make him realize that you will not fit in with his desires."

"Yes," chimed Chloe eagerly. "I have never expounded at any length on my theories of feminism, but if I were to do so . . ."

"Mr. Wery would no doubt begin to view you with the utmost alarm."

"Yes. And if I were to make it clear that I relish living in London and have no intention of rusticating on a fusty little estate in Hertfordshire and . . ."

"Do you enjoy life in London so much?" asked Hester in surprise.

"Well, no. In fact, my happiest times with Uncle Thorne have been the months we've stayed at Bythorne Park, but Mr. Wery need not know that, and I think," concluded Chloe judiciously, "that since he is the thrifty sort, I shall make it a point of remarking on the number and the cost of my gowns—and on the quantity of jewels I shall require as a married lady—with some slight exaggeration, of course."

Hester laughed outright. "You will have the poor man fleeing in alarm inside a fortnight." She sobered a little. "On the other hand, you might want to reexamine your position with Lord Bythorne. Now that we have decided he truly has your best interests at heart, there is really no point in setting his back up needlessly, is there? I mean, if he does mistreat you—"

"Oh no. In fact, when I first came to live with him and Aunt Lavinia, I quite liked him. He is so handsome, and he always shared the latest *on-dits* with me—well, some of them, anyway, for despite his own scandalous reputation," she continued austerely, "he is quite strict with me. And he never minded my attending feminist lectures, or reading your books and pamphlets. He considers them of such little account, you see," she added in explanation.

"Does he?" replied Hester, an edge to her voice.

"Oh yes," said Chloe, unheeding. "When I told him I wished to go to the lecture you gave at the Assembly Building in Westminster, he simply laughed, and asked if I shouldn't like him to take me to see the learned pig on display at the Bartholomew Fair as well."

"I see." Hester's voice could have cut glass. She rose abruptly. "Why don't you get your things together, Chloe, and I shall inform his lordship of your decision to return home with him."

By the time Chloe had retrieved her belongings and bade a tearful farewell to Sarah, and the Wendovers had expressed their regret once again for their unwitting participation in dear Chloe's defection, the afternoon was well advanced. As the earl and his little party prepared to mount the hired carriage, he turned to Hester.

"It will be well after dark by the time we reach Overcross, I fear, and there will be no moon tonight. I think we should simply proceed to Bythorne Park. We can send this carriage back and ride to your home tomorrow at our leisure in the comfort of one of my vehicles."

Still simmering from Chloe's ingenuous description of Lord Bythorne's view of her work, Hester would have liked to dispute this high-handed arrangement. She found herself welcoming his invitation, however. She did not look forward to a long ride in the ill-sprung post chaise, and a glance at Larkie's countenance told her that the older woman was fatigued, as well.

The earl sent a rider to travel ahead of them to announce their imminent arrival at the Park, and the group set off with no further incident.

The manor house at Bythorne Park was a sprawling structure of early Tudor origin. The ancient brick glowed rosily and mullioned windows glittered in the late-afternoon sunlight. Somewhat to Hester's surprise, they were greeted promptly by a smiling butler and his wife, who apparently acted as housekeeper when the family was not in residence. Inside the house, all was in immaculate order, as though the master had given notice days ago of his arrival.

Glancing at her, Thorne smiled.

"Since the Park is so close to London," he said, "I invite people here fairly frequently—or sometimes I just use it as a refuge. I keep the place fully staffed, so that I can descend more or less at a moment's notice."

"A refuge?" queried Hester.

"Mm. I am at heart a creature of the city, but once in a while the noise and the bustle get to be too much, even for a dedicated urban dweller. The Park holds many warm memories for me, so I enjoy its peace and solitude."

Hester glanced at him, again surprised. A grin curved his well-formed lips, and she found it was not so difficult after all to imagine the earl as a small boy scrambling up the trees that surrounded the house or swimming in the lake that could be seen shining in the distance.

The housekeeper Mrs. Pym showed Hester and Miss Larkin to their adjoining rooms, and these, too, looked as though they had been kept in readiness for visitors. Fresh flowers stood on the rosewood commode in Hester's chamber, and brushes, combs, and a mirror lay on a charming dressing table.

"His lordship keeps country hours here at the Park," said the housekeeper, whose face displayed only a certain discreet curiosity as she poured water from a graceful pitcher into a basin. "We shall be dining at six, about an hour from now. His lordship usually meets with his guests beforehand in the green salon. If you'll ring when you are ready to go down, someone will show you the way." She smiled, and with one last glance about the room, curtsied and hurried out with a rustle of bombazine skirts.

It was too bad, thought Hester as she removed her rather utilitarian shawl, that she had not brought something into which she could change for dinner. Although, she reflected with a laugh, there was nothing in her wardrobe at home that would not look sadly out of place in this fairy-princess bedroom. Shrugging, she availed herself of the cool water in the basin—scented, of course—to bathe her face, and the

combs and brushes to repair her hair from the ravages of
the day's travel. She reaffixed her cap firmly, and some
moments later, she followed a maidservant along the corridor, having collected Larkie along the way.

"Gracious, Hester," said that lady, her eyes wide and
sparkling, "have you ever seen such elegance? My room is
furnished with everything one could want for an overnight
stay—even cruets of scent and books on the bedside table!"

"Enjoy it while you may, my friend," replied Hester with
a chuckle, "for tomorrow we return to our cinder pile by the
hearth at Rosemere."

The ladies, having been led without incident through
broad corridors and stately staircases, were eventually ushered into a large, airy chamber furnished in the first stare of
elegance. Long windows, hung with emerald damask,
looked out over velvety parkland. Lord Bythorne sat at his
ease on a satin striped settee, deep in conversation with his
ward. He rose as his guests entered the room.

"I trust you have been made comfortable, Miss Blayne,
Miss Larkin," he inquired smoothly, expressing gratification at their affirmative response.

Chloe was simply gowned in white muslin, over which
lay a tunic of pink sarcenet that reflected the delicate color
of her cheeks. Pink ribbons threaded through her dark curls
completed her ensemble and she looked, thought Hester,
absolutely charming. Mr. John Wery must be a very undis-
criminating suitor indeed to confine his conversation to
sheep and crops while in her presence.

The girl had evidently decided to follow her preceptress's advice, for her demeanor was equally charming. She
maintained a deferential courtesy through dinner, saying little, and any discomfort she might have been suffering as a
result of her aborted escape to freedom was in little evidence as she made an excellent meal of Davenport fowls,
stuffed and roasted in butter, baked carp dressed in the Por-
tuguese way, and a variety of vegetables in appropriate
sauces.

Larkie, seemingly overwhelmed by her grand surroundings, remained subdued. Thus it was left to Hester and

Thorne to maintain a conversation that remained surprisingly convivial.

Truth to tell, Thorne was more than a little amused at the presence of the country's foremost feminist at his table. In her plain round gown, with that absurd cap tied tightly beneath her chin, and her eyes glinting shrewdly, she was as out of place as a wren in a gilded canary cage. Lord, what would his London cronies think if they were to walk into the room right now to find the Earl of Bythorne dining *à quatre* in splendor with his ward and two spinsters from an obscure village on the fringe of Surrey? They'd consider him well round the bend, of course. Not that he cared for the opinions of a parcel of jaded roués from the hells of St. James's. In addition, to his surprise, he found he was enjoying his conversation with the redoubtable Miss Blayne.

"So you do not think Byron a dark and dangerous man?" he asked idly.

"Not nearly so dangerous as he would have his readers believe," retorted Hester with some asperity. "I think him a very good poet, but he would be a much better one if he would stop all that ludicrous brooding and soul-searching."

Thorne laughed. "The ladies of the *ton* would cast you into the nearest pit were they to hear such sentiments of one of their favorites. For even though he departed this sceptered isle in disgrace—or perhaps because of it—he is still much talked of."

"Yes, I suppose they would." Hester smiled. "I have grown accustomed to ostracism, however, and it bothers me not in the slightest."

Thorne dissected with his fork the damson pie that had just been placed before him. "I understand"—he glanced at Chloe—"that you are the daughter of a peer, Miss Blayne, and your family name is an ancient and honorable one. If you had so chosen, you could have taken your place among the ranks of the privileged. Do you not regret taking another path?"

Hester considered his question, cocking her head to one side in what Thorne found an unexpectedly endearing gesture.

"No," she said at last with a spurt of laughter. "I rather consider it an escape from prison. I spent a term there—what most people would call a Season—and I was never so bored in my life. The whole time was spent in places I would rather not have been, conversing with persons who appeared to have not one idea to rub against another."

What a strange little woman she was, thought Thorne in surprise. Her eyes were really quite beautiful, but set in such a plain little face. . . . Or no, she was not in truth plain, was she? Her nose was well shaped, above a mouth that curved full and warm, particularly when she was laughing, and a round little chin that seemed created for cupping in one's fingers. It was her militant expression that made her so unattractive, he decided, plus, of course, her dowdy clothes—to say nothing of the starchy caps of linen and lace she wore pinned to hair pulled back so tightly it must make her eyes water. He smiled. Despite her best efforts, a few tendrils always escaped to curl temptingly about her cheeks.

It was a lovely color—her hair. He tried to picture it unconfined and hanging down her back. Would a man feel compelled to fill his hands with it? To run its silken length through his fingers?

Steady on, old horse, he thought, startled. Of all the women of his acquaintance, this particular female was the least likely candidate for a spot of dalliance. He pulled his mind back to what she was saying, something about the corn laws, for God's sake.

"Well, do you, my lord?" she was saying.

"Do I what, Miss Blayne?"

She clicked her tongue in annoyance. "Do you not agree that the law in its present state is positively iniquitous?"

Thorne was about to utter a pat rejoinder when Miss Blayne continued tartly, "My lord, if you are about to tell me not to worry my pretty little head about such matters, I may be forced to disembowel you." She waved her dessert fork menacingly.

Larkie gasped, and Chloe raised her head, startled. Thorne burst into laughter. "Having been forewarned, I shall do nothing of the sort. But, you must admit," he concluded slyly, "it is highly unusual for a female to express herself so vehemently on a subject that does not involve fashion or household management, or—"

"Or how to entice a husband," finished Hester, laying aside her weapon but retaining the acid in her tone.

Not that the little termagant would be able to converse sensibly on any of those topics, thought the earl. Particularly the latter. Lord, he pitied the man who found himself leg-shackled to the self-righteous Miss Blayne. He would be sliced to shreds by that double-bladed tongue inside a fortnight.

And yet, he mused, she had accomplished a miracle with his ward. Look at the chit, bending demurely over her dinner as though butter wouldn't melt in her mouth. He supposed he could count on this pleasant state of affairs only until Miss Blayne took her leave on the morrow. He shuddered inwardly, almost dreading his guests' departure.

On the other hand . . . A thought struck him, so abruptly that he almost spilled his wine into his lap. No, he thought a moment later, the whole idea was preposterous. And yet . . . He glanced pensively across the table.

"Miss Blayne, do allow me to pour you a little more of this excellent Chambertin," he said silkily.

Chapter Six

After dinner, the earl, declining to remain in a solitary state with the port decanter, accompanied the ladies to the music room, where Chloe entertained at the pianoforte. Though not technically skilled, she played with a great deal of expression and the applause she engendered was quite genuine.

Afterward, Thorne's offer of a guided tour of the manor was accepted by Hester and Miss Larkin with alacrity. Chloe trailed the group with a pretty show of enthusiasm.

"As you have probably already surmised," said the earl, "the original house was built in the time of Queen Elizabeth. The owner at that time was Henry Trent, the fourth Baron Trent. The earldom came several generations later, and in the meantime the house expanded into rather a jumble of styles." He pointed to a Restoration staircase ascending from a Jacobean corridor. "We Trents have never been known for our taste in building, as we place comfort and space above fashion."

As though to emphasize his point, he led his guests through chamber after vast chamber interspersed with breezy corridors and passageways. At last, he turned into the grand gallery, which stretched all across the front of the house. Like the other rooms, it was elegantly furnished, and was lined with family portraits.

"Here we have Henry himself," said Thorne, pointing to a stout gentleman in doublet and hose posed beside his favorite steed. "We have been given to understand that he was quite a favorite of the Queen. And, over here, behold Roderick, his son and heir. Poor Roderick evidently did not possess his father's charm of manner, for he fared poorly during the reign of James I, barely escaping with his head.

"The family fortunes, however, were repaired by his son, another Henry, who married well. Here is a portrait of him with his spouse. One gathers she must have been possessed of a very large fortune indeed."

Gazing at Lady Trent, a tall, formidable female with pinched features and a spare figure, Hester smothered a giggle.

Thorne went on to point out others of his progenitors, leading from Tudor reigns to those of Stuart to Hanover. As they reached the end of the gallery, he pointed to a large portrait featuring a distinguished-looking gentleman, a blindingly beautiful woman and a small, dark-haired boy.

"And now"—Thorne gestured—"we come to the current flowering of the family tree. My mother and father and my own humble self, aged about nine years, as I recall."

Hester studied the portrait. Thorne's father was undoubtedly a handsome man, but there was something rather forbidding about his features. His mother was obviously a diamond of the first water, possessed of golden hair, enormous blue eyes, and a smile that seemed to reach out beyond the paint and varnish of the picture to catch the beholder in its dazzling magic.

"What an extraordinarily lovely woman," she said. She glanced from the portrait to Thorne and back again.

"Yes, she was," replied Thorne, "and yes, I most resemble my father." Hester wondered at the odd glint in his eyes as he gazed at the picture, and almost as an aside he murmured, "I did inherit some characteristics from her." He turned as though to move on, and Chloe and Miss Larkin prepared to follow him, but Hester remained staring at the portrait.

"You are an only child," she stated in some puzzlement.

"Yes," replied Thorne again, his tone unpromising.

"I'm sorry—that was a rather personal remark. It's just that it is unusual that the son of so prominent a family should have no siblings."

"As I understand it, my father would have liked a large

family, but apparently Mother Nature refused to cooperate."

Thorne uttered the words lightly, but Hester sensed that the smile that accompanied them was forced. He turned once again, and this time he put his hand under Hester's elbow to steer her firmly from the gallery. She cast one last backward glance at the threesome, and was left, not with the image of two people blessed with looks and riches, but of the small, rather lonely figure of the little boy who stood stiffly between them.

The group returned to the emerald salon, where they found the tea table awaiting them. For the remainder of the evening, conversation was light and inconsequential. Chloe made it a point to comment on the upcoming dinner party with the Werys, and Thorne registered an appropriate gratification at his ward's newly acquired acquiescence. As they said their good nights a little while later, Hester was surprised by the oddly speculative expression on the earl's face as he bent over her hand.

Later, as she sank gratefully into her bed and nestled under a silken comforter, she reflected that not since she had left her family home had she spent the night in such luxury. Not that Wisseton Priory, large and comfortable though it was, could provide the sybaritic comfort of Bythorne Park.

Indeed, she mused sleepily, in the coming months, given the current state of her finances, even the creature comforts of Rosemere Cottage might suffer a decline. She snuggled farther under the comforter. If only the cloud of the mortgage payment did not loom over her, life would be sweet.

The next morning, after an ample breakfast the entire party set out for Overcross, for the earl wished to travel directly to London after depositing the ladies of Rosemere Cottage back at their home. He was unusually silent during the drive, but Chloe filled the void with questions to Hester on her feminist exploits.

When they arrived home, Hester expected that after saying all that was proper the earl would wish to be on his way. Instead, he accepted with alacrity Miss Larkin's invitation for him and his niece to fortify themselves against the trip with a cup of tea and perhaps a plate of scones. He had no more availed himself of a gulp or two of this beverage when he turned to Hester and said somewhat nervously, "I wonder if I might speak to you in private, Miss Blayne."

All three ladies present stared at him in surprise.

"Uncle Thorne—" Chloe began, her curiosity evident, but Thorne lifted his hand in a gesture of negation.

"Why—of course, my lord." Rising, Hester led the earl to a small study tucked into the back of the house. She seated herself in a small cane-covered chair and gestured Thorne to another. He remained standing, however, and after a moment began to pace the meager length of the room. It was some moments before he spoke, during which Hester sat with hands folded, displaying only a waiting courtesy. Inwardly, her mind churned with questions. What in the world could the man wish to see her about? What could he want that Larkie and Chloe were not permitted to hear? Was he about to upbraid her for her unseemly sentiments, spoken before his ward? Well, if that were the case, she certainly—

"Miss Blayne."

Hester started.

"Miss Blayne," he said again, and Hester realized with some astonishment that he was apprehensive.

"I want to express my appreciation for your coming to my rescue—with Chloe," he continued after a moment. "You have a gift for dealing with volatile young women— at least this particular volatile young woman."

Hester smiled. "Well, I used to be one myself," she said. "It is no wonder that I possess some facility in dealing with Chloe, for she reminds me very much of myself at her age."

"Really?" asked Thorne, and Hester knew a moment's irritation at the earl's apparent difficulty in picturing her as a young woman. "At any rate," he continued in some haste, "I have never known her to be so amenable, and frankly, I would give a great deal for this state of affairs to continue. I am prepared, in fact, to give a great deal toward that end."

Hester stared at him blankly.

"Miss Blayne, my household has been at sixes and sevens ever since Chloe's entrance into my life. I have lived a bachelor existence for some years and am wholly unused to dealing with young females. Until Chloe came to me, I lived in lodgings in Jermyn Street, with only Williams, my valet, to attend me. My Aunt Lavinia served as chatelaine at the Park, and I saw her only infrequently. She was kind enough to move to London when I opened up the town house on Chloe's arrival, and she has done her best to be a mother to Chloe, but the fact is—Well, my aunt has no more idea of how to deal with Chloe than I do, with what results you have seen. She is an efficient housekeeper, but not a disciplinarian."

A small flicker of apprehension began to squirm inside Hester.

"I sympathize with your plight, my lord," she said firmly, "but I do not see what it has to do with me."

Thorne's mobile brows quirked and he drew a deep breath. "I can see that you have become precisely aware of what it has to do with you. Miss Blayne, I need your help. Chloe needs your help, and you have surmised correctly. I am asking you to move into my household as a companion to my ward. Now wait," he added hastily. He flung himself into the chair next to her and grasped both of her hands in his as she prepared to rise abruptly. "Please hear me out. I do not expect you to devote your life to her, nor would your stay be of long duration. I just need to keep her from flying from the house every time I suggest something for her own betterment. As soon as her betrothal to John Wery becomes official, I'm sure she will settle down, and—"

"Lord Bythorne," interrupted Hester, "I think you have taken leave of your senses. Even if I were willing to interrupt my own schedule, which I am not, the fact that I have managed to deflect Chloe from her starts on two occasions does not mean that I have the means—or the inclination— to bend her to your will."

"I told you, I have no desire to—bend Chloe to my will. Or, at least—well, yes, I do, but it is only for her own good. Tell me, Miss Blayne, you have remained single"—Hester stiffened ominously and Thorne hurried on—"through your own choice, I am sure, but do you have no regrets? Do you ever wish for a home and family?"

"I have a home, Lord Bythorne," replied Hester frigidly. "And as for family, Larkie is all I could ever want." She shifted uncomfortably, for she knew she was not being quite truthful. While she had no desire for a husband, she felt the lack of children in her life as a permanent, aching empty spot.

"But do you think Chloe is fit for the same course?" continued the earl. "While she seems almost rabidly fervent in her espousal of your cause, I sense that she has not your— strength of purpose. She has been sheltered all her life and once my protection is withdrawn, which it must inevitably be, she will fare ill as an unmarried female."

Hester nodded unwillingly. She had come to the same conclusion regarding Chloe. While she wanted no part of forcing the girl into an unwanted marriage, she could see no other viable course for her. Damn and blast a system that refused to educate women properly so that they could develop skills with which to support themselves!

"Be that as it may, my lord—"

"I am willing to pay generously for your services, of course. What I propose is that you come to live with us for three months or until Chloe accepts John Wery's offer of marriage—whichever comes first—in return for which I will pay you five hundred pounds."

"Five hundr . . ." Hester's voice trailed into an awed gasp. Good Lord, she could pay the mortgage off altogether with that kind of money. She could repair the roof, reglaze the windows, build a new potting shed, and still have handfuls left for a new stove and Larkie's new spectacles. But, of course, the whole idea was unthinkable.

"My lord, the whole idea is unthinkable," she said firmly. The earl did not, as she expected, simply bow and return to the parlor. He remained silent and seated, gazing at her expectantly. She continued haltingly, trying for the right words to convince him of the madness of his plan.

"What would your aunt think to have a stranger foisted

on her? No, two strangers, for I certainly would not go
without Larkie. In addition, I am in the middle of a project
that is of great importance to me. I realize you believe my
writings to be nothing more than the frivolous scribblings
of a demented spinster, but they mean a great deal to me.
Nothing less than survival, to put it bluntly. I am working
on a deadline, and I could not possibly leave my work for
that long. Also," she continued breathlessly, aware she was
beginning to babble, "I have a circle of friends with whom I
meet frequently. I would be loath to forgo their companionship for such a long period of time. Last but not least, what
in the world would your friends and family say if you were
to install a writer of inflammatory pamphlets into your
home?"

"I would not dream," said Thorne smoothly, "of asking
you to give up your writing while you are in my home. I believe my hospitality could stretch to a quiet room, a desk,
and paper and ink. You would certainly not be expected to
stick to Chloe like a plaster. My aunt and her maid accompany her on most of her jaunts. Thus, you would have plenty
of time to devote to your own pursuits. I take it your friends
live, for the most part, in London? I certainly have no objection to their visiting you in my home." Thorne breathed a
silent prayer that he would not be opening his doors to
squads of wild-eyed fanatics and unbathed intellectuals. "In
fact, I should think that a sojourn in the metropolis might be
enjoyable for you. Think of the lectures—the libraries—"

"Yes, yes, that is quite true," interposed Hester impatiently, "but you must see, my lord, that the whole scheme
is utterly insupportable."

"Why?"

"I just told you why," she snapped.

"But, I believe I addressed all your concerns—except for
those regarding my family and friends. Aunt Lavinia, I am
sure, will fall on your neck, sobbing with gratitude when
you show up to take responsibility for Chloe's behavior. As
for the rest of my family, I am not in the habit of consulting
them regarding my decisions."

"No, I don't suppose you are," muttered Hester. She rose

and put out a decisive hand. "I shall consider your proposal, my lord, but I must tell you, I am most disinclined to enter into it."

Thorne grasped her hands once more, drawing her back into her chair. His smile contained a blend of mischief and errant sweetness, and Hester drew in a sharp breath despite herself. "That is all I ask, Miss Blayne," he murmured. "I promise you, I shall see to it that a stay in my home for a mere three months will make not the slightest ripple in your life. I shall put no impediment in the way of your meeting your deadline, and I shall provide every comfort for you and your companion.

"I shall not press you any further, Miss Blayne. What I shall do is send my carriage to Rosemere Cottage in a week's time. If you have decided to accept my proposal, you have but to climb aboard and the outriders will take care of any luggage you wish to bring. If you would rather not avail yourself of my offer, simply send the carriage back empty. I shall importune you no further."

The earl's smile was benign as he bent over Hester's fingers, but lurking in the back of his eyes was a gleam so unsettling that Hester snatched her hand away and sprang to her feet.

"Thank you, my lord," she murmured, finding it difficult to talk past the knot that had formed in her throat. "I shall think over all you have said."

With this, she fairly bolted from the room to the safety of Larkie's presence, though why she should feel the need for sanctuary she could not have said.

Chapter Seven

Later, after the earl and his ward had departed with mutual expressions of goodwill, Hester divulged the earl's proposal to Larkie over yet another bracing cup of tea.

"I told him I'd think it over," she concluded, "but, of course, the thing is impossible."

She lifted her gaze to the older woman, waiting for confirmation of this conclusion. To her uneasy surprise, Larkie shook her head doubtfully.

"I don't see that, Hester," she said, stirring a spoonful of sugar into her tea. "That is, three months is not so terribly long, and—well, five hundred pounds . . ." She spoke the words softly, rolling them around on her tongue as though she could taste the wealth they represented. Giving herself a little shake, she continued prosaically, "You have no other obligations on your time right now except for the book. You have that lecture scheduled next month in Canterbury, but being in London would make the trip just that much shorter, I should—"

"Larkie, you know that when I am writing, my work takes all my attention."

"Not all, Hester. It sounds as though his lordship does not expect you to dance attendance on Miss Venable. I think he just wants you around for those occasions when he gets into a brangle with her."

"From what I can see, those occasions arise fairly frequently," said Hester dryly. "But you are right." She sighed. "Five hundred pounds is a great deal of money."

"Just think of the mortgage, my dear." Once more

Larkie's voice sank to an awestruck whisper. "We could get the roof repaired—or even a new one, and—"

"Yes, I know, and the windows, and a new stove, and your spectacles, and perhaps that new bed we talked about for you."

"Oh my." A beatific expression crossed the older woman's face. "I would not ask for anything for myself, of course, but the spectacles would be nice, and a new bed would be—oh my!"

"Considering that the lacings have given way twice in the last month, I would say it's a necessity. Very well, I'll think on it."

And she did. For the better part of three days and nights she could think of little else. It was soon borne on her that she would be insane not to accept the earl's proposal, unorthodox though it might be. To have all her financial difficulties solved in one swoop, to say nothing of the pleasure of living in elegant surroundings, and to have one's every wish catered to was a compelling prospect. A three-month sojourn in London would be enjoyable, as well. Lord Bythorne had spoken correctly when he surmised that many of her friends lived there. She was a member of several intellectual societies, and since she had moved to Overcross, her participation in their sponsored events had been rare.

Her thoughts flicked briefly to Trevor. He had been highly overset when she had declared her intention of removing herself from the urban scene, his long, sensitive face clouded and anxious. His affection for her had always been obvious. Hester admitted that her only feelings for Trevor Bentham, a lettered gentleman of independent means, were of friendship, but she did look forward to seeing him again.

Yes, all in all there could be little doubt that the earl's offer of employment was well timed and perfectly unexceptionable.

Then why did she feel such a deep sense of unease at the prospect of living in his home, even for a period of such short duration? There could surely be no hint of impropriety in the situation, with both Larkie and the earl's Aunt Lavinia on the scene.

No, she decided after some uncomfortable soul-searching. It was the oh-so-charming peer himself who caused such a feeling of unsettlement in her, although why this should be she was at a loss to explain. Notorious rake though he might be, he would scarcely be tempted to the seduction of her spinsterish person. And she certainly felt no attraction toward him. He was just the sort of male she most disliked—an arrogant, chauvinistic user of women. Who had, she thought in a muttered aside, displayed his true colors the day he had shown up on her doorstep, ranting at her as though she were a scullery maid. Not, she added with a sniff, that the most menial scullery maid was deserving of such treatment.

No, the earl's good looks, his charm, and his riveting air of maleness posed no threat to Miss Hester Blayne.

The matter decided to her satisfaction, she reported to Larkie on the morning of the fourth day of her deliberations that she had decided to accept Lord Bythorne's offer.

"That's wonderful, my dear," responded Miss Larkin. "Miss Venable will be ecstatic."

"Mm," said Hester. "I hope she will not be too disillusioned at the inevitable discovery that her idol is all too human. At any rate," she concluded, "his lordship's carriage will be here in a few days. I suppose we'd better begin packing."

"Oh dear," responded Miss Larkin. "We? I did not realize—that is, am I expected to go, as well?"

"But, of course, Larkie. I would not wish to stay in a strange house without you, nor would I expect you to stay on here all alone."

"Oh, my dear," said Miss Larkin a little breathlessly. "I would much prefer to stay here. I'm afraid I am a country mouse at heart and would feel sadly out of place in the city. I would not mind staying here alone, for I have much to keep me busy—and I would hate to leave now. Who would prepare the children for the pageant? And you know I am overseeing the jumble sale for the ladies of the church. And there's—"

"Oh, Larkie, I am so sorry. I did not mean to be so thoughtless. I'm afraid I just assumed—"

"Of course, if you really need me . . ." Miss Larkin's face crumpled in dismay.

"No, of course not. I would love to have you with me, but Lord Bythorne's aunt sounds like a very nice person, and she will certainly serve to lend countenance to my visit. Actually," Hester continued in a reassuring tone, "it would relieve my mind to have you occupying the cottage while I am gone. I did hate the idea of leaving it empty for so long."

She clasped the older woman's hands in her own. "Only promise me you will write often and tell me all the village doings."

"Of course, my dear." Miss Larkin reached to bestow a kiss on Hester's cheek. "And three months is not such a very long time."

When the earl's elegant traveling coach arrived a few days later, it contained, not to Hester's complete surprise, two passengers. The first person to alight was Chloe, who tumbled down the step the moment the door was opened without waiting for the assistance of the groom just clambering down from his perch. The earl stepped out next, climbing down in a more leisurely fashion.

Chloe hurled herself into Hester's arms and greeted Miss Larkin enthusiastically.

"I do apologize for this invasion," said Thorne smoothly, without a hint of regret in his tone. "I know I said I would merely send the carriage, but when I broached my plan to Chloe, she was absolutely ecstatic and insisted on traveling down here. She made the excellent point that we should present a united front, thus minimizing the chance of your refusal."

He bent another of those melting smiles on her, and to her intense irritation she felt a traitorous heat flood her cheeks.

"However," continued the earl, eyeing the small mound of luggage at his feet, "it appears we need not have worried."

Of course not, thought Hester rancorously. There had not been the slightest doubt in the earl's mind, she realized, that she would leap at his largesse, mouth open and ready for the hook.

"Oh, Hester!" cried Chloe. "Are you really going to come live with us?"

"No," replied Hester quickly. "I do appreciate your warm welcome, my dear, but this is to be a temporary visit only."

"Oh, yes, of course. That is what I meant," said Chloe ingenuously.

"Well," said the earl, rubbing his hands briskly, "if you are ready, ladies, shall we be on our way?"

After personally directing the placement of Hester's meager belongings into the roomy storage compartments of the carriage, he handed her into the vehicle. Chloe clambered in beside her and, with a few tears from Miss Larkin and some cautionary instructions regarding Hester's well-being in the city, the vehicle rattled off to London.

Bythorne House was situated in Curzon Street. It was one of several town houses that lined that spacious thoroughfare, distinguished from the others by its size and its air of genteel elegance. It was set back from the street and hidden from the view of common passersby by a stone wall, and admittance was gained through two gates set at either end of the property. The circular drive thus provided for the convenience of guests was already open when the earl's carriage approached, and after craning his neck for a moment, the earl uttered a groan.

"Oh, my God, what the devil is *she* doing here?"

Following his gaze, Hester beheld an elegant barouche standing under the portico in front of the house. The carriage bore a crest, and its occupant had apparently already disembarked and been admitted to the house, for the coachman had taken his place on the driving seat preparatory to moving the vehicle to the stables.

Hester glanced questioningly at Thorne.

"It's Gussie—that is, my Aunt Augusta, Lady Bracken. She lives in Hampshire. Not that one would know it," he added bitterly, "for she's forever descending on me, usually to avert what she perceives as some family crisis or other. Good God!" he exclaimed, suddenly arrested. "I wonder if—" He paused abruptly before heaving a deep sigh. "Well, there's no help for it. We'd better go in."

Not unnaturally, this statement produced in Hester's breast a certain feeling of uneasiness, but, following the earl's lead, she descended from the carriage with what dignity she could muster. The front door swung open wide and an austere figure in butler's livery descended the front steps.

"'Afternoon, Hobart," said Thorne. "I see my aunt has dropped from the skies once more. Is she inside?"

"Yes, my lord," replied the butler with a nice blend of deference and sympathetic understanding. "Her ladyship arrived some fifteen minutes ago and she is at present taking tea in the gold saloon with Lady Lavinia."

After acquainting Hester with Hobart, who bustled inside to apprise the housekeeper of the arrival of the master of the house and his guest, Thorne led Hester into the house with an air of preoccupation. Crossing the polished marquetry floor of the entrance hall, from which a lofty staircase rose gracefully to the first floor, he opened the door to an adjoining chamber.

Two women were seated on a settee before the fireplace. One appeared to be of some fifty years of age, of medium height with gray hair arranged becomingly about pleasant features. The other was some years younger. Tall and thin and dressed in the first stare of fashion, she rose at the entrance of the earl and his guests. Her penciled brows rose disdainfully as she moved toward the earl.

Thorne bent to bestow a kiss on the older women before grasping the hand extended to him by the younger. "Gussie," he said heartily, "what the devil brings you to Town at this time of year? I thought you had decided to forgo the Season this year."

"Good afternoon, Bythorne," replied the woman, smiling

faintly. "What I said was that I do not plan to participate extensively, but since Bracken is here for Parliament, I decided I might as well join him. I shall attend a few functions while I am here."

"I'm sure you will," murmured Thorne. "Well, you are just in time to help me welcome my guest." He turned to the older woman. "Aunt, may I present Miss Hester Blayne? Miss Blayne, my aunt, Lady Lavinia St. John. And this is another aunt—Augusta, Lady Bracken. We are only a few years apart in age, thus we do not stand on ceremony."

Lady Bracken nodded regally, but did not move forward.

"How do you do," she said, her expression indicating that she had just bit into something sour. "Lavinia told me of your imminent arrival. Welcome to Bythorne House."

A more unwelcoming visage she never hoped to behold, thought Hester, dropping a small curtsy.

"I have rung for Mrs. Murray," said Lady Lavinia, producing a smile that eased Hester's apprehension only minimally. "I know you will—ah, here she is." She gestured toward a woman who had just entered the room, dressed in the conservative garb of an upper servant.

"Very good," intoned Lady Bracken. "I am sure you will wish to retire to your rooms to refresh yourself from your journey. Chloe," she said in minatory tones to her nephew's ward, "I know you will wish to go upstairs as well."

Dismissal was plain in her voice, and Chloe pouted ominously. Hester stepped forward.

"Yes, do please come up with me," she said. "I always feel so—unsettled in a strange house."

Her lips pressed tightly together, Chloe turned and followed the housekeeper into the hall. Thorne accompanied them.

"Perhaps," said Hester with the merest tremor in her voice, "it would have been better if on this occasion you had consulted your relatives as to your plans."

"Yes," said Chloe shrilly, "there was no need for Aunt Augusta to be so hateful."

"Nonsense," replied Thorne. He turned to address Hester. "Aunt Lavinia expressed herself to me before I left for Overcross that she was delighted that you were coming. As for Gussie . . ." He drew a deep breath. "Well, Gussie is always against any plan in which she has not first been consulted. Just leave her to me. I shall send her on her way with a flea in her ear and the next time you see her, I promise she will be all cordiality." He smiled warmly. "Do come downstairs again when you are ready, for we have much to discuss."

Once again, Thorne felt that the smile on which he had relied for all of his adult life to melt the steeliest of female hearts, was in need of an overhaul. Miss Blayne said nothing, merely staring inscrutably at him for some moments before nodding shortly. Whirling about, she moved up the stairs after Chloe and Mrs. Murray, her back stiff as a steeple.

Thorne turned angrily to rejoin his aunts, recriminations boiling on his lips. Gussie, however, was experienced in dealing with her nephew, with whom she had brangled more as a sister during their growing-up years, and she was already taking the offensive.

"Bythorne, how could you?" she cried in accusing accents as soon as he entered the room. "I could not believe my eyes when I read Lavinia's letter to me telling of your plans to introduce a notorious firebrand into the house."

"Really, Thorne," said Lady Lavinia apologetically, "I had no idea Augusta would fly up into the boughs over this. I merely mentioned—"

"But how could I not be overset by such news?" queried her ladyship in high indignation. "What in the world possessed you to invite her here? What will people say when they discover that one of the most scandalous females in the country has taken up residence in Bythorne House?"

Thorne suppressed a surge of irritation. "Gussie, Miss Blayne can hardly be considered either notorious or scandalous. She has gathered some attention to herself, to be sure, with her writings, but that is hardly cause to brand her as a scarlet woman. Besides, I need her help in controlling Chloe," he concluded simply.

"Well!" said Lady Bracken with an affronted gasp. "If you were having such difficulty in controlling Chloe, I would have been glad to have her at Summerlea."

Thorne smiled mirthlessly. "You know very well that you and Chloe do not deal well together. Do you recall the incident at Lady Pantron's ball?"

Lady Bracken shuddered. "Still, Bythorne," she returned sharply, "to invite a person of the lower orders into your home as an honored guest is bound to give rise to the most—"

"She may be possessed of some rather odd ideas," interrupted Thorne, "but I wish you would stop speaking of her as though she were some drab I hauled in off the streets. She is of perfectly respectable birth, you know."

Lady Bracken shot a glance at Lady Lavinia. "You did not tell me this."

"Yes," continued Thorne. "She is from Shropshire, I believe."

"Really?" This time Lady Bracken's brows rose nearly into her hairline. "The Shropshire Blaynes? Theirs is one of the oldest and most respected titles in the country. Are you sure about this?"

Thorne shrugged. "Her brother is Sir Barnaby Blayne."

"Mmm," said Lady Bracken thoughtfully. "To be sure, he is only a baronet, but still . . . Well, I wonder that Sir Barnaby allows his sister to make a public spectacle of herself."

"I gather he has little to say about it," replied Thorne dryly.

"But he is head of the family."

"Miss Blayne seems to care little for that. She is financially independent of her brother and she is most definitely of age. She can cry her ridiculous theories from the top of St. Paul's, if she so desires."

"How perfectly disgusting," said Lady Bracken with a sniff. "Well, be that as it may, she is an unattached female and you know what the rumor mills will do with that situation."

"Oh, for God's sake, Gussie. Did you look at her? The

woman is practically an ape-leader. She wears caps! And she dresses in gowns an impecunious governess would scorn." He declined to mention that it was his impression that the slender body concealed beneath those very plain gowns might prove well worth investigating. "I hardly think the *ton* is going to leap to any untoward conclusions about her presence in my home. In addition, with Aunt Lavinia in the house any talk of seduction and/or rapine— at least on my part—is simply ludicrous."

"I suppose that is true," said Lady Bracken grudgingly, "but, have you thought of the effect on Chloe of having a person in the house with such dangerous ideas as Miss Blayne?"

Thorne laughed. "I would hardly qualify her ideas as dangerous, Gussie. All this talk of female rights is merely that—talk. If it amuses Miss Blayne to spend her time on such a futile pastime, I see no real harm in it. I have given her permission to invite her friends here, but I hardly think the maunderings of a parcel of wooly-witted intellectuals is a threat to the fabric of society."

"But, Thorne dear," interposed Lady Lavinia with a glance at her niece, "Miss Blayne's writings have attracted quite a large audience—not just in London but throughout the country, one hears."

"Mmp," came a grunt from Thorne. "The bearded lady at Bartholomew Fair draws in the multitudes, as well, but I would hardly consider her a force for social upheaval."

Lady Bracken cleared her throat delicately. "But what will Barbara think?"

"Barbara?" Thorne echoed in a carefully toneless voice. "I should imagine Lady Barbara will wonder at the situation, just as you have, but she's an open-minded sort, and— What has her opinion to say to anything?"

"Why, her opinion must be of great consideration to you. After all, you and she—"

"Gussie," Thorne said softly. "We will leave my relationship with Lady Barbara out of this. Now, listen to me, please. Miss Blayne is a guest in my house, and if you insist on inserting yourself into this situation, I really must insist that you treat her with all the courtesy you would any other well-bred young woman."

"Well," said Lady Bracken. She glanced at her nephew from under her rather sparse lashes. "At least you agree, I hope, something will have to be done about her appearance. She dresses like a tinker's daughter. Not that we wish to have her gowned in high fashion, but . . . A simple wardrobe, I think, but one of quality."

Thorne waved a hand dismissively. "I shall be happy to leave that in your hands, Gussie, although you may get an argument from her on the subject."

Which proved to be the case when Hester descended from her chamber some minutes later. Thorne had hoped Gussie would have departed the premises before Hester made her appearance, but his aunt had remained, chatting determinedly.

"Why, there you are, Miss Blayne," murmured Lady Bracken.

Hester's heart sank. She, too, had hoped that she would not have to face the intimidating Lady Bracken again that day. Noting, however, the disdainful gaze that swept over the gray muslin round gown into which she had changed, she lifted her chin and advanced into the room.

After that first brief encounter with her ladyship, Hester's impulse had been to sweep out of the house, never to return. How dare Lord Bythorne let his aunt speak to her in that fashion, as though she were a scullery maid come to apply for a position! If either his lordship or his insufferable relative thought she was prepared to be treated in such a fashion, they were both very much mistaken. She had come here, after all, out of the goodness of her heart, and to be so insulted—well, it was not to be brooked.

After several more minutes of this sort of reflection, pacing the thick carpet of her bedchamber in affronted indignation, Hester's anger finally wore itself out to the point where she was able to take in her surroundings. Her accommodations consisted of a sitting room and a bedchamber, each furnished with an elegance that suggested it was one of the premier guest suites in the house. Her attention was caught by a writing desk set before the window. It was a little larger than one might expect in such a room. It looked as though it belonged in a man's study, in fact. Gracious, had the earl moved it here especially for her? Opening the drawers, she discovered paper and an ample supply of pens, pen knives, wipers, blotting paper, and several bottles of ink.

Somewhat mollified, she moved into the bedchamber and bounced experimentally on the bed. A soft scratch sounded at the door and she leaped hurriedly to her feet. A young chamber maid slipped into the room, carrying a pitcher of water.

"Good afternoon, miss," she said softly. "I am called Parker and I am to be your maid while you are here. If that is all right with you," she added hastily, a shy smile curving her lips.

At Hester's smile of acquiescence, Parker moved to the luggage, brought up earlier, and consisting of a single bandbox and a smallish portmanteau. If the girl thought it odd that a guest of the house should arrive with no more clothing than would outfit the poorest serving maid residing in the house, she made no sign. After pouring the water into an exquisite porcelain basin, she busied herself putting away the several gowns that Hester had brought with her. They hung rather forlornly in the splendid wardrobe that occupied nearly one whole wall of the bedchamber. Underclothing, shawls, and other accessories were likewise whisked into the capacious drawers of a nearby commode and Hester's brushes and combs were laid out on a dainty rosewood dressing table.

After being assured by Hester that she required no further service of the maid, Parker left the room with a graceful curtsy, leaving Hester to her own devices. Realizing that she could not hide up here for the rest of the day, she resolutely scrubbed her face and combed her hair into the severest knot she could manage. Affixing to it the plainest cap in her possession, she drew a deep breath and left the room to make her way downstairs. Now, facing Lord Bythorne and his ladies once more, Hester was surprised to note that Lady Bracken wore an expression of wary affability.

"Do join us, my dear," said Lady Lavinia. "I have had fresh tea brought in. And try some of these lady fingers. They are one of Cook's specialties."

After a moment's hesitation, Hester entered the room and seated herself in the chair indicated by Lady Lavinia.

"I understand," said Lady Bracken, opening negotiations, "that you are of the Shropshire Blaynes. Your father was Sir Reginald?"

"Yes, my lady," replied Hester, accepting a cup of tea from her. "Although he passed away several years ago, and my brother Barnaby now holds the title."

"Do you have a sister named Mary?"

"Why, yes. She is a few years older than I."

"I thought so. I went to school with her." Lady Bracken nodded her head as though this fact conveyed an obscure significance. Hester smiled politely.

"Well," continued Lady Bracken, "what are your plans for your sojourn in London?"

Hester stiffened. Good heavens, the woman's manner suggested that she was hatching some sort of monstrous scheme against Lord Bythorne and/or his family. Her hands clenched in her lap.

"Why, I thought I might begin by inviting the Society for the Overthrow of the Monarchy to hold their meetings here."

Thorne uttered a bark of laughter, and now it was Lady Bracken's turn to bridle.

"No need to fly up into the boughs, Miss Blayne. I was merely—"

Hester relented. After all, Lady Bracken could be forgiven for viewing with suspicion the entry of a notorious radical into her nephew's home. She smiled.

"Do forgive my wretched tongue, my lady. Truly, my only purpose in being here is to act as a sort of companion to Chloe. She and I seem to hit it off rather well, and Lord Bythorne thought—"

"Lord Bythorne thought," interrupted Thorne, "that Miss Blayne must have been sent to him by the gods."

Lady Bracken said nothing, but subjected Hester once more to a swift but minute scrutiny. After a moment, the older woman relaxed slightly and drew a deep breath.

"Well, it appears I cannot argue with a fait accompli, but"—she fixed her nephew with a meaningful stare—"what in the world are we to tell people?"

Chapter Eight

"Tell them about what?" asked Thorne blankly.

"Good God, Bythorne," retorted his aunt in some irritation. "You cannot import a strange female into your home without explanation. Even," she added hastily, "a female of impeccable breeding and even with the most excruciatingly proper chaperonage."

"Oh, for God's sake!" Thorne expostulated.

"Your aunt is right, my lord," Hester said softly, and two pairs of dark eyes swung to her in surprise.

"If your purpose in bringing me into your home is to see your ward settled properly, you must see that it is essential that there be nothing untoward in my presence here. I should have thought of this difficulty myself."

Thorne snapped his fingers. "We told the Wendovers that you are a distant cousin. Could we not continue that pretense?"

"Don't be absurd, Bythorne," interposed his aunt. "Everyone in the *ton* is quite conversant with your family background. They will recognize such a hoax instantly."

"Actually . . ." They whirled at the sound of the soft voice. Lady Lavinia, who had not spoken since Hester had entered the room cleared her throat. "Actually, I believe we are related to Miss Blayne in truth."

"What?" Lady Bracken's cup rattled in her long fingers. "That's impossible," she snapped.

"No, no, my dear. Do but think," replied the older woman. "When I was a child, I used to play with a little girl named Matilda Renfrew. I was told she was my third cousin. Later, I heard that she had married a Matthew Byrd.

Their son married Squire Mayfield's daughter, and the squire's wife, I am quite sure, was the daughter of a man named Christopher Blayne."

"Why, he is my second cousin," blurted Hester.

"There, you see?" Aunt Lavinia swung about to face Gussie and Thorne in pleased affirmation, wispy gray curls floating about her face.

"I'm not sure that has anything to say to the problem," said Lady Bracken. "Half the polite world is related to the other half in just such a fashion."

Thorne grinned. "All we have to do is spread it about that there is a relationship, albeit a distant one. That should be enough to satisfy the gabble-mongers. If anyone is ill-bred enough to ask for specifics, we shall merely stare down our noses at them."

"Indeed," said Lady Bracken acidly. "That might serve, but it will make even worse the fact that you have intro-duced a notorious feminist into your house. To think that I am actually related to Hester Blayne!"

Hester gasped. Was there no end to the effrontery of this impossible woman? At the sound, Lady Bracken turned to her.

"I do not mean to give offense, and I am sure you cannot take any for you must see how impossible a situation this is for someone in my position."

Thorne was surprised at the spurt of irritation that surged through him. "Now, now, Gussie," he said in a deceptively mild tone. "Everyone has a dirty dish or two among his rel-atives, and I'm sure no one will blame us for numbering a female among ours that actually uses her brain to think for herself and who is willing to suffer deprivation and isola-tion from her family to support something in which she be-lieves passionately."

Hester glanced at him curiously and Lady Bracken blinked. "Er, no, I suppose not. Only"—she lifted her hand in an earnest gesture to Hester—"perhaps you could go under another name while you are here. Your mother's maiden name, for example. I should think—"

"No!" said Hester explosively. "I am sorry, my lady, but

I will not hide my identity. If my presence here is an embarrassment to your highborn friends, I will be more than pleased to leave."

She rose and moved to the door, only to be intercepted by Lord Bythorne, who had risen with her. He took one of her hands to clasp it in both of his and turned to his aunt.

"I believe you owe Miss Blayne an apology, Gussie," he said sharply.

Through narrowed eyes, Lady Bracken gazed at Hester. "As I said, Miss Blayne, I meant no offense." She sighed deeply. "Well, I suppose there is no help for it, then. We shall just have to muddle through as best we can."

As an apology, Hester felt this little speech left much to be desired, but she was already regretting her own melodramatic statement. She remained silent, but inclined her head briefly. Releasing her hand from the warmth of the earl's grasp, she returned to her chair.

"Well, then," continued Lady Bracken briskly. "On to the next problem." She turned to Hester. "We shall have to do something about your clothes. Now, do not take offense—again," she added as Hester's eyes narrowed. "I am only saying that a wardrobe that might be just right for the hinterlands will not—"

"Overcross is twenty miles from London," interrupted Hester icily. "It can hardly be called the hinterlands."

Lady Bracken waved an impatient hand. "Well, it might as well be. What I am trying to convey is that if you are going to mingle in society, you will need to dress the part."

Hester drew a deep breath, and Thorne could have sworn he saw icicles forming on her lips. "Lady Bracken, I have no desire to do so much as take a cup of tea with your exalted friends. My purpose in being here is to facilitate Lord Bythrone's dealings with his ward. I believe that can be accomplished with a minimum of mingling."

"Oh, but it cannot!" exclaimed Lady Bracken, ignoring her nephew's smothered chuckle. "If you are a guest in the house, you will certainly be expected to partake in Bythorne's social activities. There is the Wery dinner party next week, for example."

"But, I have not been invited to the Werys'," said Hester, endeavoring to maintain her fragile grip on her patience, "and I certainly have no desire to—"

"Ah, Miss Blayne," put in Thorne, laughter still apparent in his voice, "I must beg to interfere. If there is any occasion on which I shall require your presence, it is the Wery dinner party. Just because Chloe has agreed to attend, does not mean she will comport herself with any degree of amenability while she is there."

Hester shivered with rage and humiliation. How dare Lord Bythorne laugh at her! If he thought—

"Please," said the earl in a vastly different tone after regarding her fixedly for some moments. "I realize we must seem like the veriest fribbles to you, and I'm sure you realize that Gussie is not suggesting there is anything lacking in your dress." He glanced sharply at his aunt. "It is merely that we inhabit a different world—and I agree, it's a superficial one. However, for a few months you will be a part of that world. I would not wish to subject you to the censure of its inhabitants, as frivolous and false as they may seem. I shall," he concluded, "of course be prepared to stand the ready for any, er, refurbishment deemed necessary for your wardrobe."

Hester exhaled the breath she had been about to expel in a burst of vituperation. She prided herself on being an eminently fair person and in the earl's words she discerned what appeared a sincere effort to be kind, as well as a measure of truth. She was forced to admit that the gown she was wearing, while perfectly adequate for a shopping trip to the village or tea at the vicarage, was sadly out of place in the drawing room of Bythorne House.

She was a plain woman. In fact, she had been known to speak at some length on the folly of the current preoccupation with fashion. On the other hand, something deep and feminine within her warmed at the thought of dressing, for just a little while, in gowns she knew to be becoming to her. Something quietly elegant in colors that suited her. Would my lord Bythorne view her in a new light? Not that she cared, of course. On still another hand, while she had talked herself into accepting Lord Bythorne's munificence in return for a few months of her time, she was damned if she'd be beholden to him for the clothes on her back.

With great dignity she turned to Lady Bracken. "I am willing to accept your rationale, my lady. I shall obtain more suitable clothing. However"—she swiveled to stare levelly at the earl—"I shall provide my own wardrobe. You are paying me handsomely, my lord, and I shall purchase anything I need from the stipend we agreed upon."

"Ah," said Thorne, completely at a loss. Transforming the determinedly grim specimen of spinsterhood before him into anything resembling fashionable correctness would cost far more than five hundred pounds. Never in his wide acquaintanceship with the female sex had one of them ever turned down the sort of gift he had just proposed. "But—" he began, only to be forestalled by a gesture from his aunt, accompanied by a stare of such significance that he was made aware that she had the situation well in hand.

He bowed to Hester in an exaggerated gesture of acquiescence.

Arrangements were made for her ladyship to accompany Hester on the morrow to various select modistes. Chloe descended from her room to join the party at that point, and the conversation then turned to more general matters. By the time Lady Bracken rose to leave, she and Hester found themselves in reasonable harmony with each other.

After her departure, Chloe, professing anew her delight at Hester's presence, declared her intention of showing her about the house. As they left the drawing room, Thorne placed his hand under Hester's elbow and drew her aside.

"I want to express my own appreciation that you have come to us," he murmured.

A little flustered by this unexpected closeness, Hester mumbled a vague reply.

"And now, I must take my leave of you. I shall probably not see you for the rest of the day, for I am going to my club, where I shall take dinner. Before leaving, however, I wish to ascertain that you have everything you need for your comfort here."

"Oh, yes, my lord," replied Hester with as much calm as she could muster.

"And while I think of it," continued the earl, "my friends call me Thorne."

"But—"

"And since we are related, I do think it would be more appropriate if you would call me that, too. And I shall call you Hester."

"I don't think—"

"Very well." He bent his intimate smile upon her. "Now that we have that settled, I shall bid you good afternoon." He lifted her hand and brushed her fingertips with his lips. They were warm and surprisingly soft and the contact was as brief as the shuttering of an eyelash, but Hester started as though he had bitten her.

Irritated by this untoward reaction, she bowed stiffly. "Good day, my lord. Enjoy your evening."

Which will no doubt be spent, she concluded silently, in a hell, finishing up discreetly in someone's candlelit boudoir. She sniffed. How fortunate that she did not care one way or another how the profligate lord spent his nights.

Several evenings later, Hester stood before her mirror viewing herself with pardonable satisfaction. After what seemed like months of endless shopping expeditions with Lady Bracken and Lady Lavinia she now possessed a wardrobe of ensembles that were acceptable, if not precisely *le dernier cri* of fashion.

Tonight, in honor of her first appearance among the denizens of the *beau monde* at the Werys' dinner party, she had donned one of her new gowns, an apricot silk trimmed with gold floss, worn with an overdress of cream-colored net. In Madame Celeste's modish establishment, Hester had been sure the gown would be much too dear for her purse, but was pleasantly surprised at its reasonable price. The other gowns brought out by Madame, after an exchange of glances with Lady Bracken, proved also to be well within her budget.

She examined her image in the mirror. The ensemble

was one of the most becoming creations she had ever owned, she admitted to herself as she twisted experimentally and watched the heavy folds swirl over her trim figure. Parker had swept up her hair in a skillful arrangement, and Hester had placed over it a frothy lace cap with silk ribbons tied jauntily under one ear. The maid had objected violently to this addition, but Hester remained firm.

"I wish to establish my position firmly, Parker. I shouldn't want anyone to think I have come to London on a husband hunt."

"I'm sure nobody would think any such thing, miss, but you're far too young for caps. And," she added as an afterthought, for she and Hester had rapidly established a friendly rapport, "if you was to attract a husband, would that be such a bad thing?"

"No, I suppose not," replied Hester with a laugh, "if I were in the market for one—which I am not."

Giving one last twitch to the offending cap, she thanked Parker once more for her efforts and descended to the drawing room.

There was only one occupant in the room when she entered. Lord Bythorne stood before the hearth, one arm flung negligently along the mantelpiece. His evening dress consisted of the conventional dark coat, embroidered waistcoat, and light-colored satin breeches, but he exuded an aura of predatory maleness to which some women, no doubt, would be helplessly attracted.

"Good evening, Hester," he said.

"Good evening, my lord," she replied with a meaningful emphasis on the latter.

"Oh, but I thought we agreed on Hester and Thorne." What Hester had begun to think of as The Smile curved his lips, further reinforcing his prowling creature-of-the-jungle aspect.

By God, he had been right, thought Thorne. Properly dressed, the Blayne female was quite attractive. No, more than that. In the silky outfit that perfectly delineated her every curve, she was downright delectable. Except for that ridiculous cap, of course. Did she think it provided some sort of barrier between her and wicked, unattached males of evil intent? He wondered what else lay beneath the revealing folds of her garment. A banked passion, perhaps, just waiting for the right touch to unleash it? He sighed. Unfortunately, it would not be his touch that would set her problematic appetites free. Dalliance with a gently bred female living under his own roof formed no part of his plans. One had one's standards, after all.

"It was you who agreed, my lord." The gently bred female's voice was pure flint. "We are far from being on a first-name basis."

Thorne merely smiled lazily. "You will find, Hester my dear, that I am a rather tenacious sort. If you—"

"Hester!" The word came in a pleased tone from Aunt Lavinia, who had just entered the room. "You look simply splendid, my dear. Come, let me look at you."

Smiling, Hester pirouetted before the older woman. "Thank you, Aunt Lavinia. I am feeling rather splendid, and I owe it all to your good taste."

Thorne's brows rose. Evidently, he reflected, his aunt had experienced no difficulty in proceeding to a first-name stage with his guest. Indeed, the two ladies seemed to have become fast friends in the short time Hester had been in residence at Bythorne House. He was pleased, for he had felt a bit guilty about hauling Aunt Lavinia into town from the Park. The estate had been her domain for a long time, and he was sure she missed it. A companionable female in the house would make her sojourn here much more pleasurable.

Chloe entered the drawing room just then, gowned in white satin under an overdress of her favorite pink. A wreath of rosebuds twined in her dark curls and a delicate flush tinted her cheeks. If John Wery indeed spent all his time with her in talking of crops and sheep, reflected Thorne, the youngster must in truth be the veriest blockhead. Perhaps he should have a word with the lad on how to win the female heart.

"I was going to wear my pearls," Chloe was saying to Hester, "but Pinkham said, 'Youth is its own ornament.'

She always says that. Personally, I think youth can stand a bit of help. What do you think, Hester? Aunt Lavinia?"

Both ladies laughed.

"I think Pinkham is right," replied Hester. "You look like the first blush of spring."

"Perfect," agreed Aunt Lavinia.

"Thank you. Oh, but, Hester, you look marvelous!" cried Chloe. "Who would have thought Aunt Augusta would have such an instinct for what looks good on one. That gown makes you look years—" She halted, clapping gloved fingers to her lips.

Hester burst into laughter. "Never mind, Chloe dearest. In my dotage as I am, I appreciate the compliment."

"I only meant," said Chloe, still much flustered, "that you look beautiful. Doesn't she, Uncle Thorne?" She cast him a glance of frantic appeal.

"Indeed," said Thorne gravely, "you and Chloe will be the loveliest young women present this evening."

Hester was not deceived, and from the glint of something wicked that flashed in the earl's eyes, she was sure that his compliment was double-edged.

Her suspicion was confirmed very soon after arriving at the house leased by the Werys in Grosvenor Street. When they entered the spacious drawing room, it became obvious that there was not another female in the room under fifty years of age. Lady Wery, a short, voluble matron whose plump figure was sadly unsuited for the current fashion of high waists and puffed sleeves, was all affability as she greeted the guests at the head of the first-floor stairs.

"Lord Bythorne, we are so pleased to see you—and Lady Lavinia, too. And, of course, dear Lady Bracken. How nice that you could join us." She paused and added archly, "I'm sorry Lady Barbara had other plans for the evening. It would have been quite a family party then, would it not?"

Hester pricked up her ears. Lady Barbara? No one had mentioned a Lady Barbara. Was she a relative? Judging from Lady Wery's tone, Hester rather thought not. A prospective relative, perhaps? Was Lord Bythorne, the confirmed rake, about to tumble into parson's mousetrap? The idea seemed somehow startling, but even the staunchest of bachelors must succumb to tradition, she supposed, particularly if he were a peer with the succession of his line to consider.

Behind Lady Wery, her husband, Sir George, stood beaming complacently, equally corpulent and equally pleased to welcome Lord Bythorne and his ladies into his home.

Lady Wery's greeting to Hester was courteous, if a little puzzled, and she introduced the younger woman to those in the immediate vicinity. One of these, a Mrs. Fenton, expressed her pleasure at meeting a cousin of Lord Bythorne, no matter how distant, but maintained an inquiring frown.

"Have we met, Miss Blayne? I do not recall seeing you before, but your name is familiar."

To Hester's astonishment, Augusta swept forward. "Why, Horatia, of course you recognize the name. This is the well-known feminist, Hester Blayne. Perhaps you have read some of her writings. Or attended one of her lectures. She is much in demand, you know. Bracken and I virtually begged her to stay with us while she is in London, but our house is quite small, and Hester wishes to entertain some of her friends while she is here. Lord Ormesby is coming to dine next week at Bythorne House. I wonder if you heard of his speech in Parliament last week in support of funds for the education of girls of the under class."

Mrs. Fenton's mouth fell open, but making a rapid recovery, she stammered, "Oh. Y-yes, of course. Such an honor to meet you, Miss Blayne."

Hester, who felt her own jaw dropping, managed to pin a vapid smile to her lips. "Of course," she murmured, glancing at Augusta. She surprised a sardonic grin, which was quickly erased by an expression of serene condescension.

At the end of the evening, as the Bythorne party rode home through dimly lit streets, Hester considered that she had brushed through her ordeal tolerably well. She had been treated courteously, though all through dinner she had been subjected to surreptitious glances full of suspicion and puzzled curiosity. One or two of the Werys' guests had ventured to seek her out for interested if ill-informed chats on the state of women in the realm, but she had suppressed the urge to climb on her soapbox. She replied to all questions with a cool courtesy that deflected any of the more personal questions she could see fairly burning on the lips of some of the ladies.

Chloe had been on her best behavior. She sat next to John Wery during dinner. Mr. Wery, a slender, inoffensive young man with brown hair and rather speaking brown eyes, had been attentive, and as the meal progressed, the two young people, to Hester's amusement, seemed to be enjoying each other's company. Chloe did most of the talking and Hester noted that some of her conversation seemed to be providing her would-be betrothed with much food for thought. Several times her remarks caused a startled expression to cross his face and it was some moments before he replied. By the end of the evening, the young man had fallen rather silent and his expression when he gazed at Chloe was thoughtful.

Of Lord Bythorne, she had seen little during the course of the evening, but once or twice she had looked up to find him watching her from across the room. At other times, she felt his gaze on her as surely as though he had come up to place a hand on her arm. Always, she seemed possessed of an instinctive knowledge of his precise whereabouts, whether he lounged near a doorway in conversation or sat at a table, playing cards. She found this fact irritating and wished she could dispel the feeling that she was somehow connected to the earl by an unseen, undefined bond.

Now, she glanced surreptitiously at him. His face, lit sporadically by the flambeaux that stood at nearly every doorway, seemed extraordinarily saturnine. Though he did not return her gaze, she felt that he was aware of her scrutiny, and she looked away quickly.

What was she thinking, wondered Thorne, behind those perspicacious brown eyes. He almost smiled. Certainly, Hester Blayne was an original. He had encountered her particular breed often, of course, the female gadflies who considered it their mission in life to redress all the wrongs of the world. He had found them all tedious in the extreme with their strident demands and unreasonable expectations. Hester, however, was altogether another species of the genus. She stated her beliefs calmly and rationally and proceeded to shred any opposing arguments with logic and—oddly—courtesy. Hester had argued like a man, he thought with some amusement, though he did not think she would thank him for the comparison.

Having dropped Lady Bracken off at her London residence, the carriage proceeded to Curzon Street, and when the rest of the party disembarked, Chloe and Lady Lavinia yawned and proclaimed themselves ready for their beds. Once in the house, Hester prepared to follow them upstairs but was stayed by the earl.

He clasped her hands in his and brought them to his lips. "Thank you," he said simply.

She raised startled eyes to his. "Whatever for, my lord?"

"For making this evening a pleasant experience rather than an ordeal by fire. Chloe was a different person tonight."

Hester laughed and tried unobtrusively to free her hands. The earl merely tightened his grip. "She actually talked to young John," he continued. "I think that's the first time they have ever had a real conversation. I don't know what magic you worked, but I beg you to continue weaving your spell."

"Nonsense, my lord," Hester found she was having a little difficulty with her breathing. "I merely convinced Chloe that it is in her own self-interest to start behaving like an adult. And now, if you will excuse me—it's getting late, and . . ."

She made an effort to turn away toward the stairs once more, but the earl was not through.

"Hester, if we are to stand before the world as cousins, I really think it behooves you to call me Thorne, or people will think it decidedly odd."

"I do not think—"

He smiled slowly. "I told you I am the tenacious sort. Believe me, it will be much easier simply to give in to this small request."

"But—" She expelled an exasperated breath. "Oh, all right—Thorne. Now, may I go?"

"But, I would never keep a lady against her will."

Bending, he pressed his lips against Hester's gloved fingers before releasing them. Hester uttered a strangled, "Good night, my—Thorne," and whirling, raced up the stairs like a guilty schoolgirl.

Chapter Nine

In her room, Hester found Chloe awaiting her, seated in a satin-striped chair near the fire, her feet tucked under her. The girl pulled some of the ribbons from her hair and ran her fingers through it, allowing it to fall about her face.

"I had an awfully good time tonight," she said ingenuously. "Did you?"

"Well, it was instructive," replied Hester, the corners of her mouth lifting.

"You were wonderful," breathed Chloe. "Oh, Hester, I did just what you suggested—with Mr. Wery—and it worked marvelously well. The minute he started talking about his estate, I started talking about your book—the *Apologia*. My tongue absolutely ran on wheels!"

"I noticed his somewhat dazed expression during dinner."

Chloe's laughter gurgled in her throat. "Oh, my, yes. He looked at me as though I had suddenly sprouted another head."

"Did he dispute your theories?"

"Well, actually, no. I think he was too astonished to actually think about what I was saying. Though, now I reflect on it, he did ask some fairly intelligent questions."

Hester grinned. "You surprise me."

"Yes. He reminded me that many men do not yet have the vote in this country. He wondered if we shouldn't see about suffrage for the average working man before we worry about women. I was rather impressed, to tell you the truth, for I didn't think he was so well informed."

"Really?" murmured Hester.

"Indeed. And then he went on to tell me of the efforts he has made for the betterment of the workers on his estate. I had no idea he concerned himself with such things. Hester, he has set up schools for the children—girls as well as boys!"

"Well, that is something. Perhaps Mr. Wery would not be such a bad bargain as a husband, after all." Hester directed a tentative glance at Chloe.

"That might be true—if I wished for a husband, which I most certainly do not," replied Chloe stoutly. "He does have a nice smile, though, don't you think? And tonight he actually complimented me on my appearance!"

"No!" said Hester, much struck. "Well, perhaps there is hope for him yet."

"Perhaps, but I intend to go forward with our program. Despite what he said tonight, I'm sure he must have been taken aback by my forthright declarations."

Gazing at Chloe's delicate features, flushed with determination, her eys sparkling with mischief, Hester privately wondered if her actions had not merely served to stir in Mr. Wery an appreciation for earnest young feminists.

"I was wondering," said Hester carefully, turning to a subject that had exercised her mind to some extent that evening. "Lady Wery mentioned a Lady Barbara tonight. A few other persons brought up her name as well, seeming surprised that she was not present this evening. I did not know how to respond. Is she another family member, perhaps? Should I know about her if I am to represent myself as one of Lord Bythorne's relatives?"

She kept her tone casual, and Chloe responded offhandedly. "Well, but you are one of his relatives, to be sure."

"Yes, but—"

"Lady Barbara? Oh, that's Lady Barbara Freemantle. She's the daughter of the Duke of Weymouth and she and Uncle Thorne have some sort of understanding, I believe. If you ask me, the understanding is mostly on her side, but Uncle Thorne seems inordinately fond of her. She's been out for this age, of course. She's considered a diamond and was much pursued during her first few Seasons, but she declined to accept any of the offers she received. It's my belief she was waiting for an offer from Uncle Thorne, since he was the first among her admirers, but, as he's so fond of saying, the gentleman's not for marrying—at least not for a long while—so things have just sort of drifted between them."

The young girl giggled. "Every time Aunt Augusta comes to town she does everything in her power to throw them together, for she fancies Lady Barbara as the perfect match for Uncle Thorne, but Uncle is much too sly for her. He squires Lady Barbara about to various functions, but that is as far as he's prepared to go—again as he says—toward immolating himself on the altar of family duty. And all the while, of course, he's galloping about town with his bits of muslin." She pursed her pink lips. "I am not supposed to know anything about that, naturally."

She pressed rosy fingertips to her mouth to suppress a prodigious yawn, and in a few moments took herself off to her own bedchamber. Hester prepared for bed, disdaining Parker's services. She felt oddly unsettled. She believed she had acquitted herself well this evening. With Lady Bracken's support she had survived her first exposure as a rabble-rouser in the *haut ton*. She tried to savor these little triumphs only to have her thoughts skitter in a most undisciplined fashion to the scene that had taken place some minutes before at the foot of the stairs.

She glanced absently down at her hands. They still seemed to bear the imprint of Lord Bythorne's lips, leaving a warmth that spread from her fingertips to her toes. She shook herself. Lord, what was the matter with her? She was acting like the veriest schoolgirl, fluttering over a pair of dark eyes and a smile. The man had only bid her good night, for heaven's sake.

Or no. There had been a definite message in the smiling gaze that had wrought such havoc in her breast. Incredible as it seemed, the man had been flirting with her. She seated herself at the dressing table, and pulling her hair from its unfamiliar coiffure, she began brushing it, all the while staring into her reflected image. She was not, she told herself, looking into the face of the sort of woman with whom the Earl of Bythorne was likely to engage in dalliance. Why, then, had he turned The Smile on her? And why, the thought came unbidden from deep within her, had it stirred a response so deep within her?

She wielded her brush viciously, sweeping her hair back so that every trace of curl was obliterated. Coiling it atop her head, she pinned it up under her nightcap. It was obvious, she thought with a grimace as she climbed into bed. The Earl of Bythorne was a rake, and it was the nature of rakes to flirt with every female they encountered. It was merely a reflex, like blinking one's eyes at the rapid approach of a foreign object.

As for her own untoward response, perhaps it, too, was automatic—some basic animal instinct that had welled suddenly to the surface, catching her unawares. She was only human, after all, and she could hardly be faulted for being aware of the presence of an attractive male in such close and intimate quarters.

She shrugged. It would not happen again, of course. Henceforth, she would be on guard against Thorne's base nature—and her own. She blew out the candle on her bedside table and turned a resolute shoulder into her pillow, but as she drifted toward sleep, a question niggled at her brain. Who was Lady Barbara Freemantle, and what hold, if any, did she possess over the elusive Lord Bythorne?

Returning from an afternoon of sparring at Gentleman Jackson's Boxing Saloon a few days later, Thorne was startled to discover a strange gentleman in his drawing room.

"A Mr. Bentham," Hobart whispered on taking his master's hat, gloves and walking stick. "He has come to see Miss Blayne."

The gentleman rose unhurriedly to his feet when Thorne entered the room and moved forward gravely. He was tall and slender, with sandy hair that waved smoothly above rather narrow features. He was dressed, if not in the height of fashion, with a precise modishness, and he wore his coat of Bath superfine and dove gray pantaloons with a modest flair.

"Ah," said the gentleman in a tone that seemed carefully cordial. "You must be Lord Bythorne. I am Trevor Bentham. I have come to—"

"Trevor," chimed a voice from the doorway, "how very nice to see you."

As Hester advanced toward them, Thorne was even more startled when she suffered an embrace from the unknown Mr. Bentham and kissed him on the cheek with what Thorne could only consider a tasteless display of enthusiasm.

"And have you met Lord Bythorne?" asked Hester.

"We were just introducing ourselves," said Thorne. He lifted his brows questioningly. "You are old friends, I take it."

"Oh, yes." Hester reached to touch Mr. Bentham's arm. "Trevor and I have known each other this age. He and my publisher—John Thompson—are well acquainted and when I was writing my first book—the *Apologia*—Trevor was of immeasurable help. He edited my work and offered valuable suggestions." She dimpled at him, and Mr. Bentham responded with a modest smile.

Thorne rang for tea. Hester gestured Mr. Bentham to a settee and seated herself beside him, leaving Thorne to arrange himself in a chair some distance away.

"Do you reside in London?" he asked.

"Yes," replied Mr. Bentham. "I live with my mother in Queen Ann Street, near Cavendish Square."

Thorne recognized the address as respectable, if not quite fashionable. "I suppose you have not seen Hester for some time."

Mr. Bentham's brows rose marginally at the sound of Hester's first name on the earl's lips, but he replied smoothly, "That is true. Mother's health is such that I do not stray far from home, so the only time Hester and I have seen each other recently is on her flying visits to the city."

Thorne did not miss the slight emphasis that Mr. Bentham placed on the lady's name, and smiled inwardly. Had

he struck a nerve? he wondered. Just how close a relationship did Hester enjoy with Trevor Bentham? He became
aware that Bentham was speaking again.

"We were so pleased to hear that Hester has come for an
extended visit to the metropolis. *All* her friends will be delighted." His glance flicked between Hester and Thorne. "I
was unaware that you and the Earl of Bythorne were acquainted," he remarked.

"Did you not know that we are cousins?" asked Thorne
innocently. At Bentham's expression of incredulous surprise, he continued casually. "Of course, the relationship is
quite distant, but Hester's mother and mine were great
friends and we played together as children." He ignored the
small gasp emitted from Hester's direction. "We only redis-
covered the connection, however, when my ward informed
me that she is a great admirer of Hester's work. I seconded
most heartily her invitation to Hester to make an extended
stay, and all of us here were most pleased when she accepted. It is unfortunate that both Chloe and Aunt Lavinia
are out of the house at present."

Hobart entered the room at that point, followed by a
footman carrying a full complement of tea and cakes.
These, he deposited tenderly on a table before Hester, who
rather self-consciously took up the duty of hostess. When
she offered a cup of tea to Thorne, however, he refused politely.

"I am sure you and your friend have a great deal to catch
up on, my dear, and since there are matters that require my
attention, I shall leave you all. It has been a pleasure meeting you, sir."

He rose, and with mutual expressions of goodwill, left
the room. It seemed to Hester that with his departure, something vital went with him, so that the drawing room, despite
its elegance, suddenly became rather drab and uninviting.

She shook herself from this foolish fancy and turned to
Trevor. "Now, do tell me all the news," she began. "Has
Mr. Fenwick completed his dissertation? And did—"

"You never told me you were related to the Earl of
Bythorne," interrupted Trevor. He flushed immediately, as

though aware of his gaucherie. "That is, I confess I am somewhat surprised to find you in such, er, sybaritic surroundings. I must say, I view the situation as somewhat improper, and I am surprised that you came to London at all without notifying me. Had I known you wished to visit the city, Mother and I would have been glad to open our home to you."

Hester experienced a spurt of irritation. Much as she liked and respected Trevor, she objected strongly to his proprietary manner toward her. He had always made it clear to Hester that he wished to be more than friends, and once, several years ago, had proposed marriage. She had refused him firmly and with great kindness—perhaps not firmly enough and with too much kindness, for he had apparently taken her refusal as mere maidenly hesitation. Though he had not repeated his proposal, he had persisted in his attentions, behaving as though he and Hester were in a state of semibetrothal.

Hester lifted her chin. "I did not think myself obliged to consult you, Trevor, nor do I see what gives you the right to judge the propriety of my actions. In any case, you are quite wrong. I am well chaperoned by the presence in the house of Thorne's aunt, and—what?" she asked as Trevor's features grew positively rigid with disapproval and his thin brows flew into his hairline.

"I noticed that he had the temerity to call you by your first name—I almost commented on it. But I hardly thought you would reciprocate." He sniffed. Hester's irritation disappeared in a burst of laughter, at which Trevor stiffened even further until Hester thought he might easily be pounded into the carpet with a sturdy mallet.

"I'm sorry, Trevor," she said through the chuckles she was unable to suppress wholly. "But you are being ridiculous. Lord Bythorne is quite respectable."

Trevor snorted.

"At least where his family is concerned," amended Hester. "And this is his family home, for goodness sake. I am well chaperoned here by his aunt—and the presence of his ward, of course. And there is Lady Bracken, his aunt and a pillar of propriety if ever was. She does not live in the house, but she is a frequent visitor and has welcomed me most graciously."

Hester was forced to bite her tongue a little on that last, but she maintained her expression of mirthful disdain.

Trevor, apparently deciding on a prudent retreat, assumed an injured air. "No need to fly up into the boughs, my dear. I was merely expressing my concern. We are certainly more than just friends, after all, and that being the case, I certainly believe I have that right."

The laughter drained away from Hester as though a plug had been removed from her toes. She spoke carefully. "I do appreciate your concern, Trevor, but it is quite as unnecessary as it is unwarranted." She forced a smile to her lips. "I think we must agree to disagree on that point. Now, do tell me about Mr. Fenwick."

Trevor pursed his lips, and for a moment it looked as though he meant to continue the discussion at hand, but apparently thinking the better of such a course, he smiled ruefully.

"No, he has not finished his work. When last heard from, he had decided to abandon his comparison of the poetry of Ovid and Pindar for a critique of the plays of Aeschylus. He is much taken with his new project, though, as you might apprehend, Miss Yelping is much overset."

Hester smiled in instant comprehension. Mr. Jasper Fenwick and Miss Henrietta Yelping were members of the discussion group to which Hester and Trevor belonged. They had been at odds with each other for years, and Miss Yelping, in an effort to prove her intellectual superiority had some years ago begun an appraisal of various Greek playwrights. To have Mr. Fenwick now devote his energies to one of those writers must have sounded an all-out call to arms.

Rolling these matters about in her mind brought the squabbles and foibles of other members of the rest of her set to mind, and suddenly she was flooded with a sense of being anchored once more. It was here she belonged, among people who relished above all things lively arguments over intellectual esoterica. She had allowed herself to be momentarily drawn into Lord Bythorne's orbit, but she was only a small, passing comet in his glittering firmament. In less then three months, she would have returned to her own quiet corner of the universe, and in the meantime, she had her friends to remind her of her direction in life.

She bestowed a brilliant smile on Trevor that quite took that gentleman's breath away.

"Yes, I can quite imagine Miss Yelping must be livid. I suppose that Mrs. Mayville is supportive, as always?"

They chatted for some minutes longer, and after the proper interval for an afternoon call had elapsed, Trevor rose.

"I must take my leave," he said regretfully, and kissed Hester rather lingeringly on her cheek. "Do come see us. Mama would be pleased, I'm sure."

Murmuring an insincere reply, Hester saw her visitor on his way with a promise to attend the next meeting of the group, to be held the following week in the home of another of its members.

She had no sooner closed the front door behind Trevor when she perceived the earl running lightly down the stairs, to be met by Hobart at the foot, with coat, hat, and walking stick.

"You are leaving us, my—Thorne?" she asked.

"Mm, yes. I have a dinner engagement at White's, with cards afterwards."

And a little something on the side after that, thought Hester before she could stop herself.

"I wonder if I might have a word with you before you leave," she said calmly.

"As many as you like, my dear," Thorne responded courteously, gesturing her into the gold saloon, just off the entrance hall.

"Well?" he asked blandly as he entered the room behind her. A spark of unholy amusement lit the depths of his dark eyes, and she felt herself flushing angrily.

"I am not your dear," she retorted tartly. "And what was all that nonsense about our mothers being great friends?

And playing together as children? If your mother so much as knew of the existence of the wife of an insignificant baronet from Shropshire, I should be very much surprised."

"As should I," he responded coolly. "I shall be the first to admit the whole scenario was a faradiddle. All right, I told an absolute bouncer, but it was all in a good cause, don't you agree? We wouldn't want Trevor to jump to any erroneous conclusions, now would we?"

"My lord—"

"Thorne."

"Oh, very well—Thorne—I do not require your dubious assistance in reassuring Trevor."

"But, your reputation, Hester." Thorne opened his eyes very wide. "You are my cousin, after all, and it is my duty to protect your reputation."

"My reputation doesn't need protecting," snapped Hester. "Even if I were living in the same house with you *sans* chaperon, it would suffice that *I* knew our relationship to be innocent. I do not care what others may think!"

"Ah."

Hester caught her breath as the devil's light returned to Thorne's eyes. "But, would it be innocent?"

In the moment of appalled silence in which Hester simply gaped at him, Thorne lifted a hand and twitched the cap from her hair. Gasping, she clapped both hands to her head, but it was too late. In one swift movement, Thorne slid his fingers through the knot she had created beneath it. Hairpins rained to the carpet, and heavy coils of hair tumbled over his hands to fall about her shoulders.

Hester uttered a small whimper of protest, but it went unheeded.

"It is as silky as I thought it must be," said Thorne almost wonderingly. "It feels like a sable pelt I once held in my hands as a boy."

Hester gasped in shock and pushed vigorously against him, but his hands had slipped to her shoulders, where he continued to stroke the waves of hair that now cascaded in abandon. She stared up at him and immediately regretted this action, for she felt she was falling into his gaze, a mesmerizing whirlpool that seemed to draw her into his very center. He stroked her cheek tenderly before lowering his head, and the next moment, his lips covered hers. She was, she acknowledged as a flaming heat swept through her, in the hands of a master. His mouth was warm and his kiss practiced. If he did not stop in the very next few seconds, she was not sure her legs would continue to hold her up.

But he did not stop. He lifted his lips from hers only to bring them to rest again, this time against her closed eyes, then to her jaw, then downward, creating a trail of delight along her throat before returning again to her mouth, which he coaxed open with the tip of his tongue. As he tasted her, she heard herself moan, and with the last of her will, she pushed against him once more. When he would have ignored her, she thrust harder, and this time he released her, very slowly.

Hester drew a deep, shuddering breath, and with more strength than she knew she possessed, she reached to tidy her hair.

"Well now," she said prosaically, pleased that her voice bore only a trace of breathlessness. "You do that very well, Thorne." With great effort, she infused her tone with the inflection of an adult chiding a small boy for breaking into a forbidden cupboard. "And I can't say I didn't enjoy it, but it won't do, you know. Please don't do that again, or I shall have to take measures."

If she had dashed a cup of cold water into his face, Thorne could not have been more astonished. He stepped back abruptly and for several moments stood staring at her, his mouth open. He whirled on his heel then and strode from the room. In a moment, she heard the slamming of the front door.

Chapter Ten

"Hester, please." Lady Bracken gasped as she spoke. "This must be the tenth bookstore we have entered this afternoon. We are in Hatchard's now, and if they don't have your wretched book here, you may be sure it is no longer extant."

Hester turned to her companion with some compunction. "Oh, Gussie, I *am* sorry! After all our shopping, and then for me to drag you all over town on a book hunt. You must be exhausted. Come, let us recoup in that tea shop across the street."

Gussie accepted the suggestion with expressions of gratitude, and in a few moments the two ladies sat opposite each other at a small table. Hester regarded the older woman with amusement. In the fortnight since Hester's arrival at Bythorne House, her ladyship had unbent markedly toward her nephew's guest. Particularly after the Wery dinner party, she had behaved in a manner that was positively friendly. Just the other day she had insisted that Hester call her by the nickname used only by her nephew, her husband, a select group of relatives, and very old, very dear friends. She had listened with some attention to Hester's beliefs, even admitting that she had read snatches of the *Apologia*. It was Hester's private view that Gussie went so far as to subscribe to some of these radical theories, for if ever a woman was born to fill a higher position than that of a mere reflection of her husband's status, thought Hester, that woman was Augusta, Lady Bracken.

"What is it again you're looking for?" asked Gussie, accepting a cup of steaming liquid from their waiter.

"It is a collection of arguments against the slave trade that Mr. Wilburforce made in Parliament and elsewhere."

"Ah. But hasn't the slave trade been abolished?"

"Yes, but I am looking for references to support my own argument that many of our own citizens are held in virtual slavery to masters who hire them to work long hours in factories for wages that barely keep them in bread and clothing. Why, do you know, Gussie, that the average worker in England—"

"Lady Bracken!" said a musical voice. "Yes, I thought that was you. I had heard you were in town."

"Barbara!" cried Gussie in a pleased voice, swiveling about in her chair. "How lovely to see you. Can you join us?"

Hester turned to behold one of the most beautiful women she had ever seen. Tendrils of golden hair escaped from a charming villager bonnet, the blue ribbons of which exactly matched eyes of a smiling azure. Her nose was straight and perfect as was the full mouth that curved upward in an expression of warmth. The vision settled into a third chair at the table with a whisper of silken skirts.

"I can stay but a moment," she said. "I am here with Sally Merton and her aunt." She gestured to where two ladies smiled and fluttered their fingers in greeting.

"Do let me present my, er, cousin, Hester Blayne," said Gussie. "Hester, allow me to introduce you to Lady Barbara Freemantle, a very dear friend of our family. And yes," she added in response to Lady Barbara's quizzical expression, "you have heard the name before—at least, if you are cognizant of the current feminist movement."

"Of course," replied Lady Barbara. "I am so pleased to meet you, Miss Blayne. You must know, I am a great admirer of your work."

"Indeed?" asked Hester in some astonishment.

"Yes. I purchased a copy of your *Apologia* when it was first published, and I attended a lecture you gave in Gloucester not long afterward. I was most impressed—not only at the content of your dissertation, but at your courage in coming forth to speak out."

Hester, who had experienced an instant, irrational antipathy toward Lady Barbara, now, not unnaturally, found herself warming toward her.

"That is most gratifying, Lady Barbara. Have you considered speaking out yourself? Surely, someone of your stature—"

Lady Barbara laughed. "Oh no. Unfortunately, I am not possessed of a single spark of moral fortitude. If asked, I'll certainly share my opinion, otherwise I simply mill along with the herd. I tend to my crocheting and my gardening and the odd good work now and then. But, do you reside in London now, Miss Blayne? I understood you to dwell some distance from town."

Gussie interposed with a slightly expurgated version of Hester's presence at Bythorne House.

"Well, I hope your visit will be an enjoyable one." Lady Barbara rose. "And now, I must be off, as I see Sally and Lady Bilkham are ready to depart. Shall I see you at the Debenham ball?" she asked Gussie.

"Oh, yes. I collect all the world and his brother will attend," replied Gussie with a laugh. "Thorne will be there as well. Perhaps you could join us for dinner first."

"That would be lovely. I haven't seen Thorne for this age. I've heard," concluded Lady Barbara, her eyes sparkling with laughter, "that he has been somewhat heavily occupied of late, if rumor is to be believed. Really, he has the most exquisite taste in opera dancers."

She left then, waving a graceful hand in farewell. Hester turned a surprised stare on Gussie.

"Lady Barbara does not seem to mind Thorne's, er, opera dancers?" she asked. An instant later, she flushed. "Oh, I do beg your pardon. It is certainly not my place to ask such a question, only Chloe said—"

"Oh, yes, it's true," remarked Gussie in some haste. "Barbara and Thorne have had an understanding for years, but she is a realist. She knows that Thorne's little flings are nothing to concern herself with. He would not consider marriage with any of his *chères amies,* of course." She leaned forward confidentially. "It is my belief that in speak-

ing so, Barbara is assuring Thorne that she will not interfere with his way of life after they are married."

"How—how very singular," said Hester faintly.

"Oh, no," replied Gussie earnestly. "It is the way of the
world, to be sure."

Hester fell silent. Mystified, she contemplated Gussie's
words. Good God, how could Lady Barbara not feel rage
and jealousy at Thorne's behavior—if he had truly professed his intention of marrying her? If it were herself—if
she held any man in high enough regard to consider marrying him, she would be devastated at such contempt for her
feelings. She would be prepared to scratch his eyes out, as
well as those of his current inamorata.

Sipping her tea, she recalled yesterday's episode in the
gold saloon at Bythorne House. The memory of Thorne's
touch lingered on her body. Her lips still seemed swollen
from the feel of his mouth on hers. She should have fought
to protect her virtue, of course. He must think her the veriest wanton. But all she could think of at the moment was
that she must conceal the shocking response that had shot
through her the moment he had caressed her cheek in that
intimate gesture. She would rather be nibbled to death by
ducks than let Thorne know that she was so deeply attracted to him. The attraction was solely sexual, but that did
not matter. She was not ashamed of her carnal instincts—
they were a part of the human makeup, after all, but she had
no intention of giving in to them.

As for Thorne himself, despite his overwhelming physical charisma, she still disliked the man. He was amusing,
but charm was a rake's stock-in-trade, and she was not to
be taken in. No, it mattered not how his eye gleamed with
humor, or how engagingly that one feather of midnight hair
curled over his forehead, Hester stood in no danger of los-
ing her heart. She was no schoolroom miss, and she knew
that one breath-stealing kiss did not a lifetime relationship
make. And she would settle for nothing else—with a man
who measured up to her standards, thank you very much.

To be sure, it was somewhat lowering to realize that this
edifying little reflection was purely academic. The idea that

the Earl of Bythorne could be seriously interested in a plain maiden of meager attributes was laugable. Indeed, since yesterday's encounter, his demeanor toward her had been distant to the point where she felt virtually invisible in his presence.

She sniffed. What a very good thing that Lord Bythorne's opinion of her counted for naught. Less than naught.

By the time she and Gussie had finished their tea and settled themselves in the carriage for the journey home, Hester felt herself once more firmly in control of her destiny. When they encountered Thorne just pulling up before the house in his curricle, she was able to greet him with a cool equanimity.

It was an emotion not shared by his lordship. His first urge on beholding Hester being handed down from his aunt's carriage was to stride up to her and shake her by the shoulders until that stupid cap she was wearing flew off into the gutter. He had learned to expect an interesting variety of reactions of his kisses, but never, not even as a stripling attempting his first amatory explorations at Oxford, had a female treated him to such utter disinterest. "You do that very well!" for God's sake, as though she were a governess complimenting a backward student on the marginally acceptable accomplishment of an assignment.

Who the devil did she think she was, this spinster with so little to recommend her, this plain little female with her ludicrous theories? Well, it served him right for even thinking of amusing himself with a bluestocking. What in God's name had possessed him to first plunge his hands into the heavy satin fall of her hair, and then to gather her into his arms for a kiss that had sent him into a spiral of wanting?

For, if he were to be honest, the spinster had more than confirmed his surmise. Underneath that cap, below that puritanical exterior, burned a flame just waiting for the breath that would stir it into a firestorm of passion. He had sensed her response, and was just beginning the enjoyable process of coaxing it skillfully into a breathless acquiescence, when she had pulled back. Dammit, she had as much as admitted that she found his embrace stimulating—much, however, as she might find the taste of a strawberry parfait!

Well, he had learned his lesson. There would be no more dalliance with Miss Prunes and Prisms. There were uncounted women in London who would be pleased to welcome the Earl of Bythorne into their arms and into their boudoirs. He would waste no more time with the likes of Hester Blayne and her perverted ideas about the place of women in the general scheme of things.

He approached the ladies as they moved toward the house. Hester paused when she saw him, dipping her head to one side to gaze up at him from beneath her bonnet. Her brown eyes were wide and bright, putting him in mind of a vixen he had encountered once outside his uncle's chicken coop—all innocence and charm, and liberally adorned with feathers. He laughed suddenly, and when after a moment she joined him, he felt oddly relieved.

"No, no, I mustn't come in," Gussie was saying. "I have an appointment in less than half an hour with Monsieur LaCosse. I am thinking of getting a crop." She patted her curls. "And he is going to advise me."

She bestowed a kiss on Hester's cheek and threw a careless wave to her nephew before remounting her carriage, and in a moment it rattled off along Curzon Street.

Upon entering the house, Hester moved hastily toward the staircase, but Thorne stopped her by the simple expedient of grasping her wrist.

"I would like to speak to you, if I might," he said, almost shyly.

"Oh, no," replied Hester with a little gasp. "That is, I must—"

"I shan't keep you above a moment." Without waiting for a reply, he propelled Hester into the library and after seating her in an elegant straw silk armchair, settled himself in a wing chair nearby. Casually, he crossed one leg over the other and surveyed her. When she lifted her brows questioningly, he laughed a little self-consciously.

"I was just wondering what magic you possess to have

turned Gussie into one of your most ardent supporters. I expected that she would treat you with a reasonable degree of courtesy, but she seems to have welcomed you into the family with open arms. And Chloe! Lord, I hardly recognize the chit these days. I don't think she's started a brangle with me once since you have been here. What is your secret?"

Hester became aware of the flame that danced in the depths of his coal dark eyes. Accompanying, as it so often did, the blinding effect of The Smile, it produced a feeling of breathless discomfort in her breast. She knew a spurt of relief that he evidently had not brought her here to discuss last night's untoward episode. She flushed. "If Gussie shows any partiality for me, I'm sure it is because of my sister. She told me that she and Mary were almost bosom bows in school. As for Chloe—well, I've merely convinced her that it is in her own best interest to behave prettily toward Mr. Wery."

"Hmm." Thorne grinned warily. "I'm not so sure I like the sound of that. I trust she is not planning some truly awful devilment."

"Well, she is—but, I think in the end she will find she has defeated herself. For, I must tell you, I am convinced that marriage is the best situation for Chloe, and Mr. Wery should be given the chance to prove that he is the best candidate for the position of groom-to-be."

"This all sounds very mysterious, but I am prepared to let you have your head."

"Why, thank you, sir." Hester nodded her head with an air of great condescension.

"Oh, very well." Thorne threw up his hands. "I will admit freely that I really have no choice in the matter. As long as we appear to have the same goal where Chloe is concerned, I bow to your judgment."

Hester nodded again, but wisely held her tongue.

"It is unfortunate," she said instead, "that you had no one to turn to in your immediate family when Chloe came to you. That is," she continued as Thorne stiffened, "Gussie has her own brood to raise." She hesitated. "I meant, if your mother were here—"

She halted, startled, as Thorne's harsh laughter interrupted her.

"My mother! Good God, I can think of no one who would make a worse model for a young girl on the brink of womanhood."

"But—but, she was so beautiful," said Hester in astonishment, thinking of the woman in the portrait. "She had such a warm smile."

"Oh, didn't she just!" Thorne's lips curved bitterly. "Just ask every man in London with whom she came within luring distance."

"Oh!" Hester gasped a little. "I didn't mean—"

Thorne shrugged. "I should not be so hard on her. She was what she was, after all."

Hester could think of no response to make to the implication of his words. Noting her expression, he smiled wearily, "You are not a part of our world, Hester, and for that you should be grateful. Women of my mother's sort were—and are—as common in the *ton* as bees in a rose garden. Although," he said consideringly, and Hester was chilled by the flatness of his tone, "few of them had the drawing power of Mama. She invited love—demanded it—and no one to whom she appealed for it could deny her. Not just men, of course. Everyone—man, woman, and child, responded to that blinding smile, that winsome charm that said, 'I am special. I am warmth. I will be sustenance for your soul'!"

He gazed before him, and Hester sensed that he was watching a small boy, seeking that warmth so many years ago, giving a love that was never truly returned.

"It was not to be wondered at, I suppose, that she turned to other men for worship. Papa paid homage at her altar for as long as could be expected, but he, too, was a product of the world in which we live. He was constitutionally unable to remain faithful to one woman for long, and he was far less discreet in his liaisons than Mama. The pair of them were a byword in the *beau monde*."

"Oh!" Hester said again, choking on the word in her dismay. At the sound, Thorne looked at her quickly. He laughed, and Hester thought she had never heard such a mournful sound.

"My dear, do not take on so. To be sure, I suffered some torment of soul when I discovered the existence of first one, then another, of her lovers, and a veritable legion after that. In fact, I was forced to trounce young Weatherby Minor rather severely during my first week at Eton after wearying of his puerile jibes on the subject. After that, I was troubled no further. And, really, it was all so long ago."

He stood abruptly and drew in a sharp breath. "You must forgive me. I don't know what possessed me to maunder on so about the travails of my childhood. It is not my habit to do so, I assure you."

Hester was surprised to feel her fingers curl like rakes into the flesh of her palms. Dear God, what kind of monster could take the open, unconditional love of a little boy and turn it back on him so that he would become the damaged man she saw before her. For there was no doubt Thorne still felt the hurt Hester had inflicted so many years ago. Hester became aware that he was speaking again.

"The Debenham ball?" she asked blankly, confused by his sudden turn of subject. "Oh. Yes. Gussie mentioned it this afternoon—or no, it was Lady Barbara—Freemantle."

Thorne's eyes lit, and Hester knew a spurt of irritation at the dismayed spasm this stirred in her own interior.

"Barbara! I did not know you and she had met."

Hester relayed the story of her afternoon encounter with Lady Barbara.

"Splendid!" exclaimed Thorne. "I've been meaning to introduce you myself, for I knew you would hit it off. I'm glad Gussie invited her to dinner. We can all proceed to the ball together."

Hester smiled a faint agreement, determined to produce a

headache on the evening in question. She had acknowledged to herself that she would be little more than a nonen-
tity in the Bythorne household during her stay there, but
somehow the idea of appearing in the shadow of the magnificent Lady Barbara Freemantle was more than she could
bear. No, she would remain safely in her room on the night
of the Debenham Ball. She needed to spend her time more
productively, anyway. With all her shopping and visiting
with Gussie, she had fallen sadly behind on the book. Yes,
she would busy herself with her work, thus remaining almost
totally unaware of Lady Barbara's presence in Thorne's
house and in his life.

Alas, her virtuous intentions came to naught. Gussie's
plans for a small dinner party to be held at Bythorne house
quickly evolved into a rather grandoise affair, and Hester
was called in to participate from the start. After compiling a
list of those to be invited, which, to Hester's astonishment
included the Duke of York, ("Oh, yes," Gussie had responded airily to Hester's choked inquiry, "the duke and
Bracken have been friends since they were boys. He's extraordinarily condescending, you know, to his cronies.")
Gussie had turned to the all-consuming question of What to
Wear.

"If it were just the ball, we could get by with your blue
silk and my Russian satin, but with the dinner party—well,
there is no help for it, we must apply to Madame Celeste
for new gowns for each of us."

"Oh, I don't think—" began Hester.

"Nonsense. None of the things you have purchased recently is even remotely acceptable for a truly elegant evening
affair."

"Gussie, when I began the nonstop shopping spree on
which I seem to have been engaged ever since I arrived in
London, I had no intention of becoming part of the social
scene. I see no necessity—"

"Hester," responded Gussie with awful majesty, "if you
are going to recite that tiresome litany about being a simple
woman of the people, I shall be forced to—hit you with

something. Did we or did we not agree at the outset that you are family? And that being the case, you cannot simply sit in a chimney corner while your wicked stepsisters—or cousins, or whatever—regale themselves at parties and balls. What would people think? And don't you dare tell me—again—that you don't care what people think. You are going to appear at the dinner party, *and* the ball and"— she cocked her head in an odd attitude of appraisal—"and you are going to dress bang up to the nines."

Thus, some evenings later, Hester stood before the mirror in her bedchamber, gazing at herself in the mirror with undisguised astonishment.

Parker had labored mightily over her appearance, creating a coiffure that would have done justice to an illustration in *La Belle Assemblée*. Despite her vociferous protests, she had been denied her cap, and Monsieur LaCosse had been called in and given carte blanche to work his will on her mahogany tresses. He had attacked with combs, brushes, and worst of all, scissors, and the result was a mass of glossy curls that tumbled from a chignon atop Hester's head to cluster about her neck and cheeks in silky tendrils. The effect, thought Hester dazedly, was pure magic. Her eyes had become much bigger and her neck appeared positively swanlike.

As for her ensemble, which consisted of a gown of orange blossom crepe underneath a tunic of gossamer sprinkled with spangles, it clung lovingly to curves she hadn't known she possessed. It also, Hester considered with guilty delight, displayed entirely too much of her bosom. Her efforts to drape her shawl of spider gauze over the expanse of bared flesh only served to accentuate nature's bounty. It was a great deal too bad, Hester thought in irritation, that nature could not display a little more discretion in her dubious gifts.

Her fingers touched the pearls that lay about her neck. The necklace was her one good piece of jewelry, inherited from her mother. Feeling oddly nervous, she stood smoothing her skirts one last time.

"Oh, miss," said Parker behind her, "you do look a fair treat." She handed Hester her reticule and followed her to the door, brushing imaginary lint from the gown and twitching a recalcitrant curl into place before opening the door to allow her mistress to leave the haven of her chamber for the perils of the social swim.

Downstairs, Hester found she was the last of the family to enter the drawing room. Gussie, garbed in an ensemble of Venetian silk, topped with a massive, feathered turban, sat with her head close to Chloe, who wore a charming confection of peach sarcenet and creamy tulle embroidered with golden acorns that glinted in the firelight. Thorne had taken up his usual position before the hearth, looking absurdly magnificent in satin breeches, a dark coat and lacy cravat from which winked a single diamond.

Hester had the odd impression that his eyes darkened to an even deeper jet as she entered the room, and his gaze swept over her appreciatively. Chloe jumped up from her chair.

"Oh, Hester! You look wonderful. You will take the shine out of all of us, won't she, Aunt Gussie?"

Gussie nodded consideringly. "Indeed, my dear, you show to great advantage."

Hester decided to ignore the silent, "Who would have believed it?" that she could hear in Gussie's tone. Indeed, she could hardly believe it herself.

Before she could seat herself, the first dinner guests arrived. She had met Lord and Lady Sebford at the Wery party and was able to converse with them with equanimity. A steady stream of personages were announced then, most of whom were strangers to Hester. It was with some relief that she noted the entrance of Lady Barbara. Before she could move in her direction, however, the young woman was appropriated by Thorne, who greeted her warmly with a kiss on the cheek.

Slipping an arm through his, Barbara moved among the growing throng and eventually bumped up against Hester, who was by then conversing with a lady to whom she had been introduced earlier, but whose name had by now fled from memory.

Barbara, however, had no such difficulty. "Mrs. Tufts!" she exclaimed prettily. "I was hoping you would be here tonight. I understand you just returned from the Continent. I am so anxious to hear of your travels. Did you see Byron?"

"Goodness, no," replied Mrs. Tufts. She was short, plump, and rather red of face and her spurt of laughter put Hester strongly in mind of a guinea fowl in distress. "We did not travel to Greece," added the lady. "Though in any event, we certainly would not have sought him out." She sniffed, and the feathers in her headdress quivered indignantly.

At that point, Gussie appeared at Barbara's elbow with a lean, fair-haired gentleman in tow.

"Hester," said her ladyship purposefully, "I wish you to meet one of my dearest friends. Or, rather, his aunt and I— that is—" She drew in a deep breath. "Hester, may I present Mr. Robert Carver? Robert, Miss Hester Blayne."

At the sound of his name, Barbara turned suddenly, catching Mr. Carver, who was at the moment midbow, on the chin with her reticule.

"Oh!" she exclaimed, her cheeks flooding with crimson. "I do beg your pardon. I . . ."

To Hester's surprise, she trailed off and fluttered her hands in an unwonted loss of composure.

"Good evening, Lady Barbara," said Mr. Carver, a touch of frost in his voice. "It has been a long time." He bent over Hester's extended hand. "Miss Blayne, my pleasure. I have read all your works—even the novels, and I wish to express my admiration not only for your writing talent, but your sentiments."

Hester glanced wonderingly between Lady Barbara and Mr. Carver, but the two seemed to be determinedly ignoring each other. "Why, thank you, sir," she replied to the gentleman at last. "It is rare to meet a man who espouses the view that women are not fairly treated in England."

Mr. Carver smiled, and Hester was struck by how very

nice a smile it was. "I suppose that is true. I have my mother to thank for my enlightenment. She was a staunch believer in the equality of the sexes, and watching her in operation, I could only conclude that had she been born a man, she would have made an excellent field general."

Hester laughed in return. "The same can be said of many women, to be sure."

After a moment or two more in general conversation, Robert Carver moved on to circulate about the room. Hester hesitated a moment before turning to Barbara, who had stood silently during their exchange.

"Are you and Mr. Carver acquainted?" she asked at last.

Barbara started. "Oh. Yes. That is, his brother, the Earl of Wickham, and my brother are great friends. I have known him off and on since I was in leading strings. We—ah—saw quite a bit of each other several Christmases ago when he spent an extended period of time at Whitebrothers Abbey—my home." She uttered a short, brittle laugh. "I had thought he was my friend, as well, but events proved otherwise." Abruptly, she raised a gloved hand in a spasmodic gesture. "Oh, look, there is Sylvia Moreland. You must come and meet her."

Grasping Hester's hand, she pulled her through the growing throng.

Hester greeted Mrs. Moreland, and a great many other persons before dinner was announced, including the Duke of York—who proved to be just as jovial and expansive as Gussie had predicted. Knowing she would be unable to remember half the names she had just heard, she was grateful to note when she entered the dining room that she was seated next to Mr. Carver. Thorne was seated farther down the table, next to Barbara.

Observing Thorne's dark head bent over the spun gold of Barbara's elaborate coiffure, Hester was forced to admit they made a stunning couple. Why, she wondered, had they not married long ago? From what Gussie had told her, Hester could only assume that it was Thorne who resisted the union. Barbara, said Gussie, had been ready to accept his proposal, should it ever come, for donkey's years.

Watching him as he laughed warmly into Barbara's eyes, it was hard to believe that he was averse to taking her as a wife. She was the perfect choice, after all, blending breeding with beauty and a knowledge as to what was expected of her as the wife of a man who had no intention of giving up his outside interests for a triviality such as the marriage ceremony.

And why, she wondered further, was Barbara willing to wait submissively for Thorne to propose? It was perfectly obvious she could have any man in the kingdom. Was she so wildly in love with Thorne that she was willing to wait until he finally decided to commit himself? Or had she simply made up her mind it was Thorne she wanted to marry, and was unwilling to admit defeat?

She shuddered inwardly, thanking whatever gods were charged with the fates of unmarried women that she had escaped the necessity of enslaving herself to the whim of a man.

She turned to Robert Carver, on her right, who was speaking again of her feminist activities.

"Of late," he said, "I have been holding meetings in my home for a small group of kindred spirits. I hesitate to refer to us as intellectuals, for that seems a little pretentious, but we enjoy good books and good conversation. I wonder if you would care to join us some evening. That is, if Lord Bythorne would not mind."

"It sounds quite delightful. Thank you, I should love to attend one of your meetings. And, may I say that, though I'm sure Thorne would not object, I am not governed by his feelings in such matters."

"Ah. But he certainly cannot enter into your feelings, or your activities—"

"You are quite correct, Mr. Carver," said Hester with some asperity. "Lord Bythorne is singularly unenlightened concerning the ability of a woman to govern her own existence, but, fortunately, I am in no way accountable to him for my actions."

"Well," replied Mr. Carver softly. "You seem to have escaped falling under his lordship's legendary charm. You are, I believe, unique among the members of your gender."

He cast a sardonic glance down the table to where Barbara was regaling Thorne with a tale he seemed to find amusing in the extreme. Noting a certain rigidity in his expression, Hester asked, "Barbara says you and she have been friends for some years."

"Does she?" he asked casually. "I think, perhaps, friends is too strong a word. Acquaintances might be better—and fairly distant ones at that."

Despite the coolness of his tone, Hester was startled to note a distinct flash of derision in the gentleman's eyes.

Chapter Eleven

Hester had little opportunity to ponder the implications of Mr. Carver's remark, for the rest of the evening was a blur of activity. After dinner, the guests proceeded to a brilliantly lit town house in Upper Brook Street, where Hester was introduced to yet another contingent of the *beau monde*. To her surprise, she was much sought-after as a dance partner, a result, she was sure, of Lady Bracken's efforts.

She had forgotten how much she enjoyed dancing, but after several country dances, and two or three waltzes, she felt that her spirit had taken wings. Flushed and breathless, she stood in conversation with a group of ladies and gentlemen who prior to that evening had been totally unknown to her. She had expected to be shunned by polite society for her radical beliefs, but there was little overt reaction to her name. She was greeted with smiles of amused tolerance by some of the gentlemen and there was a bit of buzzing among the ladies, who sent sidelong glances of curiosity, but Hester was accustomed to being viewed as an oddity of nature. By and large, however, it was as though most of the persons here had never heard of Hester Blayne and her scandalous behavior. Yet another example of the redemption to be obtained under the banner of the Bythorne name, no doubt.

On the other hand, she mused ruefully, perhaps most of the persons present were truly ignorant of her activities. The *ton*, after all, had determinedly ignored the war against Napoleon until it was brought almost to their own shores. It was not surprising then, that they could manage to ignore a feminist firebrand in their midst. Still, her efforts to blend in with the matrons lining the walls of the Debenham ballroom had been fruitless, and if she were to be honest, she was enjoying herself immensely. She bestowed a brilliant smile on a gentleman who had just solicited her hand for the boulanger.

"Why, that sounds lovely, Lord Mumblethorpe. I—"

"But, you must have forgotten, my dear." The voice sounded behind her, deep and amused. "You promised the next dance to me."

She whirled to find Thorne at her elbow. Lord Mumblethorpe, whose portly form was contained in corsets that creaked with each movement, bent an indignant stare on the earl.

"I say, old man, this is out-and-out piracy. Have a notion to call you out, demmed if I don't."

"Now, now, Mum, you don't want to do that. I have a prior claim, after all—relative and all that."

Without waiting for a reply, Thorne whisked Hester onto the dance floor. There was little opportunity for conversation during the complicated figures of the dance, but when the last strains of the music had died away, Thorne led her to the refreshment table. Procuring punch and lobster patties, the two made their way to a small chamber just off the ballroom.

"My, that was lovely!" gasped Hester as she sank down on one of the little chairs scattered about the room. "I was afraid I had forgotten the steps, but it all came back to me."

"But you are an excellent dancer, my dear. Has it really been so long since you attended a ball?"

"Good heavnes, it's been ages," replied Hester, deciding for the moment to ignore Thorne's highly improper, "my dear." "In fact, aside from a few country assemblies, I don't think I've so much as set a toe on a dance floor since my Season."

"You had a Season?" Thorne's brows lifted. "Not that it is to be wondered at, of course," he added hastily. "I am merely surprised that we did not meet."

"Oh, we may have," Hester responded airily. "I met so

many people, I am sure I would not have remembered a fraction of them."

Touché, Miss Blayne, thought Thorne, grinning inwardly.

"For, of course," continued Hester, "my family, though out of the way in many respects, made sure that all the daughters had their moment of glory. At least, while my mother was alive. We were rather pinched for funds after Mary and Cecilia were brought out, but I was trotted out in my turn. I stayed with my Aunt Aurelia, in Portland Square."

She glanced up at him, her eyes twinkling mischievously. "I'm afraid the whole project was an unmitigated disaster, for I must tell you, my lord, I Did Not Take."

"You surprise me," said Thorne solemnly. "Do you mean to tell me that the gentlemen to whom you were introduced did not listen attentively to your views? For I should imagine you treated one and all to a thorough exposition of your philosophies."

"How did you guess?" Her mouth curved upward in a warm chuckle and Thorne wondered if she was aware of the magical effect of her smile. Probably not, he concluded, for she seemed totally ignorant of her charm. "I was positively grim—and thin and mousey. I wore all the wrong clothes, of course." Her smile faded. "In short, I was almost guaranteed to fail in attracting a husband, or even a modicum of attention."

"Well, you are more than making up for that lack this evening. Perhaps you are what is referred to as a late bloomer."

"Very late," remarked Hester dryly. "In any event, I know well to whom the credit for my sudden surge of popularity belongs. Gussie has been very busy on my behalf— and I wish she would not."

"You do not enjoy being solicited for every dance?"

"Well, of course, I do, but I know it is not for myself, which is always lowering. And, to be truthful, keeping my mouth shut is becoming a strain. It has been all I could do not to prick some of the balloons of pomposity that crowd the room tonight."

"Well, when you finally give in to the urge, do call me. I could use a spot of entertainment."

Thorne found himself relishing the militant sparkle that rose to her eyes. Hester Blayne, he mused, might be a thorn in the foot of society, but she was never boring.

"You would like to see me pilloried for my beliefs?" she asked a little sharply.

"No, of course not. Do not twist my meaning. It is only that I have never been a lover of pomposity myself, and rather looked forward to the sounds of balloons popping all over the dance floor."

Hester was forced to laugh. "That is what you say now, but I wonder what your reaction would be if I started discoursing to you right now on the woeful injustice being done to women."

Thorne looked about. "I suppose a case might be made for the women of the poorer classes, but I see no injustice here. Every female in the place looks well-fed. Their gowns cost enough to feed a starving family for a year and their jewelry could fill the treasury of a small country."

Hester clicked her tongue impatiently. "That is just the sort of thinking I most abhor. The women in this room are, in the main, simply the visible representations of their husband's status. They have no identity of their own, and their only function in life is to oversee the running of their lord's house and bear him children."

"But, what is wrong with that?" he asked innocently, almost holding his breath in anticipation of the fire he knew would rise in her eyes. Lord, she was almost beautiful when she was truly aroused to anger.

"What is wrong with it?" she echoed on cue. "No human being should be the—the chattel of another. It is degrading, and—" She halted abruptly and glanced at him sharply. The animation died from her features and her face became closed. "Oh, I see. You are merely amusing yourself. How very predictable of you, my lord. And now, if you will excuse me—thank you for a lovely dance, but I believe I shall return to the ball."

She rose, and with a whisper of silken skirts, moved

from the room, her head held high and her back very straight. Thorne gazed after her, breathing in the scent of violets that lingered after her. He knew an unaccustomed feeling of shame at his behavior. She was so very earnest, after all, and it had not been kind of him to mock her. He sighed, if only she were not so vocal in her foolish theories, flirting with her might be a pleasant diversion. As it was, one had merely to poke a little fun at her passion and she came all-over sensibility and affront.

He strolled back into the ballroom in search of Lady Barbara. Now, there was a female who knew to a nicety how to please a gentleman. She was totally lacking in prickles and knew precisely what was expected of her.

He stifled the sense of loss that struck him for the merest instant as he caught a last glimpse of Hester wending her way through the throng in the ballroom—a feeling that he had just let something valuable slip through his fingers.

"What do you think, Hester? Can I wear this bonnet with the primrose muslin?"

Hester looked up from the desk situated in her sitting room as Chloe entered the room. In her hand she carried a charming Gypsy straw bonnet, embellished with cherries and trailing matching ribbons. On her head she wore a villager hat whose ribbons of pomona green precisely matched the gown she was wearing.

Hester put down her pen. "Well, the villager is certainly a good choice, but the Gypsy has perhaps a trace more dash."

"That's what I thought, too," replied Chloe, tossing the villager on a chair to replace it with the Gypsy.

"Where are you off to?" inquired Hester.

Chloe's features puckered. "Oh, it is too tedious, really. Some of my friends have got up an expedition to Richmond. It sounded like such fun, but then John—Mr. Wery got wind of it and practically invited himself along. I just know the whole afternoon will be ruined."

"Dear me," said Hester, surprised. "I thought you and Mr. Wery had come to a better understanding over the last few days. Did he not dance with you twice last night at the ball?"

"Yes, but just for the country dances." She grimaced. "He thinks the waltz too daring to be engaged in by very young girls. Good heavens, it's been popular now for several years and you may see schoolgirls practicing it with their dancing masters."

Hester smiled. "I think Mr. Wery wants to impress you with his concern for your reputation."

"He'd do better," snapped Chloe, "to impress me with his ability to waltz." She heaved a lugubrious sigh. "If only he weren't so unutterably boring one might be able to bear his company a little more easily."

"How is your campaign going—the one designed to give him a disgust of you?"

Chloe gave a despairing sniff. "Not well. Would you believe, he has apparently decided there is a great deal of merit in my views on woman's education. Now, instead of prosing on about sheep, he bores on about his schools. Not that I am not interested in his efforts," Chloe said hastily, "but one would like to converse just once in a while about—oh, fashion and gossip."

"Of course," remarked Hester gravely. "But, I thought you were going to talk about your craving for jewels and your determination to live in London."

Chloe brightened. "Oh, that's going much better." She giggled. "Last night, when he complimented me on my pearls, I bemoaned the fact that I am not old enough yet to wear the emeralds that my mother left me. Then, I went on at some length about all the gewgaws I look forward to wearing when I am a married lady. The poor man looked positively green by the time I ran out of breath."

"That sounds promising," agreed Hester with a laugh. "I predict that he will soon take you in such aversion that he will refrain from calling on you at all. I am sure you will be relieved when he no longer seeks you out at dances or pleads a space on your outings to Richmond."

Chloe's face fell a trifle. "Oh. Well, yes, I certainly do look forward to that day." She rose from the chair into which she had flung herself and smoothed her skirts. "I had better make myself ready, for he will be here shortly." She glanced out the window. "Oh dear, it looks as though it might rain later. Pinkham has a new way of doing my hair that I mean to try." She laughed self-consciously. "John said last night that he likes it when I pile it atop my head. I think that is the first real compliment he has ever paid me, and I mean to see if I can make him produce more."

She ran from the room and Hester was left to shake her head. There was no doubt that young John Wery was among the worthiest of young men, but he had a great deal to learn about winning the heart of a fair lady. It was too bad, really, that it was the rakes of the world who seemed to possess the keys to those hearts.

Hester considered her prime exhibit. He had no morals and no compunction about taking his pleasure where he might, and there was not a woman at the ball last night who was not aware of this fact. Yet, the silly creatures fairly threw themselves at his feet as he strolled among them, each hoping she would be the next blossom to be plucked and later flung aside. They knew that his intentions were not serious, that he was not interested in marriage, and yet they encouraged his advances—married and unmarried females alike. There were even those among them who believed that they could reform him. How was it he was able to engender the burning conviction in each of their breasts that she was the one woman in the world to whom he would turn for permanent companionship?

Lady Barbara Freemantle was apparently one of that number, and, to be sure, it looked as though she had an inside track to that much desired outcome. But, Lord, what made them all think he was worth the effort? She herself seemed to be the only female in London who could see the charming peer for what he was, a lecherous, uncaring, breaker of hearts. She only wished that she possessed the physical attributes that would lure him to her. She would very much enjoy breaking his heart, assuming there was one to break, of course, which she very much doubted.

Some minutes later, she was obliged to shake herself free

of a fantasy that involved moonlit assignations in scented gardens and candlelit boudoirs and the vision of a hard, muscular body bent over hers under rumpled bedcovers.

Gracious, perhaps she did need a man, after all! Her thoughts drifted to Trevor Bentham, who was hers for the asking. Somehow, however, the thought of lifting her lips to his in that moonlit garden did not send sparks fizzing through her veins as they had a few moments before when another figure filled her fantasy. And then there was Robert Carver. On the drive home after the ball, Gussie had made it more than evident that she had introduced her to Robert with a definite purpose in mind. Robert Carver, said Gussie in an unspoken but unmistakable message, was the perfect match for Hester.

Hester had accepted Robert's invitation to come to his house for a meeting of his discussion group, not because of Gussie's patent manipulation, but because she genuinely liked the man. She would, she decided, avail herself of Robert's company and simply see what developed. There could surely be no harm in that—and perhaps something very good would come of it. She was certainly not, as she had averred so often, in the market for a husband, but there was something to be said for masculine companionship—in judicious doses.

In the meantime, Trevor would be collecting her that evening to take her to a meeting of The Friends of Greek Literature, to be held at the home of Mr. Jasper Fenwick, critiquer of Ovid and Pindar. She looked forward to the outing, not only because she would be greeting old friends, but because it would mark a return from the dangerous world of Lord Bythorne and his amoralities to her own secure environment.

In the event, however, that circumstance was to be postponed. Shortly before dinner, when Hester, Lady Lavinia, and Lord Bythorne had gathered in the gold saloon, a commotion in the entry hall sent them peltering out in inquiry. There they found Chloe standing in the center of the hall in the shelter of John Wery's arms. Her maid Pinkham stood to one side twittering distressfully. Both young women were in an advanced state of disarray. Chloe's Gypsy hat hung down her back, the cherries torn away from their moorings, and the pomona gown was mud-stained and torn.

"Good God!" exclaimed Thorne. "What happened?"

Chloe, pale and shaken, turned blindly toward him. "Oh, Uncle Thorne!" She put out a hand to him, but she did not leave John's side. "There was an accident. A terrible accident. Oh, it was so dreadful! I thought we were all going to die!"

John led her to a chair placed at the edge of the marquetry floor and tenderly desposited her in its cushioned depths. He straightened, then, and turned to Thorne, as Lady Lavinia hurried to Chloe's side.

"It was a carriage accident, sir. I believe Ch—Miss Venable has suffered no real injury, but she has sustained a great shock. Perhaps if her maid could take her upstairs?"

"I will take her," said Hester sharply. "Pinkham appears to be greatly distressed as well."

"Oh!" Pinkham squeaked, apparently startled at the idea anyone would consider her state of mind. "I am quite well, miss, thank you. It's only—"

"John!" Chloe gasped and, clinging to her aunt with one hand, gestured wildly with the other. "Do not leave! I have not had a chance to thank you properly."

"What in God's name—?" interposed Thorne sharply. "What happened?" he repeated.

Chloe, by now somewhat restored, turned a glowing face to the earl. "Oh, Uncle Thorne. John was magnificent! If it were not for his quick thinking—and his strength—we would all be stretched out lifeless on the road to Richmond!"

John flushed to the roots of his wispy brown hair. "It was nothing like that," he assured Thorne hastily. "We were driving in a carriage belonging to Fred Wilkerson, one of our party. There were seven of us in the vehicle, which was a tight squeeze, so I volunteered to sit on top, along with one of the other fellows who was in the group. We had nearly reached our destination, a picnic ground not far from the river, when the sky darkened. Thinking it was going to rain soon, we decided to turn off the main road toward Wandsworth, where we could stop for refreshments at an inn there. We had not gone far along this route, when the weather turned very nasty, indeed."

"Mrs. Salburt, Helen's mother, was with us," put in Chloe, "and she began screeching like demented crow."

"Yes," said John, "well, it began to thunder and lightning, and the horses began to grow extremely restive. Finally, as luck would have it, lightning did actually strike a tree, just as we were driving beneath it."

"I never heard such an awful sound in my life," said Chloe, going quite pale at the memory. "I thought the world had come to an end."

John smiled crookedly. "It very nearly did—for us, at least. A tree limb was broken off and it struck the coach driver, knocking him from his perch to the ground. The horses, of course, took the whole thing very much amiss—"

"Maddened by fear," whispered Chloe dramatically.

"And they bolted," finished John in a remarkably prosaic tone. "Fortunately, I was able to maneuver myself into the coachman's position and tried to bring them to a halt. However, I was able only to slow them considerably before we eventually plunged into a ditch."

"He was absolutely magnificent," breathed Chloe, her eyes wide and awestruck. "After the coach finally halted, no one else had the slightest idea of what to do, but John leaped down and, after assuring that the rest of us were unharmed, directed the groom to help him unhitch the horses from the carriage. John Coachman came hurrying up a few moments later, none the worse for wear, and John sent him to a nearby house for help." She uttered a deep, quavering sigh. "Then he hired another coach at the village posting house and brought us all home safe and sound."

She turned adoring eyes to her rescuer.

"Well!" exclaimed Thorne, expelling a forceful breath. "It seems as though you are the hero of the hour, Mr. Wery. Let me offer you my congratulations for bringing a very sticky situation to a happy ending."

John flushed furiously, all but digging his toe in the carpet, and said nothing. Hester noted that Chloe was still in a high state of excitement.

"Let me help you upstairs, my dear," she said, gesturing to Pinkham as she did so, and in a moment the little cavalcade made its way up the staircase toward Chloe's bedchamber. John spoke to Thorne in a diffident voice, and Hester caught his last words as she and Lady Lavinia propelled Chloe upward.

"If I might have a word with you in private, sir."

Chapter Twelve

Upstairs, Hester dismissed Pinkham, recommending that she get herself into a hot bath and then to bed. Aunt Lavinia, her expression a bit startled at this unusual solicitude for a servant, acquiesced in a faint voice, merely requesting that she order one of the other maids to bring up hot water for Chloe.

Chloe, unheeding, allowed Hester to assist her in removing the tattered Gypsy bonnet and stained pomona muslin.

"Uh!" she said. "It's soaked. I'll never be one of those females who damps her petticoats just to display her figure. What a dreadfully uncomfortable way to spend an evening."

"I daresay," agreed Hester solemnly. "In any event, you are fortunate you came to no further harm than a ruined gown and bonnet."

"Oh yes," cried Chloe, returning to the theme that had occupied her mind since the disaster near Richmond. "Oh, Hester—Aunt—I wish you could have seen John in action. He was just like one of the heroes in Mrs. Radcliffe's novels."

"My!" said Aunt Lavinia, much impressed. She hurried away to open the door for a maid staggering under a can of hot water, and soon Chloe was immersed, sighing with contentment, in a steaming bath.

At this point, Aunt Lavinia succumbed to Hester's urging that she seek her dinner. There was really no need, said Hester, for both of them to minister to the stricken damsel.

As she stepped from the tub into a lawn nightshift, Chloe was still talking about John's daring exploits.

"I truly did think we were all going to be killed, Hester.

The coach seemed to be pitching in all directions at once, and when we finally did come to rest in the ditch, we were tossed at such an angle! I didn't know if I was on my head or my ears. Kitty Fairchild had fallen on top of me, and, as I said, Mrs. Salburt was screeching fit to wake the dead."

"It was fortunate that John was with you," murmured Hester. "Even," she added with a smile, "if he did practically invite himself."

Chloe flushed. "That *was* an unhandsome thing for me to say, wasn't it? But, I didn't really mean it, of course. Oh, Hester, I didn't ask him to call tomorrow. Do you think he will?"

"I believe it to be more than likely," replied Hester, thinking of the words she had overheard just before coming upstairs.

Below, in Thorne's elegantly appointed library, Mr. Wery was just bringing himself to the point of his request for a private audience with the earl. He drew a deep breath.

"In short, my lord, I request your permission to pay my addresses to your ward."

More beautiful words he had never heard, thought Thorne relievedly. The next instant a flash of compunction shot through him. Had Hester been right? Was he simply throwing these two young people together to suit his own ends? Was sober, stiff John Wery really right for eager, impetuous, volatile Chloe?

Unbelievingly, he heard himself say, "Are you sure you want to do this, John? Chloe is, of course, an excellent match, but—you and Chloe are very different in style. She spends a good deal of her time swooping about in the boughs, and the least little thing sets her off. For example, do you think, on your own, you would have been able to handle her just now? I'm quite sure I could not. It would not have taken much to send her into hysteria."

"Oh no, sir," replied John earnestly. "You did not see her earlier. She bore the chaos of the carriage wreck with great fortitude, making sure the other girls were safe before she would exit the vehicle herself, and soothing them—and

Mrs. Salburt—in their fear and excitement. It was only when the crisis was over that she became, er, flustered."

"Really? You amaze me."

"It's true, sir. And—yes, I know she is somewhat volatile, but of late I have seen a seriousness of purpose that I had not observed before. She is quite interested in social issues, you know."

"Yes, I know."

"I must say, she seems inordinately interested in the decoration of her person with expensive jewelry—"

"Chloe?"

"Yes, but I am sure that is just the enthusiasm of youth for trivialities. Also, she says she prefers to live in London, but I sense she is not sincere in that."

"No, I believe you are right," said Thorne, a little puzzled. "She seemed to enjoy our stay at the Park, and several times expressed her preference for the countryside over the city. Well," he concluded, his conscience fully satisfied, "if—"

He was interrupted by the entrance of Hobart.

"You have—or rather Miss Blayne has a visitor, sir. Mr. Bentham."

"What the devil—? Oh, yes, I remember now. Well, show him into the drawing room and notify Miss Blayne of his arrival." He turned once more to John. "Now, as I— What *is* it, Hobart?" he asked the butler, who remained in the doorway, clearing his throat in some agitation.

"Miss Blayne is with Miss Chloe, sir. I am not sure she would wish to be interrupted."

"Oh, for God's sake. Just—No, never mind. I'll go up myself. John—"

"It's all right, sir, I'll see myself out. I would not wish to disturb Miss Blayne if she is ministering to Chl—Miss Venable." John's voice took on a reverent tone as though he were referring to a temple menial attending a discommoded Vestal.

"Thank you, my boy," returned Thorne in an avuncular tone. "And as to that other matter, you have my whole-hearted permission to pursue your suit."

John's smile widened to what could only be called a radiant grin.

"Thank you! Thank you, sir. I hope to speak to you again on the matter very soon."

"Such is my hope as well, John—my very devout hope." Bidding John a brief good evening, he hurried upstairs to tap on Chloe's door. A moment later, Hester appeared.

"Oh dear," she said in reply to Thorne's announcement. "I had forgotten all about Trevor. Well," she said, looking back over her shoulder, "Chloe is dozing. I prepared her some warm milk, and I think she is probably asleep for the night. I hate to leave, though, in case she wakes up."

"I suppose Aunt Lavinia could sit with her, if you think it necessary," said Thorne halfheartedly. His lips curved in a half smile. "I have some news I wished to discuss with you this evening." He was surprised at his reluctance to see Hester leave the house. He felt an unexpected need to tell her of John Wery's request. Not that he needed her counsel regarding Chloe, of course, but he rather looked forward to simply talking things over with her. "And you have not yet dined," he added awkwardly.

Hester, too, knew a moment of hesitation. She had been looking forward to this outing for some days, but now, at Thorne's words, the thought of going out for the evening was strangely unwelcome. Conversely, the notion of staying home for a quiet chat with the earl held considerable appeal.

"I think it would be unwise for me to leave the house," she said mendaciously. "Aunt Lavinia could cope with Chloe, of course, but I think she would rather not."

"I agree."

Hester smiled. "I'll just go down and explain to Trevor. I'm sure he will understand."

"I do not understand," said Trevor, upon receiving Hester's brief explanation of the evening's events. His thin nose pinched unbecomingly. "We have had this engagement for over a week. Everyone is expecting you tonight. I cannot believe you would desert your friends to hold the hand of a pampered young miss who—"

"Trevor, please," responded Hester tartly. "I am hardly deserting my friends. I was planning to invite everyone here for a small collation in a few days. I shall send notes around tomorrow. In the meantime, it would be remiss of me to leave the house tonight. My reason for coming to London, as you will recall, was to assist my cousin with his ward. She underwent an extremely trying experience this evening and I just now got her to sleep—with a great deal of difficulty, I might add. If she should awake, I feel I should be at hand to, er, render assistance."

"Then, I suppose there is no more to be said." Trevor turned on his heel and exited the drawing room. Sighing, Hester sank into an armchair before the fireplace and gazed into the flames. She fell into a rather unpleasant reverie, from which she was aroused a few minutes later by the entrance of Thorne.

"Ah. You elected to stay home this evening. I trust your friends were not overly disappointed."

"No, of course not," Hester said quickly.

"Good. It appears dinner has been awaiting us for some minutes," he said, smiling. "Shall we?"

Hester knew a moment of discomfort when she realized that Lady Lavinia had already taken her meal and retired for the evening, thus she and the earl would be dining *a deux*. Her fears were allayed some moments later, however, when it became obvious that the earl's conversation was to be entirely unexceptionable. Thorne told her of his recent conversation with John Wery and accepted her felicitations with gratification.

"I should imagine he will pop the question any day now, and with any luck, Chloe will be married by year's end."

"You think she will be amenable?" asked Hester, a shade of doubt in her voice.

Thorne paused, a forkful of mutton pie poised halfway to his mouth. "Of course. Don't you?"

"Well, her feelings for him seem to have changed markedly, but . . . She was so adamant before . . . Oh, I'm being nonsensical. Of course, she will accept him. He is her perfect, gentle knight, after all."

Their conversation turned to other topics then. From a discussion on the poetry of Coleridge to an exhaustive survey of the Prince Regent's failings as a ruler to the likelihood of paved roads in the future as far north as York, they talked through an excellent dinner—although later, Hester could not recall what they had eaten.

Afterward, they adjourned not to the drawing room, but to Thorne's study on the ground floor, where, said Thorne, he wished to show her a collection of miniatures he had just begun to acquire. They were as yet unframed and he had not decided where to hang them.

This was the first time Hester had entered the earl's sanctum, and she would, perhaps, have been surprised to know that she was the first female he had ever invited to set foot in this haven he had created in the heart of his fashionable town domicile. It was a pleasant room, furnished not in the first stare of elegance, but with comfortable, sometimes shabby chairs, tables, and footstools. A well-used chess set reposed on a plain wooden table near the fireplace and a navigation globe stood in a corner. A small brass telescope stood on a tripod in front of a pair of long windows. Shelves bearing a varied assortment of curios ranked about the room, including what appeared to be the nest of a very large bird, positioned next to an exquisite jade figurine.

Observing her expression of faint wonderment, Thorne laughed. "You may be forgiven for supposing you've stumbled into a lumber room. I wanted at least one room to be just mine, and I brought a lot of stuff from the Park that I've collected over the years. That"—he gestured to the nest—"was brought back from Africa by my Uncle Pointdexter. He says he personally snatched it out from under an infuriated blue-footed oryx. I was twelve years old at the time and had no idea then or now what an oryx might be, blue-footed or otherwise, but it apparently exercised a strong fascination for I have kept it by me ever since."

"And no wonder," said Hester, examining the huge mass of straw, leaves, and other construction ingredients, at whose identity she preferred not to guess. "And this?" she asked, picking up the figurine.

"Ah, that was my own acquisition. I found it in, of all places, a little shop in Cairo. Lovely, isn't she?" he asked, moving closer to trace the cheek of the little oriental goddess with his fingertip.

"Oh!" she exclaimed. "You have been to Egypt. How I envy you!"

"Yes, it was one of the few places one could travel during the recent unpleasantness with Napoleon, and since the end of the war, I have visited the continent several times."

"I hope to go there myself someday. It has always been a dream of mine to travel."

"To Paris, perhaps?"

"Yes, and to Rome and Venice and into Greece—perhaps even Turkey."

"Ah. Do you wish to participate in the revolution there, too?"

"Too?" She twisted to look up at him. "Do you consider me a revolutionary?"

He led her to a comfortable chair by the fire. "Are you not?" he asked, pouring wine for them. He handed her a glass and settled with his own in a nearby chair, regretting the words as soon as he had spoken them. He had no wish to encourage Hester to climb on her hobbyhorse at the moment. Though she was attractive when fired up, she was also at her most tedious when her bluestocking instincts took over her conversation. To his surprise, she broke into laughter.

"If you could see your face," she said with a chuckle. "Behold the male in all his splendid indifference."

"Well, we can't all be gadflies." He spoke calmly, but he was somewhat nettled. Just because he did not share her propensity for churning up the status quo, did that make him a conscienceless clod? "Tell me," he said, leaning forward, "how did you become so devoted to—to righting all the wrongs of our society?"

"Goodness!" she said, startled. "Surely not all the wrongs—just a selected list. I guess," she continued thoughtfully, "it started many years ago with two of my friends, one of whom I went to school with, the other the daughter of our village apothecary. The father of my school friend was a renowned scholar and he trained her to be his assistant. She helped in his research and transcribed his notes—that sort of thing. He was an enlightened man, and allowed her intellect free rein, and by the time she was twenty, she was as knowledgeable in her father's field as he. No one knew this, of course, and her contributions to his expertise went unrewarded. When he died, he was in the middle of what he thought of as his greatest work, one that he had counted on bringing enough money to provide his daughter with a comfortable dowry. Jennifer—that was her name—was left virtually penniless. She was fully capable of finishing the work herself, but the publisher would not hear of it.

"Without a dowry, she was unable to attract a husband who could be counted on to support her, of course. Her situation was quite desperate for a while until she contrived to acquire a position as governess in a family with several children. She now resides in Hereford—we still correspond.

"The other—Elizabeth Whitcombe, the apothecary's daughter—was bright and keen of wit. She developed an early interest in her father's business, but received no encouragement from her family to learn more about it. In fact, Jeremiah Whitcombe reached the point where he threatened Elizabeth with bodily harm—more than threatened, I gathered—if she did not stop hiding herself away with his books on pharmaceuticals instead of helping her mother around the house.

"She was married at her father's insistence when she was nineteen to a farmer, an unlikable block who, needless to say, had no sympathy for her fierce desire for learning. Her brother, who had no interest in running the shop, but had a burning desire to follow a career at sea, inherited the business, of course. The last I heard of him he had lost it because of a growing addiction to the bottle. Elizabeth," she added tonelessly, "died a year ago giving birth to her sixth child."

Unthinking, Thorne reached to cover Hester's hands

where they lay clenched in her lap. She jerked them away, raising one to dash the tears that had risen to her eyes.

"Don't you see?" she cried. "The stories of Jennifer and Elizabeth are repeated a thousandfold all over the country. It is not fair that a woman's mind must be bound into a tidy little parcel and stuffed into an unwanted marriage—or stultifying penury for the rest of her life."

She drew a deep breath and continued more calmly. "To say nothing of the fact, as Mary Wollstonecraft so often averred, that the nation is being deprived of a resource it can ill do without."

Despite himself, Thorne found himself stirred by her passion. For the first time in his life, he considered the vast population of females in the realm who were persons in their own right, but who could never live the lives of their choice. Most of them, to be sure, if given a choice, would undoubtedly still prefer to rely on a man for their livelihood and to make the important decisions in their lives. For some, however, such as the redoubtable Hester Blayne and those of her sisterhood, who were capable of so much more, it was, he was forced to admit, eminently unfair that they be permanently—what was it?—"cribbed, cabin'd, and confined."

"And so," he said softly, "Hester Blayne mounted her pulpit to right this monstrous wrong."

She stiffened. "I imagine it is all vastly amusing to you, my lord, but I am in no mood to see my life's work derided."

She made as though to rise. Thorne stayed her by grasping her wrist.

"I'm sorry, Hester. I was not speaking facetiously. It has taken a great deal of courage for you to turn your back on your family and what would no doubt be a comfortable life in order to uphold your convictions." He spoke with unaccustomed awkwardness, and Hester was touched despite herself.

"Um. Well." She felt a little awkward herself. "Yes, it has been a little difficult, but I would not have it any other way." She smiled joyously. "I am free, you see, and that compensates for the scrimping and the snubs and the hostility and—and all the rest."

"And now," continued Thorne, smiling, "you have embarked on other reforms as well. Don't forget I was present during your instructive discourse to Lord Pickering the other night on shorter working hours for children, or—no, no—" He held up a hand. "No labor at all for children under fourteen."

Hester returned his smile, and the mischievous twinkle that Thorne was learning to relish appeared in her eyes. "You learn quickly—for a man. But yes," she added, her expression serious once more. "There seems no end to the inequities besetting the poor and helpless of England. But, slowly—very slowly, things are getting better. Because of Mr. Wilburforce, we are no longer involved in the iniquitous slave trade, and, of course there's Mr. Bennet's work—that's Henry Gray Bennet—do you know him? He's the second son of the Earl of Tankerville, and an outspoken proponent in the House for the abolishment of the use of climbing boys. I have participated in his committee from time to time."

"Mm, yes, he is chairman of the Select Committee now, is he not? I understand he tried to bring up a bill in the House this year, but it was too late. Perhaps he will try next year."

Hester's brows lifted. "I did not know you followed the reformists's progress."

"Not precisely with bated breath," drawled Thorne, "but even the most dedicated hedonists among us must be touched by the plight of little boys being forced up smoky chimneys for hours on end. Particularly when there are other methods, just as cheap, of cleaning them."

"I am glad to hear you say it, my lord." Hester smiled. "Perhaps you would like to accompany me next month to one of Mr. Gray's meetings."

"I think not, but I would, with your permission, like to attend the gathering you intend to hold here next week."

Hester's gaze dropped to her lap, where her fingers busily began to pleat her skirt. She had not told the earl of her plans to invite her friends to Bythorne House, and realized that he must consider her to be taking gross advantage of his hospitality. "I did not mean—that is Aunt Lavinia considered that you would not—"

"That I would not mind," he finished smoothly. "Of course, I do not. I told you at the outset, Hester, that you must feel free to invite whomever you wish here. I assume that among those present will be Mr. Bentham?"

Unaccountably, she flushed. "Yes, and Robert Carver as well, and—and Lady Barbara expressed an interest in attending."

"Barbara?" Thorne's brows flew up into his hairline. "Now you do surprise me."

"Well, I must admit, I was a little surprised myself. I was speaking to Aunt Lavinia about the gathering, in front of Lady Barbara, and I invited her mostly as a courtesy. She accepted with a good deal of alacrity, in fact."

"Well, well."

"I hope you will not hold it over my head, Thorne," added Hester, laughing, "if you find yourself married to a crusader."

"I beg your pardon!"

Thorne's tone was so frosty that Hester was momentarily taken aback. "That is, I understood from your aunt—both your aunts—that you and Lady Barbara were—are—"

"Allow me to tell you, Miss Blayne, that my relationship with Lady Barbara Freemantle is of no concern to anyone save myself and, of course, Lady Barbara."

Hester stiffened. "Yes, of course. I did not mean to intrude on your private life, my lord."

Thorne abruptly unbent. "And now we're back to 'Miss Blayne' and 'my lord,' aren't we? I wish my relatives were not quite so busy on my behalf. I suppose I shall marry Barbara someday, but I do not propose to become leg-shackled for some time to come."

"You do not wish to marry her?" asked Hester curiously. Immediately, conscience-stricken, she clapped her fingers to her lips. "Oh dear, I'm sorry. I didn't—"

"I do not wish to marry anyone," he said casually, "but

in my position, it's inevitable, I'm afraid. Barbara is as likely a candidate as any—and I'm sure she feels the same way about me. I like her, which is more than I can say for the procession of simpering misses my aunts have paraded before me for the last ten years or so."

"But, to marry someone for whom you have no more than a liking . . ." persisted Hester, appalled at her own gaucherie. She had no business prying into this man's matrimonial intentions, for God's sake. Why was it so important to her to ascertain his feelings on the subject?

He merely glanced at her in some surprise, however. "But, surely that is all one can expect in such a union. Ah," he continued, his voice tinged with amusement. "You speak of a more tender emotion. Love, perhaps? I did not know you were such a sentimentalist, my dear."

Hester flushed again. "I do not believe that marrying for love can be called merely sentimental," she said, pressing her lips firmly together.

"Perhaps not, but it is certainly unrealistic," replied Thorne in a bored tone.

Hester rose. "I do believe I pity you, Lord Bythorne. To be so heartless—totally devoid of passion, either socially or personally, is a great tragedy."

Thorne, too, stood, and moved to stand before her. Lifting his hand, he ran a finger along her cheek. "Oh, not totally devoid, I think," he said lazily, an unholy light flaming at the back of his dark gaze. He shifted his hand to cup the back of her head, but she stepped back abruptly.

"Goodness, the evening has quite fled, my lord. I must look in on Chloe, and then I believe I shall retire. I have enjoyed our conversation, and now I shall bid you good night."

With a rustle of her skirts, she turned and left the room, leaving Thorne with his hand still upraised. It felt, he mused regretfully, oddly empty.

Chapter Thirteen

It might have been expected that soon after John Wery's declaration to Lord Bythorne, an Interesting Announcement would have been issued to society at large via the *Morning Post*. Such, however, was not the case. When Thorne informed Chloe of John's stated intentions, her reaction was a wide, indignant stare.

"But, Uncle, of course I am not going to marry him! Have I not told you so over and over?"

"But—but, what about his dramatic rescue? The other night he was your champion on a white charger."

Chloe's cheeks flushed with pink. "Oh yes, I admire him tremendously for what he did. My opinion of him is much improved. Even if I thought him the most perfect of men, however, I have no intention of marrying."

"Oh, my God!" The cry came from Thorne's heart. What the devil was he to do now? "Hester!" He fairly bellowed her name.

"Miss Blayne is away from home, sir," said Hobart, materializing at his elbow. "She and Lady Lavinia were to meet Lady Bracken at the Egyptian Hall—to view the current exhibition—of items from the South Seas, I believe. Lady Lavinia said they would be home in time for dinner."

Thorne was forced to curb his impatience. Why the devil had Hester picked this afternoon to jaunter about town looking at old bones? She had come to Bythorne House to help him get Chloe buckled. Why was she not here in his hour of need?

Not that she'd been around much of late at all. Not since their little *tête-à-tête* in his study the other evening. Her attitude toward him had been chill to the point of glacial, in fact. How was he to know she would take snuff at a little harmless flirtation? She had virtually asked for it with that gratuitous puffery about his lack of passion.

Love! He snorted to himself. He might have known a female whose head was so permanently planted in the clouds would view the institution of marriage through a pink haze.

He simply had to stop indulging in late-night chats before the fire in intimate little chambers with Miss Prunes and Prisms. The thought left him feeling strangely forlorn. He pondered their conversation. It certainly had held no hint of dalliance—which was unusual of itself. Normally, he had only one thing in mind when he sat down for an amiable coze with a female. Yet, he had enjoyed simply talking with her—talking almost as he would to a friend. Though, to be truthful, not many men of his acquaintance could discourse as interestingly on as many subjects as Hester, a fact that would ordinarily have sent him fleeing a woman's company. He had never met anyone quite like her, he admitted to himself. He was forced to admit her presence had wrought a change in him.

He now found himself looking at his world with new eyes. The old apple woman on the corner, for example. With the kind of education available now only to privileged males, might she have grown up to make a dramatic contribution to, say, the medical knowledge of the day?

He had been born to a life of wealth and privilege—but hundreds of thousands had not. What might some of them have become had they been blessed with his opportunities?

Even among the women of his own class, were there some who might have qualified as crafty financiers—as cabinet ministers? He laughed softly as he thought of Gussie meting out justice from the bench. And he thought of Hester. A picture of her garbed in parliamentary robes rose before him. Hmmm, perhaps not so hard to imagine, after all.

Still . . . He sighed. It was just too bad she was so damned straitlaced.

*   *   *

It was too bad Lord Bythorne was such an incorrigible rake, thought Hester for the hundredth time as she wandered through the chambers of the Egyptian Hall. Ordinarily, she would have been engrossed very quickly in the displays of ancient artifacts about her, but today she seemed unable to marshal her thoughts into a proper channel. Despite her best efforts, they tended to drift back to the moment a few nights ago when she had swept out of Thorne's study.

She hadn't wanted to. At least she was honest enough to admit that. Her knees had turned to soup the moment he had touched her cheek, and it was all she could do not to lean into the embrace she was sure would have followed. Dear God, what was the matter with her? She had had plenty of experience in turning aside unwanted masculine attention. She knew it was not her fatal desirability that encouraged men to take liberties, it was her outspoken feminism. For some men that was a signal—nay, an open invitation for any sort of presumption. Apparently, my lord Bythorne was among their number. Or, perhaps it was simply that he was congenitally unable to confront any female without making an attempt on her virtue.

She sighed. How very tiresome, to be sure, for she had been enjoying their discussion. He had showed a side that she had not thought existed. The man could actually be sensitive to the misery of others, it appeared. Could there be some hope for him? She rather thought not, if he could not rid himself of his unfortunate propensity to molest every woman that crossed his path.

Well, she would soon be removed from that path. John had requested permission to court Chloe, and after his heroic performance at the carriage wreck, there seemed little doubt that Chloe would now welcome his suit. The betrothal would probably be announced within a few weeks and Hester Blayne, feminist, could return to her home, her writings, her speeches, and the purposeful routine of her life.

She would, she told herself, be glad to settle down again in the quiet backwater that was Overcross. Not that she hadn't enjoyed her little fling in the metropolis, but—the thought bubbled to the surface at last from where it had lain waiting to be noticed—she had become entirely too fond of Thorne's company of late. It was one thing to acknowledge his carnal attraction for her. She could deal with that. But when mere conversation with him could fizz through her veins like champagne, then it was time to sound the retreat. Nothing could be more disastrous than to form a real attachment to a man whose sole purpose in life was, apparently, the seduction of as many women as he could schedule into his hedonistic life.

Not, of course, that she had anything to worry about in that direction. His feeble attempts at flirtation had been no more than an automatic reflex—a response to a challenge, for, of course, rejection was not to be countenanced. The Earl of Bythorne, in the unlikely event that he should turn his thoughts to marriage, would set his sights much higher than her unseductive self. To the desirable Lady Barbara Freemantle, in fact.

Clutching these and other equally salutary thoughts to her bosom, Hester returned her attention to the Ancient World. Later, she and Lady Bracken and Lady Lavinia refreshed themselves with tea and cakes in a nearby pastry shop. Thus, the afternoon was far advanced when the little party returned to Curzon Street. There they were greeted by a scene of rampant disharmony. Even as they entered the front door, they could hear the sound of voices raised in the music room, just at the top of the flight of stairs to the first floor.

"I won't!" came an all-too-familiar cry, and the three ladies exchanged glances of consternation before hurrying up the steps. They entered the music room to find Chloe seated on a piano stool, weeping copiously into a lace-edged handkerchief. Above her, like a swollen thundercloud brimful of lightning, loomed Thorne.

"Chloe," he was expostulating, "Wery will no doubt be appearing on our doorstep at any moment, and when he does, by God, I expect you to—"

"Thorne!" exclaimed Hester. "Chloe! What in the world is to do?"

"Good God!" chimed in Lady Bracken. "You sound like a pair of Billingsgates. I shouldn't wonder the whole neighborhood isn't a party to your row."

Lady Lavinia said nothing, but gasped audibly at the scene before her.

Chloe, upon observing Hester's entrance, leaped to her feet and ran to fling herself on her preceptress. "Oh, Hester!" she cried. "I'm so glad you are home. Oh, dear heaven, was anyone ever so beset as I?"

"Oh, for God's sake!" snorted Thorne. "If ever I saw a Tragedy Jill." He turned to Hester. "Where the devil have you been?"

Hester stiffened in umbrage, but Thorne immediately lifted a hand in apology.

"I'm sorry," he said. "It's just that I've been so bedeviled—" He drew a long breath as Hester disengaged Chloe from her bosom and led her to a chair by the window. "I told my totty-headed ward," he continued, "of John Wery's intention to ask for her hand and she—she refuses," he concluded in disbelief.

"Oh dear," said Lady Lavinia, and all three ladies swung to gaze at Chloe in varying attitudes of incredulity.

"Good God, gel!" exclaimed Lady Bracken. "What nonsense is this?"

Chloe broke into a fresh paroxysm, sinking to her knees and burying her face in Hester's skirt. Looking over her head, Hester met Thorne's gaze and she jerked her head almost imperceptibly toward the door. He opened his mouth as though to protest, but immediately clamped his lips shut.

"Come, Gussie," he said instead, interrupting that lady midtirade. "Aunt Lavinia," he added, gesturing both ladies toward the door. Gussie was still talking when he led them from the room.

Hester bent over Chloe. "There, there, my dear. It's all right. They're all gone and now we can have a comfortable coze." She drew a clean handkerchief from her reticule and began mopping her protégé's cheeks. Within a few mo-

ments, Chloe had stopped crying, although she occasionally
erupted into spasmodic hiccups.

"What am I going to do now, Hester?" she asked dole-
fully. "I did just as you suggested. I've gone along with
Uncle Thorne's wishes, and I've talked feminism to John
and babbled on about jewelry and London town houses and
here I am, on the verge of betrothal. Oh, Hester!" Her eyes
welled again. "I just can't bear it."

"Well," Hester replied in a prosaic tone, "there's nothing
that says you have to—bear it, that is. If you really feel you
cannot marry Mr. Wery, all you have to do is tell him so."

Chloe swiveled around, her tears forgotten, to stare wide-
eyed at Hester. "B-but, what about Uncle Thorne? And
Aunt Gussie? And how am I to tell John—?"

"I think you may safely leave your uncle and aunt to
me," said Hester briskly. "As for John, you must simply
say, straightly and forthrightly, 'I am sensible to the honor
you have bestowed upon me, Mr. Wery, but I am afraid we
would not suit.' If necessary, repeat the phrase until the
gentleman fully understands that you're not going to marry
him."

"You make it all sound so easy."

"Well, and it is. You must merely maintain your dignity
throughout."

Chloe fell silent for a moment, twisting her handkerchief
in her lap. When she lifted her head at last, she bent a coaxing smile on Hester. "Could you not talk to John for me?"
she asked. "I know it's perfectly chickenhearted of me, but,
oh, Hester, I just do not know how to face him—to break
his heart in such a manner and still keep my—my dignity."

"Oh, no," replied Hester promptly. "That would not do at
all, I'm afraid. It would be most unbecoming in you. If
you're going to break his heart, my dear, you must do it to
his face."

Chloe cast her eyes down again. "I suppose you're right.
Oh, how could Uncle Thorne have led him to believe his
suit would be acceptable?"

Hester smiled. "Perhaps because he so dearly wished it
to be so. And, you must admit, Chloe, you gave us all rea-

son to believe your feelings toward Mr. Wery had undergone a profound change."

Chloe's startled glance flew to Hester's face. "Oh, but they have! I admire him tremendously. But"—she blushed to the roots of her hair—"that does not mean that I am in love with him—or that I wish to marry him. I would think Uncle Thorne, above all people, would understand that," she concluded bitterly. "He apparently thinks the world of Lady Barbara, but I don't see him down on his knees before her proposing marriage."

"That's true," replied Hester a trifle unsteadily. "But, men, as you have perceived by now, are not blessed with a great deal of empathy."

Chloe said nothing, but heaved a profound sigh, and the two ladies remained in unspoken communion for a few moments.

"Well, then," said Hester at last. "Perhaps you had better repair to your room. Mr. Wery may be upon us soon, and we do not want him to discover you in such a lachrymose state."

Chloe pulled herself up from her knees with yet another soul-wrenching sigh and allowed herself to be led into the hall and up the stairs. Having deposited her into Pinkham's waiting hands, Hester returned downstairs, to find Thorne and his aunts awaiting her in the drawing room in a state of high indignation.

"Well, have you managed to talk some sense into the little twit?" were Thorne's first, unpromising words.

"No," snapped Hester. "I feel I will be doing well at this point to talk some sense into you."

"But, Hester," put in Gussie, "you're the only one she will listen to, and if you cannot convince her to receive Mr. Wery's attentions, what are we to do?"

"Please, let us sit down for a moment," said Hester with an admirable assumption of calm. "There is really no reason for despair."

Lady Lavinia twittered distressfully, but seated herself as requested, and after another few moments of expostulation Thorne and Gussie did likewise. Hester took a deep breath.

"I have suggested to Chloe that, since she still feels adamant on the subject of matrimony, she will simply have to refuse Mr. Wery when he comes calling."

"What!" bellowed Thorne. "Good God, is that your idea of a solution to this tangle?"

"Yes, it is," replied Hester coolly. "At least, a temporary one. The thing is, I believe Chloe is at least half in love with John Wery, and even though she doesn't understand her own feelings, it will not take much to push her over the precipice—so to speak. She has held for so long, buckle and thong, to her notion of a celibate life, that it is very difficult for her to—to realign her thinking. If you will all bear with me—and with Chloe—I believe we will still see her betrothed to John in the not-too-distant future."

"You're talking in circles," growled Thorne. "I say it's time I put my foot down on Miss Venable and all her foibles."

"You have tried that, my lord, with a singular lack of success. Now, if you will just let me—"

She was interrupted by the sound of the front door knocker, and all activity was suspended as the four conspirators waited with stilled breath. In a few moments, Hobart entered to announce that Mr. John Wery had come to call on Miss Chloe. At his words, acrimony broke out once more until Hester held up her hand, bringing it down with a slap on a small occasional table at her side. Once more, a startled silence fell on the room.

"Please," she said in a low, fierce voice, "we do not have time for further discussion. I ask you to trust me in this." She spoke to all of them, but her gaze went to Thorne, who stared back intently for some moments.

"Very well." He stood. "What do you want us to do?"

"But, Thorne—!" exclaimed Gussie while Lady Lavinia contented herself with an unintelligible series of "Oh, dear me's."

"I asked Miss Blayne here to help me," Thorne said to his afflicted relatives. "I see no alternative at this point but to let her get on with whatever she's planning."

He turned to Hester, his visage calm, but with a minatory look in his eyes. "What do you want us to do?" he repeated.

"Thank you, Thorne," said Hester simply. "I would like to speak to Mr. Wery for a few minutes—alone. Then, I will call for Chloe to come down to receive him. I promise," she added with a smile that was almost mischievous, "I will Explain All later."

Thorne did not return the smile, but turned to usher his aunts from the room.

Hester sat down and folded her hands, and in a few moments John Wery was ushered into the room. If he was surprised to behold Miss Blayne awaiting him instead of his inamorata, he displayed no sign of it, but, greeting her courteously, he seated himself nearby.

"I know you have come to call on Chloe," began Hester, and John nodded, his brows lifting quizzically.

"Yes, I was given to understand that she is at home to visitors." The statement was almost in the form of a question.

"Oh yes," said Hester, "but I wanted to have a word with you before she is apprised of your presence here."

"Ah," said John, his obvious puzzlement increasing.

"Mr. Wery, I realize we do not know each other well, but I have become friends with Chloe—and—and with Lord Bythorne. You already know that his lordship smiles upon your suit, as do I." Hester drew in a deep breath. "In fact, the only person not in favor of the match is Chloe herself."

"What?" exclaimed John. "But—I was given to understand—that is—"

"Please, believe me, Mr.—may I call you John, please, for I feel that you and I are about to become much more closely acquainted."

"Certainly," John replied a little wildly. "But—"

"Please, believe me," said Hester again, for she had rehearsed this speech rather carefully. "Chloe holds you in the highest regard, and I am afraid it is my fault that she is prepared to refuse you this afternoon—if you should still care to declare yourself."

"Your fault! But, I thought you said—" John ran trembling fingers through his mouse brown hair.

"My fault because I seem to have inspired Chloe to take up the feminist cause."

"Well, yes, I have heard her speak of you most admiringly, but—"

"I am afraid she misunderstood some of my writings to indicate a belief that women should not marry."

"Uhh-hh," said John, an expression of wary comprehension beginning to spread across his features.

"Yes," said Hester. "She has apparently decided that she must devote her life to the cause, and plans to spend the rest of her days writing and lecturing."

For a moment, John said nothing, and Hester watched him intently. After staring into space for a few seconds, John appeared to gather himself together.

"I must confess, Miss Blayne, your words come as a shock to me. It had not escaped my notice, of course, that Chl—Miss Venable's sentiments toward me were, er, less than enthusiastic, but last night . . . Well, the carriage incident seemed to bring us together, and I thought—"

"John, why do you wish to marry Chloe?"

For a moment, he simply stared at her.

"W-what?"

"I said—"

"Yes, I heard you," John said hastily. "I mean, why? That is, why do you ask, Miss Blayne?"

Hester smiled. "As in, 'What possible business is it of yours, Miss Blayne?'"

He flushed. "Well—er, yes."

"I ask only because I think I can help you, but first I wish to ascertain your feelings for Chloe."

John stiffened. "Well, naturally, I hold Miss Venable in the highest esteem." Apparently perceiving that Miss Blayne required a little more exposition on his part, he rushed on. "She is lovely, and—and lively, and up until now, I had thought we would suit admirably as man and wife."

Hester sighed. "Did you ever tell her that—the part about her being lovely and lively?"

He gave an affronted gasp. "Of course not! Do you take me for a complete here-and-thereian?"

"Absolutely not," she replied dryly. "But, never mind that now. Do you love her, John?" she asked gently.

John blanched visibly, as though he had been accused of planning to sell Miss Venable into white slavery.

"I—I just told you, I hold her—"

"Yes, yes." Hester waved an impatient hand. "But, that is not the same thing, is it? I want to know how you really feel about her."

"I—I do not wish to contemplate my life without her," said John gruffly. "I like being with her, and I feel—oh, empty when I am not. I like just looking at her, but I like it even more when I can hold her in my arms during the dance."

"And—?"

"Yes," he said miserably. "I do love her. But what has that to do with anything if she does not return my affection?" He rose, his expression bleak. "I really believe I should leave, Miss Blayne. I see no point in distressing her with my declaration if it is unwelcome to her, nor do I wish to subject myself to the humiliation of her rejection."

Hester's eyes glinted with satisfaction. "Sit down, John. All is not lost. Trust me, for I have a plan."

John sank slowly back into his chair, his aspect dubious and his demeanor unwilling.

"In a few moments, I shall notify Chloe that you are here, and when she comes down, you will make your proposal."

At this, John leaped to his feet again as though bitten. Hester merely held up an admonitory hand, and as she continued to speak, his attitude lightened considerably. When she finally paused to draw breath, a slow, wary smile lit his eyes.

"I think one of us must be a little mad, Miss Blayne, and at this point I am not willing to hazard a guess as to which one it is. However, I shall do as you wish. I, too, it appears am about to join the ranks of your adherents—whether for good or ill, we shall have to see."

Chapter Fourteen

A few moments later, when Chloe entered the drawing room, John awaited her alone. Chloe was pale and still obviously distraught, but Pinkham had managed to obliterate most of the tearstains from her cheeks. She smiled wanly when John brushed her fingertips with his lips, and allowed herself to be drawn to a small settee near the window.

"Miss Venable," began John. He spoke softly, searching her face intently, "I trust you have recovered from our adventure yesterday afternoon."

Chloe started and glanced down at her hands, one of which still lay in John's grasp. "Oh, yes, of course. Although, of course, the whole thing will forever remain in my memory." She assayed a quick glance at him through her lashes and blushed at the expression she found there.

"Miss Venable," said John again, "dear Miss Venable, I believe you are aware by now that I have spoken to Lord Bythorne and—"

"Goodness!" exclaimed Chloe. "Has no one rung for tea? How very remiss of Hobart not to have seen to it."

Pulling her hand from his, she rose abruptly and went to the bellpull. On her return, she seated herself a little way away from him. Hobart entered the room almost immediately, leading anyone to suppose he had been lurking immediately outside the door. Chloe, in a trembling voice, ordered refreshments, and when Hobart had bowed himself from the room, she turned to John and spoke brightly.

"I must send a note around to Sophy Salburt to inquire about her mother. The poor lady was in such a sad state when we arrived home, that I'm sure she must have gone into severe palpitations."

"Yes, she did seem overset. Miss Venable—"

"I must own I was surprised when it came on to rain yesterday, for I do not think there was any forecast. And today the sun—"

"Miss Venable," said John gently. "Chloe. I did not come here today to discuss the weather conditions in southern England." He picked up a small, straight-backed chair and placing it directly in front of her, sat down. This time, he took both of her hands in his. "I do not mean to distress you, my dear girl, but I have come to ask you to be my wife."

"Oh-hh-h!" moaned Chloe in dismay. She bit her lip. "Mr. Wery, this is so very sudden, I—" She glanced up to catch his gaze on her. "Well, no, I guess I cannot say that, can I?" She tugged at her hands, and he released them without a struggle. Chloe took a deep breath.

"Mr. Wery, I am conscious of the deep honor you do me, but I fear we should not suit. I have elected to devote my life to the cause of feminism and equality for women." She uttered the words in a rush and stared apprehensively at him.

John pushed back his chair and stood. For a moment, he looked down at her. "And you do not think you could fit a husband and family into your program?" he asked with a smile.

"No! That is—I must tell you Mr. Wery, that I view the institution of marriage as little more than a form of slavery."

"Ah." John moved the chair back a little and reseated himself. "Perhaps, if—"

At this inopportune moment, Hobart entered the room, followed by a footman, who carried an ornate tea tray. An awkward silence prevailed as the footman arranged cups, saucers, and a plate of biscuits on a table. After the two men withdrew, the delicate Meissen clattered loudly as Chloe poured tea and offered John a biscuit, which he refused.

"I am sorry—"

John looked up quickly at Chloe's almost hysterical tone.

"I seem to be inordinately clumsy this afternoon. It's just that—" She gasped a little and uttered a high-pitched burst of laughter. "I do not think I have ever been alone with a man for such an extended period of time. And I know my aunts are upstairs waiting to pounce on me after you've left. They will want to know how our interview went, and when I tell them—" She burst into tears, and John, a look of consternation on his face, put down his cup and sank to his knees before her.

"Don't," he said, patting her hand ineffectually. "Don't do that. I never meant to discommode you. Oh, Chloe—" Gently, he put an arm about her and drew her head onto his shoulder. "I shall not importune you. If you do not wish to marry, I—I shall respect your wishes."

Startled, Chloe drew back, her eyes wide and her tears studding the long sweep of her lashes. "You mean—?" she asked breathlessly.

John withdrew a handkerchief from his pocket and began drying her eyes. His gesture was so avuncular—not at all loverlike—that Chloe relaxed against him.

"All I want is for you to be happy, Chloe. I am sorry that the idea of marrying me does not fulfill that wish, but I will respect your decision."

He rose. "I shall not stay for tea, I think. I will leave you now, Chloe—my dearest Chloe."

Chloe's pink mouth made an O of astonishment.

"But, I want you to know that if you should change your mind, I—I will be waiting."

He stooped to pick up her hand and once more kissed her fingers lightly. He turned then, but stopped abruptly when he got to the door. He whirled about. "I forgot—you look lovely today—as always."

Then, he was gone.

Chloe fell back into her chair. "Ohh-hhh-hh," she said softly, pressing her fingertips to her lips, and it was many minutes before she rose to leave the room herself.

To her surprise, there was no pouncing. In fact, neither

of her aunts seemed to be on the premises, nor was Uncle Thorne. She ran lightly up the stairs and tapped on Hester's door. Upon receiving permission to enter, she fairly flung herself into the room, where Hester sat at her desk, writing.

"Oh, Hester," she cried, "this has been the most wretched day of my life!"

"Come, now," Hester replied briskly. "It could not have been that bad. Tell me what transpired."

"It was awful! I refused his suit, and he was s-so noble— so brave! He s-said," she wailed, "that he wished only for my happiness!"

"Well, now, there is nothing in that to turn you into a watering pot, my dear. You see, I told you that all you had to do was refuse him."

"But, I have broken his heart!"

"Nonsense. Hearts do not break so easily. I'll warrant that by this time next month he will have formed an attachment to some other pretty young miss and will have a hard time recalling your name. So, you see how well it has all turned out."

"How can you be so unfeeling, Hester?" Chloe fairly gasped in her indignation. "He said he will be waiting for me if I change my mind."

"Oh, they all say that," replied Hester prosaically. With a bright smile, she turned back to her desk. "Now, if you'll excuse me, my dear, I must get back to work. If I do not finish this chapter today, I shall become woefully behind schedule. I hope you don't mind?" she added, her eyes already on her page.

"No, of course not," replied Chloe stiffly. "I have a few things to attend to myself."

With a petulant rustle of skirts she turned on her heel and stalked from the room.

Hester gazed for a few moments at the closed door, and smiled.

Dinner that evening was a fairly subdued affair. Lady Bracken did not dine with them that evening. Lady Lavinia seemed immersed in thought, and Chloe toyed listlessly with her food. It was thus left to Thorne and Hester to maintain a desultory conversation.

"Did I hear you say something about your giving a lecture soon?" Thorne asked Hester.

"Yes, indeed. I have been invited to speak to a gathering of ladies in Seven Dials. The lecture is sponsored by Sir Gerard Welles and will be held at the Blue Boar Tavern."

Thorne frowned.

"Good God, you can't possibly go there."

Hester looked up from her plate, startled. "Why not?"

"Because—You must know what an unsavory area that is."

"Yes, I know, but I shall have Trevor with me, and—"

"Ah," said Thorne in a withering tone. "You set my mind at rest. What could possibly befall you in the company of the stalwart Mr. Bentham?"

Hester flushed. "I scarcely think anything at all is liable to befall us, but I assure you we will be accompanied by a full complement of coachman, groom, and probably a footman or two."

Thorne's frown did not diminish. "I still cannot like it."

"I am sorry for that, my lord, but you must know that your likes and dislikes do not form the basis for my decisions."

Thorne opened his mouth, but Chloe, who had so far taken no part in this discussion, now piped up. "I am planning to attend the lecture as well, Uncle Thorne." Her mouth set mulishly as she delivered this information.

"Absolutely not," said Thorne flatly.

Hester sighed. She had not been given the opportunity to speak privately to Thorne about her recently conceived plans for Chloe's future. Dear Lord, left to his own devices, he would make mice feet of the whole thing! She cleared her throat.

"But I'm sure Chloe would benefit from such an outing." She sent the earl a significant glance, but since he was glaring at Chloe, the look went considerably wide of the mark.

"What benefit could Chloe possibly receive from mingling with a set of malcontents and radicals?" Thorne at last twisted to look at Hester full in the face.

"I'm sure it would prove most instructive. She will observe firsthand the life of a crusader—the problems—the people one encounters."

Thorne opened his mouth once more, but paused, suddenly arrested. The significant glance had phased into a look of such steely austerity that he nearly choked on his fricandeau of beef.

He waved his fork dismissively. "We'll discuss it later," he said, and Hester breathed out a small gust of relief.

Later proved to be some two hours after dinner, in the drawing room, where Thorne and Hester and Aunt Lavinia had gathered. Chloe, having refused her first proposal of marriage, and having been virtually snubbed by her preceptress, and subsequently having undergone a thundering scold from her guardian and a tearful, reproachful monologue from her aunt, felt that she had endured enough for one day and retired early with a headache.

"Now then, Hester," said Thorne, fortifying himself with a glass of port. "Let us have a round tale, if you please. I have, I think you will agree, behaved with admirable circumspection, but—"

"Circumspection!" echoed Hester. "The first thing you did when you arrived home this afternoon was to rake poor Chloe down like a schoolmaster."

Thorne merely grinned. "If you think that was a rake-down, you have never seen me at the top of my form." The grin faded. "You must admit, she deserved much worse. I have spent the better part of a year carefully nurturing a relationship between that infuriating little widgeon and a perfectly acceptable candidate for her hand. And now, just when I thought matters were coming to fruition, she blows my whole scheme right out of the water. I hope you have something cheerful to tell me concerning the situation."

"Well, I think I do," replied Hester calmly. She leaned forward. "As I said before, I believe Chloe to be on the verge of falling in love with Mr. Wery, if she has not begun to do so already. She merely needs a little judicious nudging. Nudging," she repeated with a minatory stare at Thorne, "not flaying with a broadsword."

Lady Lavinia chuckled, but sobered almost immediately. "But, if she has refused Mr. Wery, how is he to pursue his suit without setting up her back even further."

Hester sat back. "That's just it. He will not pursue his suit at all."

"Oh, for God's sake!" Thorne threw up a hand in exasperation. "Is this what you call a plan? What is he to do? Retire to the country, hoping that absence will make Chloe's heart grow fonder?"

"No, of course not." Hester replied coolly, but she was forced to keep a firm grip on her temper. "My plan is to ensure that Chloe will encounter Mr. Wery nearly everywhere she goes. I have instructed the young man—he has agreed to be guided by my counsel, by the way—to treat her in a friendly, courteous manner, paying her pretty compliments from time to time, just as he will all the other young ladies present. In no way is he to hint that he is pursuing Chloe. Quite the contrary. From what Chloe has said, tales of young Mr. Wery's exploits during the carriage incident have engendered a great deal of admiration among the young female population of the *ton*, and—"

"Oh!" cried Lady Lavinia. "You intend that Chloe should be made to perceive Mr. Wery's worth through the eyes of her contemporaries. How very ingenious, my dear."

Thorne merely snorted. "What will happen is that Chloe will be excessively relieved to be rid of John's attentions and will further immerse herself in—The Cause," he finished in dramatic accents. "I shall never get the chit married off."

"If that is the case," responded Hester serenely, "you no longer need my services. I shall be happy to return to Overcross, my lord, if you will—"

"No!" said Thorne hastily. "No, no—there's no need for that. All right," he said, capitulating. "I suppose I have nothing to lose at this point by complying with your Byzantine little plot."

"Thorne." Lady Lavinia spoke in accents of gentle reproof, "you could be a little more gracious. Hester has gone out of her way to take on your problems, and it seems to me that she has done wonders with Chloe already. I see no reason why her plans should not culminate in a very desirable conclusion."

Thorne turned to look at Hester.

"Please accept my apology, Miss Blayne," he said grudgingly, putting Hester strongly in mind of a schoolboy called to book for his misdeeds. "Now, what would you have me do?"

"Nothing," replied Hester in a firm voice. "Cease your exhortations to Chloe, and behave as though you have accepted defeat on the Wery front. If she should speak to you of him, be noncommittal—disinterested, even, as though you have come to the realization that the doings of Mr. Wery are no longer of any consequence to you."

"Very well," said Thorne. "I place Chloe's fate—and mine, so to speak—in your hands."

Hester merely smiled, wishing that his words inspired her with a greater degree of confidence than she felt.

It was almost a week before Hester's grand scheme went into actual operation. On a balmy evening in May, she stood in the music room in Bythorne House, greeting guests who had arrived for a meeting of the Friends of Ancient Writing. The name had become something of a misnomer over the years, for, though many of the members labored over treatises on Greek playwrights and Roman poets, so many reformers had begun appearing at these gatherings that the group had become a sort of central clearinghouse for those who sought to bring about social change.

The room was beginning to fill when Lady Barbara Freemantle entered. Uttering a pleased expression, Hester hurried to greet her.

"Lady Barbara! I was hoping you would come!"

"Oh Lord, Hester," replied the young woman, "could we dispense with Lady Barbara? My friends call me Barbara, and now that you have lured me into your den of wild-eyed firebrands, I think the time for formality is long past."

Hester grinned. "Very well—Barbara, welcome to my set." She swept an arm around the chamber. "Where would you like to start? Ancient literature? Prison reform? Aid to young streetwalkers?"

"Mm. The streetwalker issue sounds promising. I was reading something on the subject in the *Ladies Magazine* the other day, so perhaps I can pretend I actually know what I'm talking about."

Hester led her to a group of comfortably upholstered matrons who had given much of their time and effort to providing alternative employment to the uncounted denizens of London's brothels. They were patently amazed to find the daughter of an earl in their midst, but their initial flutterings soon gave way to gratified acceptance, and after a few moments, Hester moved away.

"You didn't tell me *he* was going to be here," hissed a voice at her elbow. She whirled to find Chloe, her hand at her breast, staring at the doorway in horror. Turning, she beheld John Wery entering the room. There was an indefinable change in his appearance since the last time he had appeared in Bythorne House. It might be assumed that he looked on the failure of his recent courtship of Miss Venable as a sort of liberation, for he was garbed in much more fashionable attire than his usual plain-country-gentleman dress. His hair had been cropped, emphasizing the planes of his face and even seeming to increase the size and brilliance of his eyes. There was certainly no question that he was standing straighter these days. He glanced around and catching sight of Chloe, smiled, but did not move toward her.

"Oh yes," replied Hester casually to Chloe's comment. "He expressed an interest in my work, so I invited him. I was not sure he would appear, but I am glad he has come."

"Oh, but, Hester, how could you?" Chloe fluttered a hand in distress. "It will be so awkward."

"Oh, I think not. You have encountered him once or twice already since you refused his proposal, have you not? His manner seemed unexceptionable."

"Yes, I suppose it was," said Chloe with a faintly dissatisfied air. "He certainly did not present the air of a rejected suitor. In fact, if I did not know him better, I would say that he was actually flirting with Cynthia Morevale at Lady Meecham's rout. And Charlotte St. John, as well. Not that the silly twits weren't giving him a scandalous degree of encouragement."

"Mmm. Perhaps you don't know John as well as you thought."

"Apparently not," snapped Chloe. "His own mother might not recognize him in his fashionable new togs. Even his hair . . ."

"Yes, that style becomes him, I think. Do not you?"

"Perhaps, but I vow, I cannot like it," Chloe responded with a sniff.

Hester smiled. "How fortunate for him, then, that he need no longer concern himself with your approval."

Chloe made no reply, but with a twitch of her skirts whirled on her heel and marched off in the opposite direction from the young man in the doorway. A moment later, she could be seen in animated conversation with a pallid gentleman of poetic demeanor.

Hester glanced around the room, realizing almost at once for whom she was unconsciously seeking. Though he had expressed his intention of joining her gathering this evening, Thorne had not been home for dinner and she had seen nothing of him during the evening. Not that it mattered, of course. She was merely a little disgruntled that he would not keep a stated appointment. How very like him, she thought.

But no, it was not, was it? Charles, Lord Bythorne, might give the impression of careless disdain for the mores of society in general and the feelings of others in particular, but she had come to know this was not so. Where his family and true friends were concerned, he displayed a caring commitment that bordered on the autocratic.

Hester's lips curved in a smile. Well, perhaps more than bordered, for his attitude surely cut a wide swath in that territory. He had expressed on several occasions his determination that she would not make her proposed speech at the

Blue Boar. Her mouth firmed. There was no denying she took a barely acknowledged pleasure in this indication of his newly born friendship for her, but she would not allow him to dictate her actions.

She shook herself a little as she noted the entrance of a newcomer.

"Trevor!" she cried, making her way toward him. "I have been waiting anxiously for your arrival."

Which was not quite true, she told herself, but it should be.

She paused in her greeting to acknowledge the presence of another gentleman, who had entered the room behind Trevor. Robert Carver stood diffidently just inside the door, his eyes lighting as he beheld his hostess.

"Mr. Carver! How nice of you to join us. May I present Mr. Trevor Bentham?"

Courteous greetings were exchanged between the two men, but is was soon obvious that Trevor Bentham had not come to Bythorne House for polite intercourse. At the earliest opportunity he drew Hester aside.

"I have called here several times within the last few days," he said severely, "and was told on each occasion that you were out." The last words were uttered in such an accusatory tone that Hester was forced to smile.

"Well, I have been out a great deal, Trevor. Really," she said with a laugh, "I had no idea the amount of clothes required to dress one small *tonnish* miss. My life seems to be an endless round of shopping with Chloe ever since I arrived in London."

"Ah," said Trevor in a tone of deep reproach, "that she who carries the lamp of enlightenment for women should be reduced to the role of companion for a spoiled young woman."

This remark put Hester so out of charity with him that she was forced to bite back a stinging retort. Instead, she called to mind the duration and depth of her friendship with him and said calmly, "It is nothing of the sort, Trevor, as I believe you well understand. I have come to look on the Trents as my friends as well as my relatives, and I do not feel I am demeaning myself in coming to Thorne's assistance. I know you would do the same for anyone who needed yours. Now, if you will excuse me, I must see to my guests."

The rest of the evening passed smoothly. After a short business meeting, several readings were given of one of the more obscure writings of the poet Gray, which led to a rather lively discussion on certain current events. The guests were then offered a light collation in the blue salon, and it was not long before they began moving toward the exit.

In the periphery of her consciousness, Hester had been aware that Robert Carver and Barbara had come together several times during the evening, only to draw apart again almost immediately, like snowflakes eddying in a blizzard, but now they stood in a far corner of the salon in a confrontation that seemed to render them oblivious to their surroundings. Barbara frowned and her face was delicately flushed, Robert's pale and tight.

As Hester watched interestedly, Barbara lifted her hand in a beseeching gesture. Robert grasped it and looked as though he would have lifted it to his lips. Instead, he released it an instant later with what looked like an exclamation of disdain and turned away, leaving Barbara to stare after him, blinking back distressful tears. Hester would have gone to her, but she was stayed by a voice at her shoulder.

"Hester, I must have a word with you."

She turned to behold Trevor. He was apparently in the grip of deep emotion, for he placed his hand on hers and gazed deeply into her eyes.

"I must leave, but first, I would speak with you"—he breathed intensely—"in private."

Sighing, she led him out of the salon into the music room across the corridor.

"I wish to apologize," said Trevor rather portentously.

Hester relaxed a little. "That is kind of you, my friend, but unnecessary. I know that you—"

"It is just that I am concerned about you, in this house of worldly pleasure." He gestured vaguely about him.

"Oh, Trevor—" protested Hester, laughing, but Trevor rushed on, unheeding.

"You know how I feel about you, Hester. Indeed, I hope that one day you and I will be one, and I can protect you from such unwelcome influences, but—"

"Trevor," said Hester firmly, pushing against him, for he had moved to stand very close, his hand on her shoulder. "If you think our friendship gives you the right to dictate my actions, you are very much—"

"But, you know we are much more than friends, my dear."

So saying, to Hester's astonishment, Trevor grasped both her shoulders and pulling her roughly toward him, crushed her mouth with a kiss that smelled slightly of the oysters she had served for supper.

"Oh, I am sorry."

The voice, instantly and heart-sinkingly recognizable, spoke coolly from the doorway.

Chapter Fifteen

Hester's heart somersaulted and Trevor jumped as though he had been poked with a sharp stick.

"Wh—wha—?" he croaked. "Miss Blayne and I were speaking of—that is—"

"Of course," murmured Thorne smoothly. "These intellectual discussions can become quite lively, can they not? I do beg your pardon for the intrusion."

He began to withdraw from the room, but Hester gasped, "No! That is—" She patted her hair and attempted to speak calmly. "We were quite finished with our—discussion. Trevor was just leaving."

Trevor's expression was that of a man ready to chew bricks.

"Indeed." His voice was icy. "I shall bid you good evening, my dear," he said to Hester, and with a nod to Thorne, he strode into the corridor.

"Oh my," said Thorne, his voice vibrating with amusement. "I fear I have driven away your—friend. How very unfortunate. But there will be other moments for, er, intellectual discourse."

Hester turned on him, and the glance she sent across the room raised its temperature enough to melt glass.

"I am so pleased to have provided some amusement for you, my lord—again. Not that it is surprising you find the honest affection of a good man a source of entertainment—mixed with a dollop of contempt, of course."

Thorne blinked. Good God, what had there been in his words to arouse such vituperation? Particularly since, on entering the room, his first sight of Hester locked in an embrace with Trevor Bentham had caused a maelstrom of rage to sweep over him. His initial impulse was to wrench Bentham from her and pound him into a satisfying smear on the carpet.

It was only when he observed the determined push Hester administered to her swain that the red mist faded from Thorne's vision and he was able to put the scene into proper perspective. It was, he supposed, his astonishment at the violence of his reaction that had led him subsequently to fall back on his usual attitude of bland amusement.

He saw no reason to adjust this strategy.

"But, surely your own response to his honest affection was no more cruel than my own? Can it be that the gentleman's ardor is not reciprocated?"

Hester paced the floor in an exasperated swish of silken skirts. "I hold Trevor Bentham in great affection," she said firmly. "It's just that—" She sighed. Really, there was no accounting for the agony of embarrassment she had experienced when Thorne entered the music room. Even though Trevor had been mauling her as though she were a lightskirt, she had not been cooperating in the embrace. She sighed again. "Not that any of this is your concern," she continued, "but, as I have asserted in the past, I have no room in my life at this point for any—entanglements."

"Is that what an *affaire de coeur* would mean to you?" he asked curiously. "An entanglement? And you call me heartless!"

"That's not what I meant," she sputtered. "I merely—oh, never mind." She inclined her head. "If you will excuse me, sir, I must bid good evening to my guests."

Thorne swept her an exaggerated bow as she strode past him. He gazed speculatively a moment at the vacant air, which carried the fragrance of violets.

He turned, preparing to make his way to his rooms when he was stayed by an imperative voice.

"A word with you, my lad, if I might."

Thorne sighed. "What is it, Gussie? It's getting late and I was about to seek my bed."

Gussie uttered a sound that in anyone a shade less regal

would have been called a snort. "You haven't sought your bed at any time for the past fortnight a minute earlier than four in the morning. If we were to speak of someone else's bed, of course—"

"That will do, Gussie." He led her into a small salon just off the drawing room and gestured her to a comfortable chair near the fire. "Now, what is it?"

"I wish to speak to you about Hester."

Thorne stiffened and said in a colorless voice, "If you are going to prose at me again for inviting her here, I beg leave—"

Gussie interrupted him with an impatient wave of her hand. "No, no of course not. I never prose. In any event, I am more than pleased you brought Hester to us. She has proved to be a welcome addition to the family, and in view of that fact, I have come to believe that for all her talk of feminine self-sufficiency, what she really needs is a good husband."

His attention thoroughly arrested, Thorne stared at his aunt through slitted eyes.

"I see. And do you have a candidate for the position?"

"Certainly. Robert Carver. Don't you see?" she continued as Thorne seemed momentarily bereft of speech. "He is perfect—wealthy, unattached, intelligent, a thoroughly nice man, and one who takes an interest in intellectual pursuits."

"And what makes you think this paragon is in the market for a wife? I do not know him well, but I understand he is quite happy in his single state—possibly," he added acidly, "because he has no relatives to concern themselves with the unhappiness of his situation."

Lady Bracken laughed, unaffected. "Well, that's my point. It is up to us to bring this lack in his life to his attention. I have, in fact, been working on it for some days."

"What!"

"Oh, yes," said Gussie blithely. "I introduced them, you know, and it was I who saw to it that Hester invited him to her little soiree this evening. I must say, they seem to be hitting it off remarkably well. The next step is simply to throw them in each other's way at every opportunity. Propinquity is a wonderful thing."

Thorne expelled an exasperated sigh. "Of all your ridiculous starts, Gussie, this ranks right up at the top of a very long list. For one thing, Hester has no desire to marry. For another—"

"Nonsense. Every woman wishes to marry, no matter how she might decry the fact."

Thorne, without stopping to analyze the deep repugnance he felt at the idea of Hester marrying Robert Carver, strode about the room.

"Lord, Gussie, I wish you would give up this wretched penchant of yours for organizing other people's lives. I daresay Carver may be a perfectly decent fellow, but he is not the man for Hester. Good God, she'd make his life a living hell."

Gussie turned a blank stare on him.

"Why do you say that?"

"Well—um, she'd fill up his house with malcontents— eating his mutton and swilling his wine. He'd spend half his time rescuing her from thugs and footpads in the neighborhoods she likes to frequent in her forays; and when he wasn't doing that he'd be bored to distraction listening to her catalog of things that need fixing in this country."

"Thorne," replied his aunt patiently. "She has been living with us for almost three weeks now. It seems to me we have all enjoyed her company—as well as the, er, malcontents she has chosen to invite here—whose company, by the by, include some of our most prestigious citizens. I have yet to see you racing off to rescue her, nor does she bore you with her views. Indeed, it seems to me that your mental attitude is vastly improved since she came. And, think what she has done for Chloe."

"As far as I can see, all she's done is to encourage the little widgeon in precisely the course I have spent months in attempting to eradicate."

The words sounded pettish in his own ears, and he relented. "All right, I will admit that she is endeavoring to turn Chloe's mind toward the life I have envisioned for her.

Although, I must say, the results so far have fallen wide of the mark."

"On the contrary," replied Gussie briskly. "I think her strategy an excellent one. Did you see Chloe this evening? She could not take her eyes from John Wery. And he is all she can talk of these days. You mark my words, we will see a betrothal there in less than a month. But, getting back to Hester, I expect you to do everything possible toward getting her together with Mr. Carver. I was thinking of an outing to Vauxhall. There's to be a gala there two nights hence. You could make up a party with Hester and Robert, and of course, Barbara."

"Of course," murmured Thorne resignedly.

"You could hire a boat of flutes and make it a really festive occasion."

Thorne groaned. His aunt rose from her chair and bade her nephew a cordial good night, and after she had gone, Thorne slumped into the vacated seat and stared into the fire.

Hester—married to Robert Carver. He was surprised to discover that the idea made him faintly sick—and for what reason, he could not discover. It was not as though he had plans of his own for the earnest little gadfly. He wouldn't at all mind having her in his bed, for he was sure the fire he had detected beneath her somewhat austere exterior would be worth fanning into a blaze of passion. One did not, however, seduce respectable maidens approaching middle age—particularly those that were related to one, no matter how distantly, and even more particularly ones who were under his protection.

That being the case, and looking at the situation objectively, Thorne was bound to admit that Robert Carver seemed the perfect mate for Hester. Assuming, of course, that Hester would so much as consider the possibility of taking a husband, which at this point she seemed strongly disinclined to do. Somehow, that thought comforted him.

Very well then. He would arrange the gala evening at Vauxhall and he would promote a match between Hester and Robert Carver. If she conceived a *tendre* for the fellow, so be it. If not—well, his conscience would be salved, and Miss Blayne could go back to her cottage in Overcross, free to take up the cudgels once more for the liberation of women.

And he could return to his own life. Sobriety and rectitude were all very well in small doses, but enough was enough. It was time to reinstitute his plans for the Earl of Tenby's toothsome little wife before some other enterprising fellow, Jack Winsham, for example, took steps to mount her. And the girls at Desiree's would no doubt be missing him.

He stared at the fire for another few minutes, waiting for the sense of anticipation the thought of this program should bring. What he felt, however, was—nothing, merely an odd, forlorn emptiness. He shook himself, finally. If he did not take himself firmly in hand, he told himself, he was in danger of turning into a doddering old fogram, moldering before his hearth. He rose and plodded upstairs to his bed-chamber.

Two nights later, a party disembarked on the south bank of the River Thames at the Vauxhall dock. In the boat were Lord Bracken and his lady, the Earl of Bythorne and Lady Barbara Freemantle, and Mr. Robert Carver and Miss Hester Blayne. In another craft, hauling to nearby, several musicians tootled a finish to their concert and bade the merrymakers a very good evening.

It might have been expected that the prospect of an evening in one of England's premier pleasure spots, with the promise of a concert and fireworks later on, might have evoked expressions of anticipation and merriment among the party, but it was, by and large, a rather somber group that made its way from the water to the establishment's gate.

"You did not tell me Robert Carver was going to be here tonight," hissed Lady Barbara to Hester, in much the same tone used by Chloe on the occasion of the meeting of the Friends of Ancient Literature.

Hester had become friendly with Lady Barbara during

their short acquaintanceship, and a degree of informality had sprung up between them.

"I did not know," she now replied petulantly. "It was all Gussie's doing. Good God, she seems to feel duty-bound to find me a husband, and Robert Carver is apparently the chosen sacrifice. Damn and blast!" she muttered.

"Well, I don't know why you should be so overset," responded Barbara, a touch of ice in her voice. "Robert would make any woman a fine husband."

"I'm sure he would," Hester now replied tartly, "but, as I keep telling people—to very little avail—I do not wish to marry. In any case, I cannot see that Mr. Carver has the slightest interest in marrying me, either."

The two women glanced at their escorts. Thorne bore himself with his usual courtesy, but it seemed to Hester that his mind was elsewhere. In some secluded little boudoir just off St. James's, perhaps. Robert Carver, on the other hand, was unable to conceal his discomfort. Hester almost expected him to hiss in her ear, "You didn't tell me *she* would be here!" For his attention, though he never once looked at her, was obviously on the lovely Lady Barbara.

Only Lady Bracken and her husband seemed to be enjoying themselves. Stanton, Lord Bracken, was a tall, thin man in his early forties. He was very much a political animal and seemed to know everyone in London. A surprising number of people, from many walks of life, made it a point to greet him, and he responded heartily to all. Gussie, too, nodded to acquaintances, so that their walk to the box reserved for them near the pavilion resembled less a leisurely stroll than a royal progression.

Once seated, the group settled back to enjoy a repast of punch and the thin slices of burnt ham for which the Gardens were famous. Afterward, Gussie announced that there was just time for a promenade along the paths bordering the pavilion before they would be obliged to return to their places for the concert.

Hester could not remember ever having felt quite so awkward as she did taking Mr. Carver's arm. She was quite well aware by now of Gussie's machinations, and she was sure Mr. Carver must be as well. Not that it seemed to matter to him. His eyes were on Barbara, moving along the path some distance ahead of them, her head bent close to that of Lord Bythorne.

"What?" he asked absently in response to a remark from Hester.

"I was saying, how lovely it is that the sticky buns are in bloom."

"Mm, yes, they—what?"

He turned to look at her, bewilderment writ large on his features. Hester laughed.

"So you are paying attention. I thought I had lost you altogether."

In the light of the hundreds of lanterns lighting their way, Mr. Carver could be seen to blush hotly.

"I am sorry, Miss Blayne. I must confess that for a moment my mind wandered."

"For a moment! My good man, it is obvious to the meanest intelligence that your mind has had only one destination all evening long, and it is not my humble self."

"Oh! No—really—"

Hester laughed again. "It is perfectly all right, Mr. Carver. Or, no—do let me call you, Robert, for I have quite decided that I like you very much and we are destined to become fast friends."

Robert seemed somewhat startled at this ingenuous declaration, but he nodded smoothly. "Of course, Miss Blayne, but only if I may be granted the same privilege."

"With my blessing. Now, Robert," she said peremptorily, "what is all this between you and Barbara."

Robert's bonhomie disappeared. "I have no idea," he said austerely, "to what you refer."

"To what I refer," she returned tartly, "is the fact that your attention has been glued to her like a sticking plaster all evening—and every other instance in which you have been in her company."

In the frigid silence that greeted this remark, Hester wondered if she had gone too far. Men were so protective of the ridiculous barrier they put around their feelings.

"Robert, we are friends now, remember, and I don't like to see my friends unhappy. I do not wish to pry. Well—" She dimpled. "Perhaps that's not quite true—but, my motives are pure. I only want to help. Now," she began again, encouragingly, "tell me how it is that you seem to know Barbara so well."

For a long moment, he remained silent, but at last he said tightly, "I'm sorry, Hester, but I will not discuss Lady Barbara, I—" He paused again, and from somewhere brought out a smile that was almost painful to behold. "And now, newest of my friends, may I suggest that we return to the pavilion? We have been gone for some time, and I do not wish to give rise to gossip."

"Very well," she said in some chagrin, "but I shall not give up, you know."

Robert said nothing, but placing an elbow beneath her arm, turned back toward the garden's main thoroughfare. It was in a thoughtful mood that Hester allowed herself to be escorted back to the box where the others waited. All during the concert, she kept her attention on Thorne and Barbara, her mind busy with the puzzle of the relationship between Barbara and Robert. For it had become blindingly obvious that there *was* a relationship.

Well, this was all just ridiculous. If the two star-crossed idiots did not have sense enough to bring their sundered hearts together, she would just have to help them. She glanced speculatively at Thorne. She felt no compunction about snatching Barbara out from under his nose, so to speak, for despite his courteous attentions to the lady, he obviously felt no more for her than friendship.

Hester was uncomfortably aware of a still, small voice deep within her commenting rather acidly on her extraordinary eagerness to do such a selfless bit of interfering with the lives of two people to whom she had just been introduced. Well, that was just nonsense, too. She certainly was *not* motivated by a wish to remove the beauteous Lady Barbara from Thorne's proximity. What a ludicrous idea. In fact, if she knew of a young woman who would suit, she would be the first person to encourage Thorne to settle into connubial bliss. For if ever a man needed settling, that man was the rakish Earl of Bythorne.

Somewhat to her surprise, she turned to discover that the concert was over.

"I beg your pardon?" she asked Robert, who had turned to speak to her.

"I believe the orchestra is about to phase into music for dancing," he said. "Would you care to take a turn?"

Nodding, she rose, observing that Lord and Lady Bracken, as well as Thorne and Barbara, all had the same notion. As did most of the other merrymakers thronging about them. The area before the pavilion was a solid mass of bodies and as Hester and Robert took their places for a quadrille, the crowd surged against them and they were separated.

She clicked her tongue in irritation and reached out a hand, but Robert was nowhere to be seen. With some difficulty, she began to retrace her steps to the box, but she was halted by a large obstruction. A stringent oath fell on her ears.

"Madam, if you would be so kind as to remove yourself from my foot—Oh, it's you."

Thorne attempted to dodge to one side, but was pushed against her once more.

"Good God, what a mess!" He placed an arm about her waist and drew her apart from the dancers until they stood on the perimeter of the floor. Still holding her, he glanced about.

"I've lost Barbara. Do you see her?"

Out of the corner of her eye, Hester caught a glimpse of Robert, who held a lady whose face was hidden, safe in the protection of his arms.

"No," said Hester.

"Well, let's try to get back to the box."

Their efforts were unavailing, however, as the crowd pushed them farther toward the outside of the circle of dancers. In a few moments, breathless and disheveled, they found themselves at the head of a path that lead away from the maelstrom created by the dancers.

"Lord!" exclaimed Thorne as they made their way along

the secluded lane. "I haven't seen such a crowd at Vauxhall since the peace celebrations of fourteen and fifteen."

"Uff," gasped Hester, pulling her shawl of gossamer about her. "I guess everyone in London decided to come out to enjoy themselves—all on the same night."

"The fireworks should be starting soon. The crowd will swarm to the center of the gardens then."

Thorne turned to survey her.

"You look the very devil," he said, but the oddly tender grin that accompanied his words took away much of their sting. He reached to remove her cap, which had been wrenched sadly askew. His gesture put her so much in mind of that other time he had forcibly taken off her cap that she felt a breathless flush flood her cheeks. He combed her hair for a moment with his fingers before placing the cap back atop her head. His hand brushed her cheek as it dropped again to his side and he stepped back hastily.

Patting their clothing into some semblance of order, they continued down the lantern-lit path. Other strollers could be seen emerging and disappearing into the leafy bowers that bordered the walkway, and at the end a miniature temple glowed a welcome.

"Are you enjoying yourself, Hester?" asked Thorne suddenly. "Other than being trampled by your fellow revelers."

Startled, Hester nodded. "Why—yes, of course. It's a beautiful evening, and the music was heavenly."

"Really? It did not seem to me that you were paying much attention to the music."

Hester flushed. "Oh, no—that is, yes—I was."

"Ah."

They continued in silence for a few moments.

"Gussie tells me," began Thorne again, "that she believes Chloe has suffered a reversal of feeling for John Wery."

"I believe that's true. She has not yet admitted as much to herself, but I think she will be much more amenable the next time he asks her to marry him—which, I should think would happen very soon."

"I expect you are looking forward with great anticipation to that day."

Hester glanced up, surprised.

"You must be anxious to return to your home," continued Thorne.

"Oh. Yes, of course. Not that I haven't enjoyed myself in London," she added hastily.

"Good." He turned to face her once more. "I shall miss you when you leave. You—you have brightened Bythorne House with your presence."

In the flickering light, his expression was hard to read, but Hester could find no trace of the mocking smile that usually accompanied polished words of praise from the earl. Instead, she fancied she could perceive a glow in his eyes that owed nothing to the lanterns overhead. He raised his hand again to cup the back of her head. Oh dear, was the shadowed walkway and the scent of roses that lay heavy on the air causing the consummate rake in him to revert to type?

Well, she would just have to assure him that she wasn't having any.

He lifted his other hand, sliding it along her arm until it reached her shoulder.

In just a minute, she would tell him to stop.

Gently, the earl pulled her toward him, and a breathless, slow heat began to uncurl within her.

Yes, she would just push out from those wonderfully strong arms—in another moment, or so.

But in the next instant, his head bent close to hers and his mouth descended in a kiss of such aching sweetness that her well-conceived intentions—indeed all coherent thought—fled like starlings at the approach of a hawk.

Chapter Sixteen

"I vow," declared Chloe discontentedly from her place at the breakfast table, "London has become so flat of late, I almost wish we were at the Park." She crumbled a piece of toast on her plate.

Hester lifted her head from her own breakfast of soused herring and eggs.

"Did you not have a good time last night at the Carstairs' rout?" she asked. While the others in the Bythorne household had spent the evening at Vauxhall Gardens, Chloe had attended the rout with her friend Charlotte Tisdale, accompanied by Charlotte's mother.

"It was utterly tedious."

"Ah. Who was there?"

"Oh, everyone and his brother, of course. It was an impossible crush."

"Mm, I suppose."

Hester returned to her herring and eggs. She was finding it hard to concentrate on either her breakfast or Chloe's dismal conversation, for her thoughts, despite her best efforts, drifted inexorably back to last night's events.

Or, more particularly, to last night's kiss.

What, she wondered dazedly, had happened to her in that leafy, moonlight bower? One minute, she was firm in her resolution to treat the rake to his just desserts, and the next she was a quivering mass of sensation, pressing herself against him like a limpet and twining her fingers in the soft, curling hair at the base of his neck.

He had drawn back abruptly at the sound of laughter nearby, and she found it necessary to cling to him a moment longer or she would have fallen. Oddly, he had seemed as nonplussed as she, completely bereft of his usual aplomb. He had murmured no polished, flirtatious phrases, made no sly, suggestive remarks. He had merely stood there for a moment, staring at her, while she . . . Good God, she had gibbered something inane and—

Her appalled ruminations were cut short by the sound of a sniffle.

"Chloe? Chloe, what is it?"

"Oh, nothing, only . . ." Chloe dabbed at her eyes with a corner of her handkerchief. "Oh, Hester, I am so wretched!"

Hester rose and hastened to the other side of the table, where she sank into the chair next to Chloe's. "My dear, what is the matter?"

"It's John. He is making my life miserable."

"But I thought he had accepted the fact that you are not going to marry him. I cannot believe he would make you the object of unwelcome attentions."

Chloe began to sob in earnest. "That's just it. He acts as though I were not even alive."

"But I saw him greet you very pleasantly the other night at the Winnerings'."

"Oh, y-yes—just as he does everyone else he knows. He b-bows and he smiles and then he just walks right on past me and bows and smiles at someone else. He danced twice with Charlotte at the Winnerings', and last night, he spent nearly the whole evening in conversation with Mirabelle Brent. You should have s-seen her, Hester. I never realized what an ill-bred hoyden she is—flapping her eyelashes at him and simpering in *such* an unbecoming fashion."

Hester clicked her tongue. "Some young women simply have no breeding," she said, hiding a smile.

"And then the orchestra played 'Les Petites Jouées.' Oh, Hester, he knows that is my favorite song! He glanced over at me, but then he walked up to Gwendolyn Marchbank and asked her to dance. I could have just sunk through the carpet."

"Chloe," said Hester carefully, "I am surprised to see

you so blue-deviled. Are you regretting your rejection of John's proposal?"

"Oh—no, of course not. That is—oh, I don't know. I guess I did not expect him to accept it so tamely. And then to go about flirting with every female in town—which I did not think he so much as knew how—as though he had never felt anything for me at all. Well, it is very lowering."

"I'm sure it must be. But," Hester concluded bracingly, "no doubt you will get over it. After all, it is not as though you felt any real affection for John."

"N-no, I suppose not," Chloe replied dubiously.

Hester returned to her breakfast, feeling that the matter of Chloe's future was well in hand. She wished she felt so sanguine about her feelings for the earl. She must stop this ridiculous tendency to turn into a blancmange at his slightest touch.

Hester might have been considerably surprised to know that Thorne's reflections at the moment were remarkably similar. He had decided on an early morning ride in the park, and cantering along Rotten Row, he was aware of a sensation of utter bafflement as he considered last night's incident in Vauxhall Gardens.

He had had no thought of dalliance in mind when he had swept Hester into the shadowed path that wound away from the crowd. He had turned to look at her, and suddenly his breath had caught in his throat. With that absurd cap askew and her hair tumbling out of its rigid captivity atop her head, her gown sadly rumpled, and her shawl in a twist over one shoulder, she had put him so much in mind of a ruffled bird that he was forced to smile. When he reached to tuck a stray tendril of hair back into place, his fingers brushed her cheek, and it was as though someone had reached inside him to clutch his heart, twisting it unbearably. He was swept by such an unexpected wave of tenderness that he almost gasped with it. Her nearness, the scent of her, his sudden need to pull her against him had overcome him. Such feelings were not foreign to him, of course. The proximity of a beautiful woman always aroused him.

But his desire for Hester was different somehow, wasn't it?

For one thing, she didn't possess the attributes that usually appealed to him. She didn't exude allurement, and she was endowed with neither extraordinary beauty nor the seductive charm that he required in his inamoratas.

For another thing, Thorne was not accustomed to feelings of tenderness for a woman. Nor had he ever experienced the raw hunger that had surged through him when she had pressed her slender body into his and offered her lips for his taking.

What the devil was going on? he wondered frantically. The desire she engendered within him aside, he had never known a woman whose company alone he found stimulating.

He had still not availed himself of Lady Tenby's charms, and the ladies at Desiree's must by now be wondering at his absence. Good God, it had come to the point where he felt whole only when he was with Hester, and somewhat diminished when he was not. What a ridiculous state of affairs.

In addition, the lady in question, although she seemed to find him attractive and had admitted that she enjoyed his kisses, regarded him as a combination of the worst attributes of Don Juan and Attila the Hun.

It was time he brought himself to the sticking point in the matter of marriage. He had long ago resigned himself to the knowledge that he must marry sometime, and a marriage of convenience was the most palatable arrangement, certainly. Such a union would demand nothing of him—would not lead him into the kind of relationship he had always avoided. He did not wish to wed a woman who would weep and rail at his infidelities, nor did he expect his wife to remain faithful to him—provided she was discreet. This was the way of the world, and it was the way he had always expected to conduct his domestic arrangements. He tried with only minimal success to suppress the empty, faintly sick feeling his reflections engendered within him.

It was time, perhaps, that he proposed to Barbara.

In the meantime, it would behoove him to steer clear of small, vocal, bewitching feminists.

This course of action, however, proved difficult to put into effect. The following weeks saw an increase in the already frenetic social pace of the Season. Parliament was in full swing, and the town houses of London fairly quivered with gossip and the bustling of servants and the comings and goings of the country's most select families. Every evening, the inhabitants of Bythorne House must make a choice among several balls, a rout or two, and perhaps a musicale. Days were filled with Venetian breakfasts, garden parties, shopping, and visits to the Egyptian Hall or to Somerset House to visit the Royal Academy Art Exhibitions.

As head of the household in Curzon Street, it was up to the earl to squire his little family to many of these functions. Thus, he found himself in Hester's company with greater frequency than was good for his equanimity. Oddly, the fact that Lady Barbara was also among those present a good deal of the time caused him no discomfort at all. Nor did he take any of the opportunities afforded him to make a formal declaration.

It was on an afternoon when Thorne had absented himself from his duties, however, that Hester was put in possession of the missing piece of the puzzle regarding Robert Carver and Barbara. The two ladies had just returned from a morning expedition to Leicester Square, where they had indulged in an invasion of several of the mercers' and drapers' establishments in that area.

"You really are going ahead, then, with your plans to lecture in Seven Dials?" asked Barbara, accepting a cup of tea from her hostess. "Thorne still seems very much opposed to the idea."

"Oh yes," Hester replied blithely. "Several schools have opened up in London under the auspices of various ladies' groups, and I wish to make their availability known to some of the girls who, I'm afraid, now earn their livelihoods on their backs. It's such a splendid opportunity for young women to learn not only skills such as millinery and dressmaking but mathematics and proper grammar, so that they may become—"

"Yes, yes," interposed Barbara hastily, "but, you will have to admit those are perfectly dreadful environs. I've heard that rioting has occurred during speeches made by some of our reformers. I heard that Mrs. Fry barely escaped with her life from an appearance she made in the north last month."

"I'm sure the incident was much exaggerated. In any event, the lecture cannot be held in Westminster because of that ridiculous new ruling against meetings with more than fifty persons in attendance. In addition, I shall have plenty of protection with me. Trevor will be with me, and"—she ignored the indelicate sound of derision that issued from Lady Barbara's perfect lips—"and," she continued, "I shall make sure that we are accompanied by some stout footmen and grooms. Also," she added casually, "Robert has said he will be there. Can I count on your company, too?"

"Robert?" The perfect lips screwed into an expression of dismay. "Oh, I don't think—"

"Barbara, Robert will be in town for an extended length of time. You cannot continue to blanche like a boiled bed-sheet every time you come within ten feet of him."

Despite the care with which Barbara set her cup and saucer on the tray before her, the fragile porcelain still rat-tled alarmingly. She folded her hands tightly in her lap and turned to face Hester.

"Robert and I were more than just acquaintances many years ago. We were betrothed."

Hester drew in a sharp breath, and Barbara glanced up quickly. Her gaze fell again almost immediately as she began a conscientious pleating of her skirt.

"My brother William and Robert were at Harrow to-gether, then Cambridge. He visited our home fairly fre-quently, and, of course, I was always there." Barbara smiled. "I was tall for my age, and too thin, with bony arms and legs that seemed to extend in all directions at once. Robert treated me as though I were his little sister as well as Will's. They teased me unmercifully, sometimes to tears.

Not that I couldn't hold my own," she declared with some satisfaction. "I was positively fierce!

"Then, during Michalemas one year, he came to the Abbey—and something was different. I had grown up a great deal—I wasn't thin and bony anymore, and I had several beaux in the neighborhood. Robert and I were awkward together. It was very strange and uncomfortable, but one day"—Barbara's voice softened—"it was in the midst of a house party. It had been raining all morning, and after luncheon we all went up to the attic to plunder the trunks for costumes. Some of my friends and I were getting up a theatrical. Somehow Robert and I were separated from the rest of the group. I berated him for having neglected me— and he responded with something cutting about my spending all my time soaking up compliments from every sprig within twenty miles of the Abbey. I snapped back and in a few minutes we were embroiled in a full-fledged battle. I burst into tears. Oh, Hester, I was simply appalled—and I was so miserable. Robert put his arm around me and began apologizing—and the next thing I knew—he was kissing me—and I kissed him back!"

Barbara paused for a few moments, gazing ahead of her—or rather, Hester thought, backward through time and space.

"Within a week, he had declared his love for me, and I confessed I loved him, too. We talked of marriage, though we were both too young to make any concrete plans. In addition, Robert held some silly notion that the third son of an obscure baronet could not be considered anything close to an acceptable *parti* for the daughter of an earl. Of course, I said this was nonsense. His birth was respectable, as were his prospects, and I knew my parents liked him and would consider my happiness rather than their own worldly interests."

"And they did not?"

Barbara laughed mirthlessly.

"The matter was never brought before them. About a year later, Martin Denby, the Marquess of Bentwaters, came to the Abbey. He paid violent court to me, and—and

I—oh, Hester, I never felt anything for him, but he was so very dashing. He showered me with pretty compliments, which Robert never did, and—well, yes, my head was turned. But, it was all so meaningless—and if I led him on, it was mostly to make Robert jealous—just a little. You see, once he had declared his love for me, Robert seemed to take our relationship very much for granted. I wanted to—well, shake him a little."

"And you overdid it."

"Apparently, for he grew resentful. He took me to task several times, but I merely laughed. Unheeding, I continued to accept Denby's attentions. I was so sure that, underneath his crotchets, Robert understood that I was not serious. I even thought he might realize that I really only wanted him to pay me a little of the same sort of attention. When he continued to take me to task, however, I grew sullen, and—well, the whole situation escalated until he began to grow distant. I was sure that he had conceived a disgust of me, and I convinced myself that I did not care.

"Oh, Hester, we never really had a final quarrel. That might have led to a reconciliation. We just grew farther and farther apart until, at length, he stopped coming to the Priory. I told myself it did not matter, and eventually I was able to believe that it did not. Robert left the country for several years to attend to family business on the Continent. I paid little attention to Martin after that, but I immersed myself in the social whirl, and then Thorne came along, and—"

"And it was not until you saw Robert at Bythorne House the night of the meeting of the Friends of Ancient Literature that you realized the treasure you had slip between your fingers. That is—" amended Hester. "Oh, do forgive me, I'm afraid that was the novelist in me talking. But, I think I am not far off."

She gazed searchingly at Barbara, who flushed and attempted to smooth out the punishment she had inflicted on her skirt. "No," she said in a low voice. "You are not far off."

"Well, this is a sad misunderstanding, to be sure, but it does not seem to me that it is irreparable."

Barbara lifted her head abruptly.

"And just what do you suggest?" she asked in a sharp voice. "I can scarcely walk up to him and say, 'How could you have been such an idiot as to let me go, when I am obviously the love of your life?'"

Hester laughed. "No, I suppose not, although that would certainly get his attention. I expect we shall have to work out something a little more subtle."

Barbara stared at her in astonishment. "We?"

"Well, of course. I told you, I hold Robert very much my friend, and I have come to regard you in the same light. Since both of you seem sadly disinclined to gather up the tattered remnants of your—oh. Sorry. What I mean to say, is that it looks as though you could stand a modicum of help."

"But, what about Thorne?"

"Thorne?"

"Yes, we have had an understanding for a number of years, and—"

"Barbara, do you think his heart is truly engaged? I—I would not have him hurt."

The words lodged in Hester's throat. She had convinced herself that Thorne did not really care for the scintillating Lady Barbara Freemantle, and the idea that she might be wrong was almost too painful to contemplate.

Barbara sighed. "No, he likes me well enough, and I think he feels he and I would suit in the kind of marriage he envisions for himself, but he is certainly not what you could call an eager suitor. Actually, I think that is why I have allowed myself to dangle after him in such an unbecoming fashion. I have always known that he would never really come up to scratch, but at the same time, I more or less put myself off limits to the attentions of other men."

Hester cocked her head curiously. "You did not find it insulting that he should let the world think the pair of you, er, semibetrothed, while he dashed about town with his high-priced Cyprians."

Barbara picked up her cup once more and sipped thoughtfully. "I suppose I might have if my heart were truly engaged. And, really, he had no conception that he might be wounding me. None of his flirts mean anything to him." She glanced swiftly at Hester. "I think any woman who intends to engage *his* heart must understand that."

Hester shook her head. "It looks very much as though the Earl of Bythorne has no heart to give," she said, striving to keep her voice steady.

"That may be true—although, at times I have wondered . . . Thorne's parents," Barbara continued slowly "were—"

"Yes, Thorne told me something of them."

"Ah. I never knew Lady Bythorne, but from all accounts she was an Incomparable—and much given to—pleasures of the flesh."

"As was her husband, I take it."

"Mm. Even in the climate of the time, they were notorious. It is no wonder Thorne grew up with a jaundiced view of marriage. And being gifted with more than his share of charm, nothing in his experience as an adult has served to change his attitude."

"I see. Well, in that event, it is unfortunate, perhaps, that he will have to marry someday. Let us hope that he will make a union of convenience, for it would be a shame if some young woman were to lose her heart to him only to have it broken after they were wed."

Hester had spoken in as prosaic a tone as she could manage, but Barbara once more sent her a penetrating glance. Bowing her head over the teacups, however, she said merely, "Do you go to Lady Wincannon's musicale tonight?"

"Yes. Will Thorne be escorting you?"

Barbara laughed. "Oh, no. He declared that though he would cheerfully walk through fire and swim rivers for me, asking him to sit through the 'caterwauling of yet another soprano' is just too much."

"I think Chloe feels much the same way, but Aunt Lavinia and I prevailed upon her to accompany us tonight."

"Ah—and will young John Wery be there, as well?"

Hester grinned. "I think he just might be."

As it turned out, she was correct in this optimistic prediction. The ladies of Bythorne House had no sooner settled into their chairs in Lady Wincannon's great drawing room, than John entered. Looking about the chamber, he slid quietly into the seat next to Chloe, who blushed prettily. Immediately afterward, under the interested eyes of Hester and Aunt Lavinia, he asked her to take a turn with him on the terrace, where several other couples disported themselves in the warm, summer evening.

"And after that," reported Chloe later in Hester's bedchamber, her eyes glowing, "he asked me to supper. Oh, Hester, I don't know when I have spent a more enjoyable evening."

"You found the music enjoyable, then?"

"The mu—oh, yes, of course, but I meant—Hester, you are funning me!"

"Perhaps just a little," replied Hester, smiling.

"I never knew John could be such fun to talk to," continued Chloe. "Though, if you ask me what we discussed, I don't know that I could tell you." She laughed. "We spoke of—oh, poetry, and riding, and—and our favorite flavor of ices."

"An eclectic range of subject matter," murmured Hester.

Chloe smiled engagingly, but immediately grew serious. "I must tell you, Hester, that I am—well, I'm reconsidering my refusal of John's proposal."

Hester allowed her eyes to widen in a simulation of surprise. "No!"

"Do you think I am dreadfully flighty? I mean, would I be betraying the cause if I were to marry? It would mean giving up my plans to write and give lectures—and, all that."

"You goose, of course it would not be a betrayal. In fact, as a married woman, you could do a great deal of good. The wife of John Wery, prosperous landowner, will be most influential in an area where so far little work has been done in promoting women's education. You could head committees, raise funds, dispense literature, and all manners of worthwhile activities."

"Yes, that's true. I had not thought of that. Of course," she said, blushing rosily, "I do not know if he still wishes to marry me, but if he asks me again—well, I just might say yes."

Hester reached to embrace the girl in a gentle hug. "I think you could not make a wiser decision, my dear. John is obviously a pearl among men."

Chloe blushed again. "I think so, too—and he has even said he wishes to go with us when you speak at The Blue Boar. You don't think Uncle Thorne will forbid me to go, do you?" Chloe asked anxiously.

"I shouldn't think so. His main objection seems to be one of safety rather than corrupting your young mind." Hester spoke with some asperity. "And he knows we shall be well protected."

Chloe yawned. "I expect you're right." She rose from the little wing chair by the fire and bade Hester good night.

When she had gone, Hester remained staring into the cheerful little blaze. It appeared that her tenure at Bythorne House was nearing an end. And a very good thing, she reminded herself severely. She was becoming much too fond of the Trent family in general and of my lord, the Earl of Bythorne in particular. No—more than fond, if she were to be honest.

Oh, very well, she thought grimly. She might as well admit it. She was in love with Thorne.

Chapter Seventeen

There she had said it.

Not that saying it made the idea any less absurd. Two more unsuited people she could not imagine than herself and the Earl of Bythorne. Even if she wished to marry, she would not choose a man who was the very antithesis of everything she believed in. She certainly would not so much as consider allying herself with a man whose only claim to her affection was a darkly compelling visage, a smile that turned her knees to pudding, and the ability to make her dizzy with delight at his touch.

She preferred not to consider the fact that the gentleman was also intelligent, a stimulating companion, and possessed a number of virtues, for none of them outweighed his flaws. He was a user of women who believed heart and soul that the female had no higher purpose in life than to provide the male's creature comforts. To be sure, she thought that she had detected a softening in his attitude during her visit, and his conversations with her were an exchange of spirit and wit and intelligence, but—

But—this dialogue with herself was pointless. Even if she decided the earl was her heart's desire, it would be ludicrous to suppose that he might feel the smallest interest in her—beyond, of course, that automatic response with which he had been so acutely endowed.

In her heart, she sensed that his feeling for her was different from the way he felt toward other women. Did not the fact that he actually seemed to enjoy her company rather bespeak that fact? She was sure he was not in the habit of sparring mentally with his *chères amies*, or even with Barbara, whom he evidently planned to marry some-day. He probably did so however, with many of his male friends, and he certainly did not feel a tender passion toward any of those.

Was that it? Did he think of her as a friend? Possibly. Did he think of her as the love of his life?

Fat chance, she concluded with an aching sigh.

Very well, then. She was used to disappointments in her life, and she could deal with one more. Perhaps her new-found friendship with the earl would continue after she returned to Overcross. Perhaps, she thought with a despairing giggle, he might ask her to stand as godmother for one of the children he would produce when he eventually married.

He would *not*, however, be producing those children with Lady Barbara Freemantle. Not if she had anything to say about it. *Sorry to disappoint you, my lord, but Lady B. is slotted for someone else.* The earl would just have to find another complacent, discreet daughter of the *ton* to produce his children and to adorn his house.

Having resolutely arranged the rest of her life to her dubious satisfaction, she sat down to consider the problem of Robert and Barbara. Despite their professed intentions of keeping apart from each other, Hester had not failed to notice that when they did find themselves in the same room together, they seemed inevitably drawn together. Witness the evening at Vauxhall Gardens. Hester had not been a party to the scene that had taken place between them after she had observed them in each other's arms, but she would be willing to wager a substantial sum that they did not sit down for a discussion of the quality of the orchestra.

She would just have to assure their continuing exposure to each other. That should not be too difficult, given Gussie's determination that Barbara and John be included in all the Bythorne House activities—even though Gussie's purpose was far removed from her own.

Three days passed before Hester was able to put her plan in operation. The occasion was a dinner party hosted by Viscount Halburton and his lady in honor of the betrothal of their youngest daughter to the heir of the Earl of Cashin.

As luck would have it, the housekeeper at the Halburton establishment had worked at Bythorne House in her youth, and was still friends with many of the staff. Through a complex series of negotiations and a little judicious bribery, Hester was able to ensure that Robert and Barbara would be seated next to one another at the table the night of the dinner party.

To her consternation, however, she discovered on entering the Halburton dining room in company with a glittering throng, that she had neglected to consider the partner on her other hand. Barbara had not accompanied the party from Bythorne House on this evening, but had arrived with her aunt, the Countess of Carbrooke and her young daughter. The hair on Hester's neck lifted gently as she observed Thorne taking his place on Barbara's right, while Robert, grim-faced, settled in on her left. Across the table, Gussie writhed in obvious irritation. She must have planned for Robert to be placed next to Hester and was wondering why her scheme had gone awry.

Meanwhile, Chloe and John disported themselves at the far end of the table. Hester breathed a small sigh of relief. At least things seemed to be progressing satisfactorily in that quarter.

The meal, as far as Hester was concerned, progressed in fits and starts. As she watched, leaving her own dinner partners largely ignored, Barbara devoted most of her attention to Thorne, while Robert applied himself diligently, first to his portion of turtle soup, then to the partner on his other hand. When Barbara did turn to speak to him, he replied in monosyllables until, with a resolute shrug of her shoulders, she abandoned him to his own devices.

Oh, for heaven's sake, thought Hester. This would never do. She would have to arrange something. When dinner was concluded and the gentlemen had joined the ladies after their port, she gestured to John from across the room to the seat she had been saving next to her. Before the young man could reach that goal, however, Thorne slid into the indicated chair.

"I say," he whispered, "have you noticed Chloe and John? They've had their heads together all evening."

"Yes," replied Hester, uncomfortably aware that his head was bent close to hers. "In fact, I saw them leave the room together just now. It's horribly improper, of course, but I think we may allow a couple in love a little latitude."

"They may have all the latitude they require, with my blessing, if it will result in a betrothal announcement. By the by," he said, drawing back to survey her, "you are looking exceptionally well tonight."

The appreciative gleam in his eyes disconcerted her, but his words put her in mind of a subject that had been rankling for some time.

"As well, I may," she retorted, "considering the amount of money that has been spent on my behalf."

At the questioning lift of Thorne's brows, she fanned the flame of indignation that she had coaxed into being inside her. "How could you deceive me so, my lord?"

"My lord, is it? Now what have I done to incur your displeasure, Madame Firebrand?"

"I discovered from something Gussie let slip the other day that Madame Celeste has been charging me a fraction—a very small fraction—of what my gowns are worth—and that you have been making up the difference."

Thorne had the grace to flush, albeit almost imperceptibly. "Well," he said reasonably, "how else was I to proceed? You would not agree to my simply paying for the gowns, and Madame's prices are far too exorbitant for you to have paid on your own."

"I would have—"

"You would simply have decided to appear in gowns you *could* afford—a program unacceptable to either Gussie or myself. Now, admit it," he continued before Hester could utter the protest forming on her lips, "haven't you enjoyed your new furbelows? Even a woman who has foresworn the frivolities of fashion must indulge herself occasionally in the knowledge that she is wearing something indecently expensive and wildly flattering."

Thorne's words hit so close to the mark that Hester

shifted uncomfortably. She glanced down before she could stop herself at her beguiling ensemble of pale rose Italian crepe worn under a tunic of spangled gauze. Brilliants caught the material at her shoulders and glittered at the ends of two tassels that depended from her cap of satin and Jouy lace.

"Yes, I cannot dispute the fact that Madame Celeste is a superb practitioner of her art, but—"

"We are being rude," interrupted Thorne with a great show of offended propriety. "Lady Halburton's nephew is about to favor us with one of his verses, if I am not mistaken."

"Yes, but—" Hester sputtered furiously.

Thorne waved an expansive hand. "We can discuss all this later, my dear."

"I am *not* your dear," she grated in a last, futile effort to preserve the upper hand.

Long before Lady Halburton's nephew had ceased spouting an interminable ode to spring, Thorne had vacated his chair and drifted off to the card room. So much for his virtuous declarations on the subject of rudeness, thought Hester resentfully. But, never mind that. It was time to regenerate her plot to get Barbara and Robert together. Containing herself until the last strains of the poem had been dinned into the ears of the young man's audience, she hastened from the room. She summoned a footman and ordered pen, paper, and ink to be brought to her in a small chamber she had spied farther down the corridor and in a few moments handed two notes to the footman, to be delivered immediately. She then sat back to await events.

Events, however, once more proved uncooperative. Returning to the drawing room, she observed the footman's approach to Robert, and Robert's subsequent exit from the chamber. Shifting expectantly to Barbara, she was pleased to note the glowing blush that flooded her cheeks. However, so quickly did Barbara turn, that she jarred the elbow of a young man who was carefully carrying two cups of punch. A cascade of brilliant red liquid poured over the front of her gown, and her subsequent gasp caused a flurry of activity among those close to her. In a moment, Barbara could not even be seen for the group of gentlemen that clustered about her, proffering handkerchiefs to repair the damage.

Well, damn and blast.

It would be a very long time before Barbara would be able to disengage herself from her court. In the meantime, Hester could not simply leave Robert pacing the floor in the small chamber, where her note had directed him to await the sender.

Sighing, she walked again to the small chamber. Robert was not pacing, but he gave every evidence of a man about to do so. His head swiveled abruptly as Hester entered the room.

"Oh," he said, "it's you. That is," he amended hastily, "I was expecting—"

"I know who you were expecting, and she will not be coming."

"I—I don't understand."

Hesitantly, Hester approached Robert. "I'm so sorry, but it was I who sent that note." Ignoring his startled gasp and the disbelieving crease in his brow, she continued. "Believe me, Barbara wanted to come, but there was an accident. No, no—she is quite all right—just a little damp."

She explained the contretemps that had prevented Lady Barbara from reaching his side. To her surprise, Robert spluttered angrily for some moments before replying.

"Do you mean," he said at last, "that you were trying to engineer a meeting between Barbara and myself?"

"Why, yes. Isn't that what I just said? Now, there's no need to thank me. I merely—"

"Thank you! Why you interfering little busybody! What in God's name possessed you to do such a thing? What could I possibly have to say to Barbara? Or she to me?"

Hester stared at him, dumbfounded. "But, but—"

Robert surged toward her and grasped her arm, shaking it a little. "Oh God, I suppose you meant well, but you must get it through your head that there is nothing between Barbara and me. Not anymore. Nor will there be in the future.

The two people we were all those years ago no longer exist."

Tears sprang to Hester's eyes. "Oh no, Robert, you're wrong. You were mistaken in Barbara when you left her before. She never felt anything for that wretched marquis. Don't leave her again."

In her dismay, Hester all but flung herself against Robert, tugging at him as if by sheer strength of will she might persuade him. He put up his hands to hers to bring them away from him, and she knew a sudden shame.

"Oh Lord, I'm sorry, Robert. Here, let me straighten—" The words died in her throat as she glanced up to behold behind Robert several figures who stood in the doorway. The only one that fully registered on her consciousness, however, was that of the Earl of Bythorne.

His eyes seemed to catch the light of the candles that lit the room and they glittered with the added blaze of a rage Hester had never seen there. He strode into the room, and it was then that she saw he was accompanied by Gussie, Lord Bracken, and Barbara. John and Chloe brought up the rear. Hester felt as though she had been suddenly turned to stone, and she watched, unable to so much as lift her hand as Thorne advanced, fists clenched. He halted abruptly, however, as Gussie spoke.

"Why, Hester! Mr. Carver!" she cried in a pleased voice. "I had no idea things had progressed so far between you. Are we to wish you happy?"

Beside Hester, Robert made a faint strangled sound. Barbara, her face as white as the wine-stained handkerchief she held in her hand, also uttered a soft moan.

"No!" cried Hester, at last galvanized to action. "We were not—that is, it is not as—"

"Yes, of course, Lady Bracken."

Hester whirled to face Robert, who held her hand in a bone-crushing grip. He turned to face Thorne, and when he spoke again into the silence that seemed to thunder about them, his voice was controlled, if a little breathless. "I suppose I should have applied to you first, my lord, for the lady's hand, but she assures me that she is her own mistress and needs no one's permission to wed."

"Now, see here—" began Hester, but she was over-whelmed by Gussie's tumultuous embrace. Lord Bracken, too, stepped up to bestow a kiss on her cheek, and within a few minutes, the room was filled with well-wishers from the drawing room who, with finely honed instincts, had sniffed out the scene in progress.

"This is ridiculous," Hester was saying. "We were not engaged in the slightest impropriety, and I have no inten-tion of marrying Mr. Carver."

"Nonsense," said Gussie briskly. "Now," she continued, shooing those who had come to stare out of the room, "I think it is time for us to make our departure. We can begin making wedding plans later."

"But—" began Hester once more, only to be grasped firmly by the elbow. "Your aunt is correct," said Robert, propelling her from the room. "We can talk later—but right now it would be best to vacate the premises as quickly as possible, don't you agree?"

With a glance at Thorne, Hester allowed herself to be swept into the corridor. In passing, she caught a glimpse of Barbara, standing pale and silent at the far end of the room. Her expression as she gazed at Hester was bitterly re-proachful.

In a few minutes, Hester found herself ensconced in the Bythorne carriage. Robert, whom Gussie had insisted ac-company them from the house, sat on one side of her and Thorne on the other. The passengers, who included, in ad-dition to those mentioned, Lord Bracken, Aunt Lavinia, Chloe, and John, were thus severely cramped, but Gussie fairly bubbled with self-congratulations on her successful matchmaking and plans for the coming nuptials. Chloe sat, wide-eyed and silent, and Aunt Lavinia merely contributed a sort of litanical series of murmured responses to Gussie's rhapsodies. Robert occasionally interpolated a remark, if not with enthusiasm, at least in agreement. Hester, how-ever, was almost wholly focused on Thorne, who had said nothing since striding into the small chamber in Halburton

House. She could sense the tension in the arm that brushed hers occasionally, but beyond that she could not fathom his reaction to the contretemps. Lord, surely he could not think that she had any intention of marrying Robert—or that Robert wished to marry her. He could not think that they had really been embracing one another.

Or, even worse, was he pleased at this turn of events? Did he wish to see her wed to Robert? Ridiculous! How could it matter to Thorne whether she married or remained a spinster to the end of her days?

Thorne could not believe the ferocity of his response to the scene he had just witnessed. Never in his well-ordered life had he experienced such a maelstrom of emotions in such a short space of time. His initial reaction on beholding what appeared to be a tender embrace between Hester and Robert had been one of such overpowering wrath that he thought he would be sick with it. Gussie's exclamation of pleasure at the sight had abruptly brought to mind that he was supposed to be promoting just such a denouement for Hester. Her demeanor now certainly did not indicate the presence of the tender emotion in her breast, but why else would she have been standing there pasted to him like a sticking plaster?

They must be married, of course. Again, he was surprised at the sinking sensation this thought produced within him. It must be that he had become more used to her presence in his life than he had imagined. Or, perhaps—he smiled grimly—it was similar to the awareness of one's own mortality engendered by the death of a close acquaintance. Perhaps now he would knuckle down to the inevitable and propose to Barbara. At any rate, it was no doubt all a good thing. He had become much too fond of his newly acquired cousin, and her departure from his household would provide an impetus for getting on with his own marital plans.

He would, he decided, smile on the projected union. He would render whatever assistance the happy couple required, which might, he reflected ruefully, consist of persuading the bride-to-be of the necessity of committing to the married state.

After several dubious sidelong glances at Thorne, Hester turned her attention to Robert. What in God's name was the matter with the man? How could he sit there quietly accepting Gussie's congratulations and those of Lord Bracken? Well, it was time to put a stop to this nonsense.

"Gussie," she said in peremptory tone. "Gussie," she said again as the flow of her ladyship's excited chatter remained unimpeded.

"And, of course, the betrothal party will be held at Bracken House. I think—Yes, what is it, dearest?" she asked, becoming aware at last that Hester was tugging at her skirt.

"Gussie, there will be no betrothal party and no wedding."

Gussie's eyes opened wide. "Oh, but dearest—"

"You must know perfectly well that there is a perfectly innocent explanation for what you saw. Robert and I—"

"—were caught in an extremely compromising position," concluded Gussie baldly. "If a betrothal notice does not appear prominently in the *Post* within the next few days you will be ruined."

"Gussie, you are mistaking me for someone who cares about that absurd nonsense. I—"

"Gussie is right," said a voice at her elbow and she whirled in her seat to face Thorne directly. "It doesn't matter what you were doing, you and Robert must be married."

Hester's mouth dropped open. "What! This—coming from you? You cannot mean you subscribe to this ridiculous notion."

Gussie, too, stared at her nephew in some surprise and Lord Bracken eyed him owlishly through his quizzing glass.

"I'm merely saying—" began Thorne calmly, but at that moment the carriage pulled up in front of Bythorne House.

Upon entering the house, Hester declared her intention to seek her bed. "I am tired and I have the headache," she claimed rather pettishly, "and I do not wish to continue this ridiculous discussion any more tonight. Robert—" She bent a minatory stare on her would be betrothed. "I would appreciate it if you would call on me tomorrow at your earliest convenience. Good night, Gussie—my lord," she said to Lord and Lady Bracken. "Aunt Lavinia, Chloe," she added, inclining her head, and over her shoulder, she threw a last farewell. "And to you, Lord Bythorne."

The image of his face, once again ablaze with a flash of anger, stayed with her as she stumped up the stairs, and when she reached her bedchamber, she stood for a long moment in the center of the room staring at nothing in particular before she rang for Parker.

Chapter Eighteen

Hester awoke, after a virtually sleepless night, to a disgustingly beautiful morning. The weather, she thought dismally, should at least reflect her mood. A middling typhoon might suffice, or even just a torrential rain. Oddly, it was not so much the predicament in which she found herself that had caused her to thump her pillow so restlessly through the wee small hours. She had no doubt of her ability to remain firm in the face of Gussie's importunities and Robert's misplaced chivalry. No, it was Thorne's reaction to the situation that stung. The spark of what she could have sworn was anger in his eyes had been of such brief duration that she was sure she had imagined it, and afterward—she could not say why she had been so overset at his bland agreement with Gussie's pronouncements. Had she somehow expected him to leap at Robert's throat in a fit of lover's jealousy? How perfectly absurd.

As dawn's gray light began to illuminate her bedchamber, Hester came to the reluctant conclusion that Thorne, having accepted her as a member of his family, had become just like every other male to whom she was related. He considered that it was his duty to find her a husband and get her married so that she would start raising babies and stop making trouble for everyone with her radical nonsense.

This realization produced a profound depression within her, and wearily, she rose and splashed water on her face. Well, at any rate, she was not about to become betrothed to the wrong man. She would explain to Robert today that, while she appreciated his gesture, she was *not* going to marry him. Then, she would have to make her peace with

Barbara. She recalled with a pang Barbara's white, anguished face. Lord, she should have made it plain to her immediately that she had no intention of participating in this stupid charade.

In another area of the house, Thorne, too, was in the process of setting his life in order. His night had been sleepless as well, and now, as he stood in his bedchamber looking out at the sunlight that slanted through the streets of London, he came to a decision. Today, he would propose marriage to Lady Barbara Freemantle, thus putting to an end once and for all his unbecoming fascination with Hester Blayne.

He could not fathom the unpleasant sensation that still churned through him at the thought of Hester's sudden betrothal to Robert Carver. He had already decided, after all, that Carver was a perfectly unexceptionable *parti* for his newfound cousin. True, he did feel a twinge of compunction at having allowed Gussie to maneuver Hester in such a fashion. On the other hand, Gussie was perfectly right. In allowing herself to tumble into Robert's embrace, Hester had put herself into an untenable position. She might decry the absurdity of the social commandment that said, "Thou shalt avoid the incidence of impropriety," but there it was. She had broken that commandment, and now she must pay the price.

Or, perhaps she would not find the price too much to pay. Hester obviously liked Robert. Why, after all, had she allowed the man to maul her in such a manner if she did not hold him in special affection? Was she an advocate of free love, as had been Mary Wollstonecraft before her? Well, by God, there would be none of Robert Carver's butter prints running tame in Bythorne House if he had anything to say about it. The fact that he had, indeed, virtually nothing to say about either Carver's butter prints or Hester's declaration of her intent to leave Bythorne House eventually only served to exasperate him even further.

At this point, having roused his valet at an unaccustomedly early hour, he found himself full clothed and cravated, leaving him with no other choice than to take himself down to breakfast.

Somewhat to his discomfiture, he found Hester there before him.

After awkward good mornings were said, Hester cleared her throat.

"About last night . . ." she began, and then trailed off as though she were uncertain as to how to continue.

"Yes?" Thorne's tone was unencouraging.

Taking a deep breath, Hester launched into a somewhat disjointed explanation of her presence in the Halburton's little saloon with Robert Carver and their subsequent, scandalous proximity.

"So, you see," she finished, "it was all perfectly innocent."

At the beginning of her monologue, Thorne had adopted an attitude of benevolent understanding—the pater familias who, though adamant in his determination to fulfill his duties, was prepared to listen. However, by the time she had finished, his aspect had undergone an unpleasant transformation. His face bore a thunderous scowl, and his eyes had narrowed to glittering slits.

"You were trying to arrange a meeting between Barbara and Carver?" he asked very softly in a tone of chill steel.

"Well, er, yes," Hester faltered. It had not occurred to her until this moment that the last person in the world who might understand her altruistic desire to bring two sundered hearts together was the man who himself expected to engage in a relationship with one of those hearts. "I do not suppose you are aware of their prior attachment, but—"

"No, I was not."

"But, now that you are, I am sure you understand that they belong together."

"No, I am afraid I do not."

Thorne still spoke in a tone of iced silk, but he rose abruptly to stand before Hester.

"Good God!" The phrase exploded from him. "How could you serve me such a turn? Barbara and Carver? A prior attachment? I never heard such drivel in my life. May

I remind you that my ultimate betrothal to her has been an understood fact for years?"

"Well—yes, but—"

"May I also remind you that Barbara has never given the slightest indication that my suit is anything but welcome to her."

"Yes, I know that, too, but, Thorne, it is also my understanding that—that your heart is not, er, involved, and—"

"What the devil would you know about my heart?" snarled Thorne.

Hester whitened and stepped back abruptly. At the sight of the startled mortification in her eyes, something snapped within him.

"The state of my affections is of absolutely no concern to you," he said scathingly. "Do you understand that? However, allow me to inform you that, although I may eschew your maudlin, romantical notions of love, it is my intention to make Barbara my wife—and I would appreciate it if you would simply keep your meddlesome, busy fingers out of my life. Do I make myself clear?"

For an instant, Hester could not speak. Her hand flew to her throat as though she might stay the tears that gathered there, and her body suddenly seemed turned to lead. With a choked sound, she whirled and stumbled from the room, leaving Thorne to stare after her.

She did not stop until she had reached the haven of her bedchamber. Here, she lowered herself very carefully into a small chair near the fireplace as though at the slightest jar she might break into a thousand jagged pieces.

How could she have been so mistaken in Thorne's feelings for Barbara? He might say he did not believe in the concept of love, but his outburst just now had proved otherwise. He—why, he was obviously in a perfect rage of jealously over the notion that Barbara might prefer Robert to himself. The thought tolled like a great bell within her, echoing in the emptiness that filled her. Dear God, she had never known that love could hurt so.

What was she to do now? Thorne had warned her not to interfere any farther in his life, but what about Barbara?

The idea of doing any further disservice to Thorne was not to be borne, but could she let him marry Barbara, knowing that the lady loved someone else? Perhaps Barbara would come to the conclusion on her own that she could not wed Thorne. She would certainly not do so while her beloved was ostensibly betrothed to someone else, so it would seem that the first order of business was to release Robert Carver from the results of his moment of folly.

It was many minutes, however, before she arose from the little chair to make herself presentable for Robert's impending visit.

Downstairs, Thorne set out from the house in a black mood. It was unfashionably early to pay a social call, but he felt an unsettling urgency to do something about his situation. Issuing a curt command to his tiger, he mounted his waiting curricle and set out for Weymouth House, the town home of the Duke and Duchess of Weymouth and their daughter, Lady Barbara Freemantle.

Thorne was aware that the butler who answered the door would have informed any other caller at this hour that his grace and family were not yet receiving, however, the door was flung wide to admit the Earl of Bythorne. Thorne had decided earlier to speak to Barbara before making his official request for her hand to her father. Thus, in a very few minutes, he faced the lady in her drawing room.

He was startled at her aspect, for it was apparent she had not slept well the night before. The shadows beneath her eyes stood out like bruises against the pallor of her face. She greeted him with her lovely smile, however.

"Thorne! I could hardly believe Blickster when he told me you were here. Whatever are you doing out and about at the crack of dawn?"

Thorne glanced at his watch. "I will agree that ten in the morning is unconscionably early, my dear, but hardly the crack of dawn. It is merely an indication of the import of my visit."

Barbara lifted her brows questioningly. Thorne led her to a settee by the window and drawing her by his side, seated himself.

"Tell me," said Barbara. "How—how is Hester this morning?"

"When I left her," he replied stiffly, "she seemed in excellent spirits."

Barbara's fingers twisted in the fringe of her shawl. "I noticed that when you left Halburton House last night, Ro—Mr. Carver accompanied you."

"That is true. He wished," continued Thorne, feeling somewhat harassed, "to assure Hester that his proposal earlier was genuine and to assure himself that she had accepted it."

"And did she?" Barbara's voice was a whispered scratch.

"Well—no, not right away. But he will be attending Hester later in the morning, and I believe," he concluded mendaciously, "that she will accept him."

"Ah."

"Well, she has no choice in the matter, does she? She was thoroughly compromised last night."

Barbara looked away. "Yes, undoubtedly. I—I was surprised to see them so. I had no idea there was such a degree of affection between them."

"Yes. Er, no." Thorne was beginning to feel as though he were creeping through a minefield. "It is obvious that they hold each other in esteem. In addition, as Gussie has pointed out several times, Carver is the perfect *parti* for Hester—and she seems the perfect mate for him. They share the same interests, and—"

Barbara lifted a hand. "Yes, yes, I know," she said brokenly. "I'm sure I'm very happy for them."

"Quite." Thorne took her hand, prepared to get down to the matter at hand. "Barbara," he began, sliding into the speech he had prepared on the short journey from Bythorne House. He was surprised to discover that he was perspiring profusely and that the words that had flowed so trippingly over his tongue earlier now seemed glued there. "Barbara," he said again. "You—you must be aware of the affection with which I have regarded you for a number of years."

Barbara said nothing, but nodded hesitantly and eyed him warily.

"I fact, I think I am not overstating the case when I say that you and I have enjoyed an, er, special relationship."

Barbara nodded again.

Thorne plunged on, a hint of desperation overtaking him. "Look, Barbara," he said abandoning the prepared text. "We've teetered on the brink of betrothal for donkey's years, and we're neither of us getting any younger."

At Barbara's affronted gasp, he rose abruptly. "Devil take it, you know what I mean." Taking a deep breath, he sat down again and took her hand in his. "I seem to be making a mull of this, my dear, but you must be aware of my feeling for you. And now—at long last—I'm asking you to marry me if you'll have me."

There, he'd said it. He smiled into Barbara's eyes and was a little dismayed to discover that, instead of returning it in blushing acceptance, she had turned even whiter and had dropped her gaze to her lap.

"Barbara?" he prompted. "Do you—?"

"Yes," she said suddenly with a little gasp. "Yes, I will marry you, Thorne."

He leaned forward to press his mouth on lips that were cold and set.

"You have made me the happiest man in London, my dear."

She looked directly at him. "Have I?"

Searching inside himself, he discovered that, no, he was not happy. He had known that he would not be sent into alt by her acceptance, for he had expected it, but surely he should feel more than this—this hollow chill that seemed to fill him.

"Of course you have," he said briskly. "We shall deal very well with each other, Barbara, you'll see." He rose to his feet. "Is your father at home? I'd best do the pretty before I leave—make it all right and tight."

"Yes," said Barbara in a low tone. "He is in his study. Oh, Thorne!" she exclaimed suddenly. "We are doing the right thing, are we not?"

God, what a selfish boor he'd been. Or course Barbara would be experiencing something of a *crise de nerfs* at a

time like this, and he'd been acting as though he were con-
cluding a mildly challenging business deal. Placing an arm
around her, he drew her to him and dropped a kiss on her
hair.

"Of course, we are, sweetheart. You're a pearl beyond
price, and any man would be fortunate to claim you as his
bride. I promise I'll do my best to make you happy."

Again, he did not feel as though his words were those of
a man who has just attained his dream of bliss, but it was
the best he could do. He released her and bowed himself
from the room.

It was more than an hour later, however, before he left
Weymouth House. After bearding Barbara's father in the
ducal den, he was rewarded with a gratifyingly prompt acceptance of his suit. The duke, while not precisely clasping
Thorne to his bosom, declared himself pleased at the proposed union, his words of acquiescence containing only the
merest hint of, "What took you so long?"

After that, the duke sent for the duchess to apprise her of
the glad news, and the couple accompanied Thorne back to
the drawing room, where the rest of the family, including
his oldest son and heir, two more daughters, and a younger
son home on leave from the army, were summoned to add
their voices in congratulating the happy couple.

When Thorne returned home later, the house was silent.
Hobart informed him that Lady Lavinia and Miss Chloe
had departed moments before on a shopping expedition,
and Miss Hester was closeted in the blue saloon with Mr.
Carver.

Thorne pricked up his ears at this intelligence, but after a
moment's thought decided against joining the couple. His
presence would no doubt be decidedly *de trop*. However,
on passing the doorway to the blue saloon, he heard voices
through the door that could only be described as acrimo-
nious. Pausing for a moment, he knocked peremptorily and
entered.

Hester stood before the fireplace, her face flushed and
her demeanor tense. Robert Carver stood near her. His face,
too, was noticeably strained, although he bore no other

signs of perturbation. They both swung about as the door opened.

"I trust I do not intrude?" asked Thorne.

"Not at all," responded Hester. Robert's lips tightened.

"I was having a private conversation with Miss Blayne," he said.

"Ah," said Thorne. "In that case, do forgive me." He began to back out from the room.

"Oh, don't be silly." Hester's voice was high with exasperation. "Robert, Thorne was privy to all that happened last night. All this polite backing and filling is quite useless." She moved toward Thorne. "Robert has been kind enough to repeat his proposal, and I have been trying to tell him it is all quite unnecessary and that I have no intention of marrying him."

"Well, if you're expecting me to second those sentiments," remarked Thorne, strolling farther into the room, "you're backing the wrong pony. As I was just saying to Barbara, you have no real choice in the matter."

At the sound of Barbara's name, both Hester and Robert responded noticeably. Hester appeared startled, while Robert took a step forward, his hand lifted in an unconscious gesture.

"You—you have seen Lady Barbara this morning?" asked Robert after a moment.

"You have been discussing my situation with Barbara?" asked Hester at almost the same moment.

"Yes, to both questions," replied Thorne with a spurious air of cool self-possession. Of Robert's obvious distress, he had taken little note, but he found himself almost tingling with an awareness of the tension that fairly radiated from Hester. Without quite knowing why, his breath became attenuated as he uttered his next words. "You may, by the by, wish me happy."

Hester's hand went to her throat, as it had earlier that day. "Oh!" she breathed, "You have offered for her?"

"Oh God!" The exclamation, quickly stifled, burst from Robert as though forced by a blow to his chest. Thorne stared at him before turning back to Hester.

"Yes. I expect the news will appear in *The Morning Post* in a day or two."

A sense of unreality descended on Thorne, as though he were observing the scene from a great way off. He, Hester, and Carver, all seemed players mouthing lines written for them, in a drama that would come to an end at any moment, leaving him to make his way back to the normality of life as he had known it. The life of uncomplicated hedonism he had known before he met Hester Blayne.

Hester licked her lips. "Of course, I wish you happy—my lord. When will the glad event take place?"

"We have not set a date as yet," replied Thorne smoothly. "When I left Weymouth House, Barbara and her mother were speaking of sometime early next spring."

Hester nodded. Robert moved forward jerkily and extended his hand.

"I, too, wish to offer my felicitations, my lord."

Thorne expressed his appreciation in a suitable manner. Then, crossing his arms, he bestowed a measured stare on Hester.

"Now, Miss Blayne, let us direct our attention to setting a date for your own nuptials."

Chapter Nineteen

Hester stared at him for a long moment. She felt that her knees would no longer hold her up. Oddly, other than this trembling deep within her, she was remarkably calm. The news that Thorne had proposed to Barbara should not have come as a shock, even though she had hoped to prevent it. It was, however, as she had heard sometimes happened to victims of a gunshot. She knew she had been critically wounded, yet she felt nothing. Never mind, she thought. The pain would come.

"There will be no date, my lord, for Robert and I are not to be married."

Robert stepped forward.

"Hester, this is nonsense. I will agree that neither of our hearts are engaged, but please believe me that I am most sincere in—"

"Why don't we all sit down," interrupted Thorne, "and discuss this rationally?" Pausing to ring for coffee, he settled into a comfortable chair in one of the groupings that dotted the room and motioned Robert and Hester to a nearby settee.

"There is nothing to discuss," said Hester tightly, but allowed herself to be guided to the settee.

"Now then," Thorne said to Hester in an avuncular tone, "it seems to me that Robert is behaving in a most proper fashion. You do not dislike him, do you? It has always seemed to me that you hold him in esteem."

"Yes, of course I do and yes, I like him very much. And he likes me, but that is far from being a basis for marriage, my lord."

"It seems to me that it is the only basis," returned Thorne. "Mutual esteem is the cornerstone of a successful connubial relationship." As though aware of the pomposity of his words, he shifted in his chair and continued earnestly. "Robert will make an excellent husband for you, Hester," he continued earnestly. "And you know—"

"Perhaps, my lord," interposed Robert, "you would allow me to speak for myself." He turned to Hester. "My dear, as I was saying, although we have been more or less catapulted into this situation, I believe we shall deal very well with each other. I am well able to support a wife, and I would be pleased to enter into your interests. I—I would be very proud to call you my own."

Touched, Hester placed her hand over his. "And any woman would be proud to call you husband, Robert, but I—I simply cannot marry you. Not only do I not hold you in the sort of regard that I feel is necessary for a happy marriage, but"—she shot a glance at Thorne—"there are other circumstances—of which we spoke earlier."

Robert, too, allowed his gaze to skitter to where Thorne sat, an expression of polite interest fixed to his features. "Er, yes, but I must reiterate, you are quite mistaken in that—other matter. In addition, as Lord Bythorne has pointed out, you have no choice. Despite the innocence of the occasion, you were quite compromised last night."

"Please," said Thorne, interrupting again. "Call me Thorne. And, Hester, if you call me 'my lord' one more time, I shall be forced to conclude that I have offended you in some manner."

Hester flushed and leaped to her feet. She was offended, so deeply that she thought she would bear the scars on her heart for years to come, but it was the height of absurdity to blame the earl for her own stupidity in falling in love with him.

"Very well, then, Thorne. I will say again that I do not care a button for the ridiculous imperative of society that says a woman is ruined in such situations. Even if Robert and I had been indulging in a truly passionate embrace, I do not see how I could be considered ruined. Robert, do you feel compromised? No, of course not. It is always the

woman whose purity is sullied if she allows a man to pleasure her in such a way."

Feeling a little foolish at her outburst, she sank down
once more onto the settee.

Robert rose to stand before her. "It is apparent—" he
began soberly, but was interrupted by the sound of voices
in the hall downstairs. In a few moments, the door opened
wide to reveal Gussie and Lady Lavinia.

Two pairs of bright, interested eyes swung between
Robert and Hester as the ladies moved into the room.

"Well, how nice to see you this morning, Mr. Carver,"
said Gussie, her voice lifting in a question.

"Good morning, ladies," Robert replied in a tone so
somber that not the meanest intelligence could take him for
a man just betrothed.

Gussie's mouth dropped open, but her breeding would
not allow her to broach the question that obviously burned
on her lips. An awkward silence descended on the group
until Robert cleared his throat.

"Actually, I was just leaving." He turned to Hester. "I
believe we still have something to settle between us, Miss
Blayne, but this does not seem the time or place to continue
our discussion. I shall call on you again—tomorrow afternoon."

"Oh, but—" began Hester before clamping her lips shut.
"Yes, yes of course, Mr. Carver. I shall see you out."

She whisked herself around Gussie and Lady Lavinia,
and taking Robert's arm, led him from the room.

Gussie immediately whirled on Thorne. "What happened?" she hissed.

"Absolutely nothing," replied her nephew somewhat
grimly. He had risen on the ladies' entrance to the room,
but now seated himself as Gussie and his aunt took chairs
on either side of the fireplace. "Hester is being her usual
stubborn self and Carver has not the backbone to bend her
to his will."

"Oh, Thorne!" cried Lady Lavinia faintly. "Who would
wish to marry a man who would use such methods?"

Thorne's face cleared a trifle. He laughed ruefully. "Or

what man could hope to bend that little termagant's will? Ah well, I shall keep at her, and since Carver promises to call again, perhaps we will wear her down. By the by," he continued, "I have some news of my own."

He related the stirring events that had taken place in Weymouth House that morning, which effectually drove any thought of Hester and her future from Gussie's mind. Lady Lavinia, too, pronounced herself gratified in the extreme and the next several minutes were spent in a brief, but exhaustive discussion of the probable wedding date, as well as the prenuptial celebrations that must be planned.

"But, where is Chloe?" asked Thorne at length. "Did she not go out with you this morning?"

"Yes," replied Gussie, "but we encountered Melisande Grapewin and her mother in that little apothecary shop in Bond Street—you know—the one near Locke's, and a few minutes later Seraphina Bliss entered with her cousin. The girls put their heads together and decided to go to Gunter's for ices, with Mrs. Grapewin remaining to chaperon. She should be home shortly after luncheon."

But it was somewhat later in the afternoon when Chloe returned to the bosom of her family, by which time Gussie had departed for her own home. When she arrived, Chloe was accompanied not by her friends, but by John Wery.

The two seemed to move in a haze of suppressed excitement, and Pinkham, who had, of course traveled in Chloe's wake all day, giggled in a most peculiar manner.

"Is Hester here?" were Chloe's first words on entering the house. Thorne, strolling into the hall from the library, was just in time to hear Aunt Lavinia reply in the affirmative. The little group paraded up to the drawing room.

Observing the glowing countenances of the two young people, Thorne felt a stirring of hope in his breast. Indeed, Chloe's first action when Hester entered the room was to fling herself on the older woman's breast while John stood back, blushing furiously.

"Oh, Hester! You will not believe . . . That is, we have something very particular to tell all of you." She shot a sparkling glance at John from beneath her lashes.

"Yes," said the young man, blushing. "Ladies, Lord Bythorne, Miss Venable has consented to be my wife."

Lady Lavinia, clasping a hand to her bosom, uttered a genteel crow of delight, while Hester drew Chloe into a congratulatory embrace. Thorne grasped John's hand as though it were a lifeline tossed to a drowning man and shook it vigorously.

"By God," he cried, "what excellent news!"

Chloe was babbling happily. "Melisande and Seraphina and I had just finished our ices and were promenading in Berkely Square, when we met John. He asked if he might walk with me in Green Park, and since I had Pinkham with me, I thought it would be quite unexceptionable."

"Of course, dear child," murmured Aunt Lavinia.

"Miss Blayne, you were right," interposed John, a wide grin splitting his features. "Although I was cast down when Ch—Miss Venable rejected my suit, it seemed to me that of late I had noticed a change in her demeanor toward me. I had decided to try my luck once more, and when I ran into her with her friends this morning, I knew the gods smiled on my aspirations."

He took Chloe's hand in his and pressed a light kiss on her fingers, whereupon Chloe bent on him a glance of adoring tenderness.

John made his departure soon afterward in order to impart the glad tidings to his parents, but he promised to return for dinner that night. A note was sent off to Gussie, requesting that she and Lord Bracken join the family, thus it was a merry group that came together in the dining parlor at Bythorne House that evening.

If Hester found herself unable to join wholeheartedly in the general hilarity of the gathering, she was able to conceal her feelings. She was truly happy for Chloe and young John, and took genuine pleasure in their happiness.

Gussie, with yet another wedding to plan for, was in alt. Her voluble speculations effectively masked Hester's silence, and Thorne's as well. Hester could not help remarking that, though he smiled a great deal and nodded in agreement with all Gussie's pronouncements, he contributed very little to the scene of bonhomie around the table.

"Well," said Gussie, sometime later as the family regrouped in the drawing room after dinner, "this certainly has been a day for wedding news in our family. How very singular that three of you should have become betrothed almost simultaneously." Her eyes glinted purposefully as she spoke.

"Gussie," said Hester quietly, "there are only two betrothals." She lifted a hand as Gussie opened her mouth. "I have no wish to spoil this happy occasion with another brangle. Perhaps we could discuss my situation at some other time."

She darted a glance at Thorne, who stood, stiff and unresponsive near the fireplace. Gussie, too, turned to look at Thorne, but, receiving no support from that quarter, sighed.

"Very well, my dear, but you must know I am not giving up on this. There is no doubt that talk of the incident is already circulating. An announcement must be made soon. Very soon. All right, all right," she said in response to the protest that formed in Hester's eyes. "I shan't say any more now. But"—she wagged a finger—"you may count on hearing more from me on the subject, for your attitude is quite unacceptable."

The guests departed not long after that, with John Wery spending an untoward length of time at the doorway with his beloved before making his final adieu. As the door closed behind him, Chloe waltzed dreamily about the hall.

"Isn't he wonderful?" she murmured. "I think I must be the most fortunate girl in London—no, in the country—or no—in the whole world, right now."

Aunt Lavinia sighed romantically and led her charge off to bed.

Hester set her own foot on the stairs, but was stayed by Thorne's hand. At his touch, she jerked as though stung and turned to face him, her face set.

"This has been a long day, Thorne. I really would like to retire, if you don't mind."

"I merely want to add to what Chloe just said," Thorne

said earnestly. "I only want to ask you to think seriously about Robert's offer before he visits again, and what it will mean to you if you refuse."

"But don't you see? It will mean nothing to me—especially now."

Thorne lifted his brows questioningly.

"Chloe is betrothed. Our agreement has come to an end. I shall begin making arrangements tomorrow to leave Bythorne House for a return to Overcross, and it will make not a particle of difference if I am ruined in polite circles, for I shall never see any of those people again. As for your family *amour propre*, the story of my scandalous defection will no doubt make the rounds, but by next week some other nonsense will have replaced it, and the gossips will have a hard time remembering my name."

"Leave?" whispered Thorne, repeating the only word in Hester's speech that had penetrated his consciousness.

"Of course. With Chloe's betrothal, our agreement is at an end. There is no reason for me to stay any longer and—and I am anxious to return to my home."

It was as though the floor had suddenly tilted under Thorne's feet. Somehow, despite Hester's previous protestations, her announcement had come with the effect of an unexpected blow.

"I see," he said. "Of course. That is—you have become very much a part of our family, Hester, and I—we would like to see you remain longer—perhaps until the wedding. If—"

"No!" Hester's reply was sharp and instantaneous. "No, I would prefer to leave as soon as possible. Oh!" she added. "I just remembered—my lecture at the Blue Boar next week. With your permission—"

Thorne's face darkened. "As I have just said, you are welcome to stay as long as you like. But are you still determined to speak in Seven Dials? I wish you would reconsider."

"I have considered it carefully, Thorne, and I cannot see any reason for me to change my plans. I told you, the women who will attend are the ones I most want to reach,

and I shall have plenty of stalwart masculine company."
She tilted her head and slanted a glance toward him
sparkling with mischief. "Perhaps you would like to attend,
as well?"

"Thank you," he said remotely. "I think not."

The twinkle died from her eyes. What had made her
think that he would be interested in watching her speak to a
group of lower-class women? "Of course. And now, if you
will excuse me, it's been a rather long day."

She turned and again began to make her way up the
stairs. Thorne, however, an odd expression in his eyes,
grasped her hand once more.

"This has, indeed, been a momentous day for us," he said
softly, cradling her hand in his.

"Oh, yes," replied Hester a little breathlessly. "I am glad
Chloe changed her mind, and—and I am happy for you, as
well, although—"

"Yes?"

"What I told you about Barbara's previous attachment
still holds. I don't know what prompted her to accept you,
but if you marry her, you must be aware that you have not
captured her heart."

He laughed shortly. "The state of Barbara's heart is her
concern. It is enough for me that she has promised to be my
bride. I know that I can trust her to behave with discretion
afterward."

She wrenched her hand from his. "Good God, Thorne,
what a dismal picture of marriage."

"But a pragmatic one, I'm sure you will agree. One that
you would be well to adopt in your own considerations."

"Oh, no. We are talking about the permanent relationship
between a man and a woman here, and I cannot accept the
idea of entering into such a union without love."

Thorne gazed at her for a long moment. Her brown eyes
seemed very large as she stared solemnly at him, and he
knew an aching urge to draw her to him and gently, very
gently, kiss the concern from them. The thought made him
giddy.

Actually, he had been feeling light-headed all day, like a

man suffering from a debilitating illness. He should be supremely satisfied with himself. He had secured the hand in marriage of the most beautiful woman in London, one who would make him the most perfect of wives. Very shortly, his ward, that pretty little albatross who had been a weight around his neck for so long, would be someone else's responsibility, and Hester, of whose existence he had been unaware just a few short weeks ago, would be out of his life.

He would miss her, there was no question of that. Perhaps, after she and Robert had been married for a while, she would be more amenable to seeing him—every now and then. Yes, that would be just the thing. Nothing terribly illicit, just some of her sparkling conversation on an occasional basis. And—every now and then, he would take her hair down from its pins and—He shook himself. Handsomely over the bricks, my lad, he thought morosely. The realization swept over him suddenly that as a result of his actions that day, he had lost Hester for good.

But then, she had never been his, had she?

And why did that thought send a shaft of such poignant regret shooting through him that he almost cried aloud with it? Lord, watching Chloe and young Wery billing and cooing all night must have affected him more than he thought. Hester Blayne was merely a woman, after all. Admittedly, she was a superior specimen of her sex, but it was not to be thought that she would remain in his mind after she left for any longer than it took to see her out the front door.

Still, he reminded himself, she was a toothsome specimen, as well, and it seemed a shame not to avail himself of her charms, demure though they might be.

Summoning his most winsome smile, he once more took her hand in his. "I think you would soon find," he murmured, "that such a union would have definite compensations." With his other hand, he stroked the shining silk of her hair and began to draw her toward him.

She made no resistance, but as his head bent over hers, she lifted hers abruptly. Her voice, when she spoke, was calm, but colder than a moor in winter.

"I cannot believe what you are about, my lord earl. May I remind you that you are newly betrothed? That should have some significance, do you not think?"

She stared at him for a moment with a look of such contempt that Thorne fell back in astonished shame. She said nothing more, but swinging about, she ascended the stairs, leaving him to stare after her, white-faced with shock.

Chapter Twenty

The next morning, another visitor appeared on the doorstep of Weymouth House at an unfashionably early hour, and this time the door, while opened courteously, was not quite flung wide.

"I'm afraid," said Blickster at his most austere, "that the family is not yet receiving."

"No," replied Hester serenely, "I suppose they are not. I should imagine Lady Barbara is awake, however. Please announce me to her, for I think she will wish to see me."

In this, Hester admitted to herself, she was no doubt being a bit sanguine. She was probably the last person in London whom Barbara wished to face this morning, but Hester had little doubt that her ladyship would abandon the fastness of her bedchamber quickly enough when she was apprised of Hester's presence in her drawing room.

Such proved to be the case, and in a few minutes, the two sat opposite each other in the drawing room over steaming cups of tea. Barbara's aspect was not welcoming.

"To what do I owe the privilege of this visit, Miss Blayne?" she asked, and Hester fancied she could hear shards of ice tinkling.

"Oh, Barbara, you know very well why I am here, and please do not look at me in that odious fashion. You must know that Robert and I were not engaged in—in anything remotely improper the other night."

"If you imagine, Miss Blayne, that your hoydenish behavior is of the least interest to me—"

"Now, see here," snapped Hester, beginning to be nettled. "I have come here to see what I can do to help you out of the absurd situation you have tumbled into, and—"

"That *I* have tumbled into! Well, of all the—"

"Yes. You have allowed yourself to become betrothed to a man for whom you feel only the mildest affection, allowing the man you truly love—and who loves you—to simply dangle in the wind."

At this, Barbara's face crumpled. "Oh, Hester, how can you say that?" she cried brokenly, tears welling in her celestial blue eyes. "It was you Robert was embracing at that wretched party, and you to whom he proposed marriage."

"Yes, he did, you goose, but only because of his wretched sense of honor. He is no more desirous of marrying me than he is of being transported to a penal colony, and I have no intention of accepting him, so there is no harm done there."

"Oh, is there not?" Barbara's tone was bitter.

"No, for all you need to do is to inform Thorne that you were mistaken in your sentiments. There has been nothing signed yet, has there?"

"N-no, but—"

"Good," said Hester briskly. "After that, you must go to Robert and straighten out the silly misunderstanding that has kept you apart all these years."

"Go to Robert!" gasped Barbara. "Are you mad? Not only would I not dream of so lowering myself, but he would most likely laugh in my face were I to do so."

"Good heavens, have you learned nothing? Don't you think it is time you had done with pride? Besides, I hardly think that Robert will laugh at you." She leaned forward and grasped one of Barbara's hands in both of hers. "Don't you see? This is your last chance to regain the happiness that you lost so long ago. There has been no announcement, and no marriage settlements agreed on. There is still time, but precious little of it."

"Oh, Hester, do you really think—? But it was all so many years ago. We are not the same people we were in our youth."

"You may be right, but you should at least have the chance to find out. Now listen," she began carefully.

"Robert intends to visit me today, so here is what I think you must do . . ."

At the end of another fifteen minutes and a great deal of persuasion, Hester left the house tolerably satisfied that she had done all that was humanly possible toward the reuniting of two sundered hearts.

She only wished, she reflected dismally, that she could do something about her own troubles. How could Thorne have treated her so contemptuously last night? She had tried to ease the pain of her unrequited love for him with the thought that she'd at least found a friend, but his behavior had effectively extinguished even that spark of warmth. She grimaced, sickened by the memory of the lickerish smile that had lain like smut on his lips as he caressed her. He had reduced their relationship to something tawdry and unclean. He could not have more openly declared his intention to tumble her like a street slattern. She shivered and almost gasped with the grief and a sense of betrayal that seemed to permeate her being.

How very fortunate for her that within a fortnight or so she would have left Bythorne House. With any luck, she need never see the earl again as long as either of them lived. In the meantime, she would make very effort to simply stay out of his way—and out of reach of his compulsively groping hands. From the expression on his face when she had left him last night, however, she rather thought she had no more to fear on that score.

In this, Hester was eminently correct. At that moment, the gentleman in question sat slumped in a large leather chair in White's, contemplating his iniquities. What in God's name had possessed him to treat Hester in such a fashion? He would not have approached a Covent Garden nun so contemptibly. He took a long pull from the brandy at his side. He had come to enjoy a special relationship with Hester, a peculiarly satisfying friendship. Why had he sought more? And in a manner guaranteed to destroy that relationship?

He sighed. It was true. He had come to want more than friendship from her. The few brief moments of intimacy he had shared with her had only fueled his desire to plumb the depths of the passion he had sensed within her. Yes, he wanted to bed her. Yet—somehow, he wanted even more than that. But what more could there be than that ultimate intimacy?

Not that he was liable to find out. If Hester ever so much as wished him good morning again, he would be much surprised. Another thought struck him.

Would last night's assault on her virtue provide the impetus for her to accept Robert Carver's offer? If that were the case, perhaps one good thing would have come of his appalling blunder.

Oh Lord, as long as he was in a mood for self-examination, he might as well admit he did not wish Hester to marry Carver. It would be the greatest mismatch of the century, after all. Hester needed an entirely different sort of man. One who could curb some of her more outrageous starts without breaking her spirit. One, for that matter, who could tell the difference between an outrageous start and a cause to which she had truly given her heart.

On the other hand, he must admit that there was something of the dog-in-the-manger in his maunderings. He could not have Hester on his terms, so he was pettishly determined that no other man would have her on any terms at all. For God's sake, why did Hester's choice of a mate—or nonchoice, as the case might be—make any difference to him at all? He had already determined that he would miss her when she was gone, but it would be a fleeting pang, surely.

It was more than he could—

"Lord Bythorne!"

So deep was his abstraction that the voice at Thorne's elbow caused him to start violently, splashing brandy over his coat and down his trouser leg.

"Good day, sir," said Robert Carver, drawing out his own handkerchief to assist in the mopping up. "I am happy to find you here."

Thorne merely grunted and gestured him to a nearby chair.

"You are out and about early," remarked Robert.

"I might say the same of you." Thorne replaced his handkerchief and drained what was left of the brandy.

"Yes. Well, I awoke early and could not get back to sleep." Robert leaned back in his chair for a moment, steepling his fingers before him as he gazed intently at Thorne.

"Is there something I can do for you, Carver?" asked Thorne at last.

"Er, no—that is—" Robert seemed to come to a decision. "As you know, I promised Hester that I would call on her again today to renew my suit."

"Yes, so I recall."

"Since I spoke to her yesterday, however, I have begun to believe she is right in refusing me."

"What!" Thorne rose abruptly, looming over his companion. "Of all the contemptible—"

Robert, unmoved by Thorne's violent reaction, merely lifted his hand in a propitiary gesture. Thorne sat down again, but remained in a position of rigid watchfulness.

"The thing is, I cannot help but agree with her reasons for not wishing to marry me," said Robert. Thorne started forward once more.

"But you seemed sincere in your offer."

"I was. I am. I am prepared to go forward with the wedding, but I can certainly appreciate Hester's reluctance. I cannot pretend that I love her—nor does she love me."

"Love!" Thorne fairly spat the word and Robert smiled faintly.

"I know the concept is unfashionable in the extreme. I do not speak of the emotion prated about with such facility in the Minerva Press romances, but I do believe in the existence of a certain bond between a man and a woman that transcends all others, and that bond is necessary for a good marriage. I am not putting this well," he admitted as Thorne shifted irritably in his chair. "Have you never known a woman with whom you felt alive only in her presence? And somehow incomplete when you were not with her? A woman whose welfare and happiness became of supreme importance to you? Someone whom you would give up your life to protect? And, not at the least, someone whom you cannot envision living the rest of your life without."

As though ashamed of such an unmanly burst of sentiment, Robert rose abruptly. "I do apologize, my—Thorne. I do not generally expound my private philosophies so publicly. I shall leave you now. Perhaps I shall see you later in the day."

He bowed awkwardly and turned on his heel. In a moment he was gone.

Thorne made no acknowledgment either of his statement or of his subsequent departure, but stared before him in blank astonishment as the universe rearranged itself about him. No, of course he had never felt that way about anyone. Not until he had met Hester Blayne. Was that what had come to him with her entrance into his life? Was that what had virtually destroyed his interest in other women? Did the ache in his soul that now seemed to consume him have a name? Was it truly love that he felt for Hester?

Dear God, how could that be? The knowledge had been firmly instilled within him many years ago that marriage was a convenient facade, behind which one could pursue one's own pleasure. Love was simply a sugarcoated concept, invented for the purpose of luring prey into that sanctioned union—or, perhaps, into a liaison not quite so licit.

He had developed the tidy little theory that the only relationship a man could possibly want with a woman was one of bodily pleasure. He never allowed his feeling for a female to go beyond the boundary of a few transitory moments of sexual release.

Lord, he had reduced every relationship he had ever known to one of base, animal lust. And he had tried to do the same thing with Hester. Something in him had told him that here was a special woman—a person, but he could not listen to his heart. It had, he realized, become almost a necessity that he transform what was between them to something ignoble and ugly.

And he had succeeded beautifully.

It was many minutes before he dragged himself to his feet, feeling he had aged a hundred years in the hour since he had entered his club. On the drive home, he pondered further the blinding epiphany that had overcome him within those profane portals. Robert had said something about not being able to envision life without that certain woman.

Yes! He dropped his reins suddenly, almost causing his curricle to run over a diminutive crossing sweep in his path. That was the something more he wanted of Hester! To spend the rest of his life with her—cherishing her—and sharing laughter and sorrows together through the twilight of their existence.

He almost laughed aloud. God help him, he had even come so far that he wanted to help her in her various causes. But he had ruined everything. He had shattered the tenuous rapport that had developed between them with his abortive assault on her virtue last night. Even without his display of moral degeneracy, however, and even supposing Hester had even felt anything for him, he had effectively destroyed any chance of a happy ending. He had cleverly pushed his beloved into a betrothal with another man, while managing to tumble into parson's mousetrap himself—with a woman who did not care tuppence for him.

Lord, what a coil. Unable to face the condemnation he would surely find in Hester's eyes, he turned his curricle back toward Bond Street, where he spent the rest of the morning in a punishing exercise at Gentleman Jackson's Boxing Saloon. He took luncheon with a group of friends at the nearby King's Arms, the establishment owned by the ex-champion Thomas Cribb. Being one of the select few admitted to Cribb's parlor, he stayed to put down a few heavy wets with his friends and other pets of the fancy. For all that he was aware of his surroundings, however, he might have spent his time staring at the four walls of a prison cell.

"Why, Robert! I did not expect you quite so soon." Hester, who had been in the act of descending the stairs when Robert's knock sounded on the front door, opened the door herself, to Hobart's vast disapproval. "Do come into the drawing room."

She allowed none of the dismay she felt on beholding her swain's rather grim countenance to show on her features as she led him back up the stairs. She had hoped that Barbara might have put in an appearance before now. Lord, what if she did not come? She had made no promises. At least Thorne was not about. She had no idea where he had taken himself off to at such an early hour this morning, but on the whole, was relieved that she had not found it necessary to see him.

The wrenching grief she had felt at what she could only consider his betrayal had phased into a deep, abiding sadness that she knew would be with her the rest of her life. She realized that he was not altogether to blame for his jaundiced view of women and how they should be treated. Beneath his cynical, libidinous exterior, she knew, lay a man of sensitivity and warmth, and perhaps someday he would find a woman who would lay the former to rest, allowing the latter to flourish. Unfortunately, she was apparently not that woman.

But neither was Lady Barbara Freemantle. Where the devil was she, anyway? fumed Hester as she distributed tea and biscuits to Robert. She raised her eyes to his.

"Robert, I know why you have come, and I must tell you again, that, while I appreciate your motive in asking for my hand, I must refuse you. If—"

"I think I have come to agree with you, Hester."

"If you cannot—What?" she asked in astonishment.

"I believe you may be right in your refusal to consider my proposal. I have no desire to force you into a union that would be repugnant to you, after all."

"Oh, no! Not repugnant. That is, any woman would be proud—"

"Yes, yes," interrupted Robert somewhat impatiently. "I think we are agreed that we would both make sterling marriage partners—for someone else. Not that I have anyone specifically in mind," he added hastily.

"Well, I do," Hester retorted tartly. "Now, Robert, do not deny me," she said as Robert frowned ominously.

"I am not denying you anything," he said stiffly. "I am merely saying that the—the state of my affections—or lack of—is none of your affair."

"Well, of course it isn't. That's not the point. What I wish to say—what is it, Hobart?" Hester almost screamed with annoyance as the butler entered the room after tapping discreetly for admittance.

"Lady Barbara Freemantle is here, miss. Shall I show her up?"

Hester and Robert leaped to their feet, each with vastly different expressions on their faces. Hester's features lit with pleased anticipation, while Robert might just have been informed that the hangman from the Tower had stopped to see him on a matter of personal business. He turned to Hester, his eyes fairly starting from their sockets.

"Barbara? Here? I—I must be going."

Hester grabbed his sleeve with both hands. "No, you don't. Robert Carver, you are going to remain in this room and you are going to be as charming as you can hold together. Do you understand me?"

Robert made no response, but remained where he was, goggling at her in pained reproach. Hester released him and moved toward the door, just in time to greet Barbara as she entered.

"Lady Freemantle," caroled Hester. "How lovely of you to call. See who else has come to visit." She directed Barbara purposefully toward a seat near the tea table before hurrying over to pass a message of instruction to Hobart that no more visitors were to be admitted to the house.

"Tell 'em we've all got leprosy," she whispered urgently before sending the astonished gentleman about his duties, "and send up some more tea and another cup."

After settling Robert and Barbara in their respective chairs, Hester babbled something inconsequential about the weather before addressing the matter at hand.

"I hope you will excuse me for a moment. There is

something I must discuss with Lady Lavinia. Do enjoy your tea."

Before Robert could grasp at her with both hands, as he gave every indication of doing, she whisked herself from the room. She hastened to her bedchamber, where she forced her attention to the manuscript awaiting her attention on the handsome oak desk.

She stayed there for the next hour, and it is to be admitted that she made little progress on the work in hand. Despite her best efforts, she found herself listening for a summons to the floor below. At length, she closed the door to her own chamber and firmly addressed herself to her task.

Thus she did not hear Thorne's entrance into the house some minutes later, nor his step as he made his way upstairs. No one was on hand to prevent his opening the door to the drawing room, and so it was that the Earl of Bythorne was presented with a clear, unimpeded view of his betrothed, clasped passionately in the arms of the man who was supposedly on the verge of becoming engaged to the woman he himself loved to distraction.

Chapter Twenty-one

S ince Hester was by no means engrossed in her manuscript, she had little difficulty in hearing Thorne's thunderous "What the devil!" nor the subsequent agitated
murmurings of two other voices. Hurrying from her bedchamber, she raced to the drawing room to behold Thorne
and Robert and Barbara in a vociferous confrontation in the
center of the chamber.

From the general melee, she was able to catch only a few
phrases.

"Barbara, what is the meaning—?"

"Oh, Thorne, I am so sorry, but—"

"I make no apologies, my lord, for my—"

Unable to make herself heard above the din, she obtained
the attention of the combatants by the simple expedient of
picking up the tea tray and dropping it to the floor. In the
resulting stunned silence, she surveyed the group briefly.

"Now, then, are you all willing to discuss the situation
like rational adults?" She addressed Thorne, who seemed
the most overset at the contretemps into which he had
stumbled. "I know this has come to a shock to you, Thorne,
but you must realize—"

Thorne surged toward her. "It appears you were right,"
he snarled. "But then you always are, are you not?" He ignored her uplifted hand and swung to face Barbara, who
still stood in the shelter of Robert's arms.

"I see that I have been laboring under a misapprehension,
my lady. What a good thing that my error was pointed out
to me in time to avoid a social disaster." He uttered a mirthless bark of laughter. "I think I am supposed to say here,

'You may consider our betrothal at an end.'" To Robert, he said merely, "May I offer you my congratulations, sir. While I may not applaud your methods, you have won the fair lady." He turned once again to glare at Hester. "And now, if you will all excuse me . . ."

He strode from the room.

"Oh dear," said Hester to the white-faced pair before her. "I suppose it is not to be wondered at that he would be a trifle, er, disturbed at this turn of events, but I'm sure he will recover momentarily. In the meantime . . ." She smiled questioningly.

"Oh yes!" cried Barbara, her cheeks glowing and her eyes sparkling like amethysts. "You may wish us happy, Hester."

She turned to look up at Robert, who returned her gaze with one of affecting tenderness. He then grinned at Hester. "And we owe it to you."

"Oh, yes, best of my friends," added Barbara. "I—we— don't know how to thank you. If it had not been for your intervention, I should never have practically flung myself on Robert just now and almost demanded that he listen to my apology for my behavior all those years ago."

"Nor," added Robert, "would I have come to realize that it was wholly pride that had kept us apart all these years."

"I—I do feel badly about Thorne," said Barbara hesitantly. "Although, I believe it is *his* pride that has been hurt."

"Of course, it is," replied Hester stoutly. "You will see. When he has had a chance to lick his wounds, he will come to realize that this is a very good thing, and his congratulations will be genuine."

Privately, Hester quailed a little at the remembered expression on Thorne's face. He had blamed her for the disintegration of his matrimonial plans—and he was perfectly correct in doing so. Surely, he would eventually come to realize the futility of a betrothal to a woman who was head-over-tail in love with someone else, but this would only mean that he must cast farther afield for a bride. Would he ever forgive her for meddling in his life?

She should be serenely happy in the knowledge that she had accomplished her purpose, and that two people who were meant for each other were finally together. Yes, she was pleased—but, happy was stretching it. The chill emptiness that had filled her since her ill-fated encounter with the earl the evening before was still with her, and she very much feared that it would never be wholly eradicated by the passage of time.

She looked up to discover that Barbara and Robert were preparing to depart.

"We must apprise my parents of the change in our situation," said Barbara with a laugh.

"I expect I may be turned out on my ear," added Robert, "but Barbara is of age now, and may do as she pleases."

With Barbara's assurance that his grace, the Duke of Weymouth would welcome wealthy, well-bred Robert Carver as a son-in-law ringing in her ears, Hester saw the happy couple out of the house and returned to her bedchamber to contemplate her future.

If only she could leave Bythorne House immediately—or, at least on the morrow. But she was pledged to that dratted lecture in Seven Dials the following week. She must stay until then. She supposed she could beg Gussie's hospitality, but Gussie would require explanations, which Hester did not feel she could provide. Trevor Bentham was another option, but if she took up residence with him and his mother, even temporarily, he would surely take it as a signal to pursue his courtship of her.

No, assuming that Thorne did not drive her from his home with a fiery sword—which he was much too well-bred to do, Hester would have to remain *in situ* for another five days. It should be relatively simple to keep out of his lordship's way. The family had no major social engagements during this period, so she and the earl would not be rubbing shoulders at a ball or a soiree. She would contrive to spend a great deal of time outside the house and take most of her meals in her room. The day after the lecture, she would bid Thorne a dignified farewell as she swept away from Bythorne House and out of his life.

Accomplishing her purpose was not as difficult as she might have assumed, for the earl seemed to go out of his way to make Hester's game of least-in-sight a success. He, too, was out of the house a good deal, and when they encountered one another in a corridor, or on the stairs, he acknowledged her presence with the stiffest of bows before striding past, his gaze glued to the horizon.

This state of affairs lasted until Tuesday, the day before Hester's lecture. Late in the morning, as she sat in her bedchamber going over notes for her speech, a tap on the door heralded the entrance of an upstairs maid who bore a note from Thorne, requesting her presence in the library.

Suppressing a craven urge to declare herself indisposed, she paused only to glance in the mirror for a quick patting of her hair before descending the stairs.

She found Thorne pacing before a large secretary desk that reposed along one wall of the chamber. He halted abruptly as she entered and moved to seat her before the fire that crackled in the hearth—for, though it was June, the day was cloudy and chill.

"Hester," he began with the air of a man who had prepared his words carefully, "thank you for coming down to speak to me."

Hester did not respond, but nodded warily.

"Hester," Thorne said again, then stopped. "Oh, the devil!" he said at last. "The fact is that I owe you an apology—no, two apologies. I—my behavior was abominable the other night."

"Yes, it was, rather," Hester replied. Thorne grinned suddenly.

"You are not going to make this easy for me, are you?"

"No." Hester's tone was judicious.

"I don't know what got into me to treat you like—well, like a high-priced courtesan, not to put too fine a point on it. Look, Hester—" He flung himself into the chair next to hers. "You must know that I do not view you in that light. I have been striving for an explanation for my action, and the only thing I can come up with is that I am not used to dealing with women of quality."

"'Dealing,' my lord?"

"Oh God. We are back to 'my lord.' Yes, 'dealing,' for that has been the basis of most of my relationships with women. I am not proud of the fact, but there it is."

"Are you not? Proud of it? Do you not preen yourself on your ability to keep women at a distance? To keep your feelings for them on a purely physical level?"

"Well, yes, but—"

Hester sighed. "I suppose the fact you can recognize what I can only consider a serious flaw in your character means there is some hope for you—Thorne. Perhaps, in your renewed search for a bride, you will keep that in mind."

"My renewed—? Oh. Yes. That brings me to my second apology. I'm sorry for barking at you about Barbara. It all came as a shock to me and it was hard for me to accept her—defection, but I shall admit to you now—freely—that it was all for the best. Had I known that her heart was engaged elsewhere all these years, I would never have allowed our—unspoken relationship to continue for so long. I truly do wish all the happiness in the world for her and her Robert—and so I shall tell her—both of them, at the earliest opportunity."

"Handsomely spoken," said Hester, rising. "You may consider your duty done, Thorne, at least as far as I am concerned, and I accept your apology—both of them. I really must be running along now, however. My speech—"

"No!" Thorne exclaimed, leaping to his feet. "There is much more I would say to you, Hester." He stopped again, observing the reserve with which she was gazing at him. Without thinking, he reached inside himself, pulled out The Smile and pinned it to his lips. "Hester, you and I—What is it?" he concluded, for she had become quite rigid and her fine brows had drawn together.

"Nothing. I'm sorry, but I cannot stay. I have much to do to prepare for my lecture tomorrow night."

Thorne's heart sank. He had known this is how it would be. He had at last met the woman who could teach him how to love and he had driven her away, like a madman in the desert, dying of thirst and refusing a drink of water. "Of course," he said woodenly, stepping aside to let her pass. He cleared his throat. "I had not intended to be present at your lecture, but, if you would not mind—"

"I would rather you not," she replied quickly, a look almost of fear on her face.

"Of course," he said again.

Hester stopped as she neared the door. "Oh, by the by, I have made plans to leave London day after tomorrow. I have purchased a ticket on the mail, and—"

"No! You cannot leave so soon. Not now, when—" He sagged suddenly. "Very well, but you will not take the mail. My coach will take you home. Please, let me have no argument," he added as she opened her lips. "Let me do this for you."

She paused a moment, and it seemed to Thorne that she waited for him to say something more. When he did not, she lifted a hand in an oddly forlorn gesture and left the room.

Thorne returned to the hearth and without awareness, rubbed his hands before the blaze. He remained chilled to the bone, however, which was not surprising, he thought bleakly, since all the warmth in the chamber had left with Hester's departure from it.

"Chloe, that bonnet will do nicely. If you return to your bedchamber to change it, we shall be late."

Lady Bracken stood at the foot of the stairs in Bythorne House, her voice raised admonishingly as she adjured her nephew's ward to, "Hurry along now, my dear, and do stop dawdling. Mr. Wery will be here at any moment," she added for good measure.

Chloe, midway up the stairs, turned and descended with some reluctance. "Well, I want to wear something becoming, but not too frivolous, for it will not do to—Oh! Hester, there you are!" she exclaimed as that lady appeared at the head of the stairs. "My, don't you look smart."

Hester, garbed in a sober ensemble of twilled silk, smiled

faintly. "Thank you. Do I look like a female to be taken seriously?"

She was not, she thought, precisely nervous, for she had spoken many times before large assemblages. Still, she felt an unaccountable trembling, which, if she were to be honest, she must ascribe more to the state of her heart than the state of her nerves.

She had seen little of Thorne since their interview in the library. Despite herself, she had entertained the hope that he would attend her lecture, but apparently he had taken her expressed desire that he stay away at face value.

Well, she had resigned herself to life without him. It was best to start now. It was simply hard to admit that the cure was as painful as the ailment.

With an effort, she widened the smile directed at Gussie.

"You look," pronounced her ladyship, "like Boudicca prepared to lead her troops—in a more fashionable ensemble, of course."

Hester laughed. Then as a knock sounded at the door, she hurried down the stairs.

"That must be Trevor," she said, once again usurping Hobart's duties.

But it was Lady Barbara and Robert who entered the house. Greetings were barely accomplished, however, when another carriage drew up before the house to disgorge Mr. Bentham.

John Wery arrived some minutes later. He greeted his betrothed with a light kiss on the cheek, and the group milled about in an aimless fashion until Trevor, assuming control, raised his voice.

"I think we had best be on our way, Hester. You are scheduled to speak in less than an hour, and we shall want to be early. Sir Gerard will be waiting for us." He glanced around. "Are the footmen ready?"

"Yes," replied Gussie, for she had taken it upon herself to arrange the matter. "We have four stalwarts awaiting us outside. They will be in their own vehicle, of course—and not in livery."

"Good." Trevor rubbed his hands together with an air of decision. "Shall we be off, then?"

Officiously, he swept everyone outside to be filed into various carriages. As they rolled away into the north-central area of the London environs, Hester was struck, as she had been so many times before, by the difference between the manicured elegance of Mayfair and the squalid ugliness of Seven Dials, such a short distance away. It was one of the most notorious sections of the city.

When they reached the Blue Boar, an uncharacteristi-cally large and prosperous tavern in Grafton Street, a crowd had already gathered upstairs in a spacious chamber illumi-nated by lanterns hung from the ceiling and along the walls. A promise of a lavish buffet had brought together a varied conclave of females. All were of the lower orders, from women with underfed babies on their hips, to garishly painted prostitutes, to poorly clad females whose occupa-tions were less obvious.

There was also a sprinkling of women garbed in clean if inexpensive muslins and cottons. These were protégés of Sir Gerard Welles and others who had taken up Hester's cause. They circulated among the crowd, exhorting their less fortunate sisters to take advantage of the programs being offered.

Most were clustered around a lavish refreshment table and did not lift their heads from their urgent consumption when Hester and the contingent from Bythorne House ar-rived. This, despite the fact that Mrs. Honoria Blount was addressing the room from the podium. Mrs. Blount held the unusual position of secretary to Lady Glasbrooke, who had been instrumental in opening a school for impoverished young women just a few buildings down Grafton Street.

Hester moved about the room, greeting those known to her and shaking hands with those who were not. One of the latter was a tall, dark-haired man introduced to her as Mr. Theodore Smart, a surgeon who had recently opened a free dispensary in nearby Crown Street, a few blocks away from the Blue Boar. He was an ardent believer in improving the plight of the neglected scraps of humanity who visited him in their furtive legions every day.

"I can't tell you what a pleasure it is to meet you at last, Miss Blayne," he said through a mouthful of ham sandwich. He had the air of a young man who never took the time to eat properly. "I'm afraid many of the young women I see have neither the intelligence nor the ambition to better themselves, but there are others who would be excellent candidates for the schools that are being set up. I only wish there were more of them—schools, I mean."

"Perhaps someday there will be, Mr. Smart. In the meantime, the work you do here is invaluable. I understand that many a young woman hereabouts has been saved from dying in childbirth, or some sort of barbaric abortion technique, or even malnutrition and abuse, because of your efforts."

Mr. Smart cast a darkling look about the room. "I could be doing more if it weren't for the interference of some of our more undesirable local element. The bully boys of the neighborhood have no desire to see their meal tickets getting ideas above themselves."

"You mean ideas of equality? And the suggestion that females have brains, too?" Hester smiled. "It is not merely the likes of those men—" She waved an arm toward the surly, unshaven males who were also availing themselves of Sir Gregory's culinary largesse. "Most of the gentlemen of the upper classes share that one attribute with their underclass brethren."

"However," said the surgeon with a worried glance about him, "these men are a trifle more dangerous. I must tell you, Miss Blayne, they are very much opposed to your proposed lecture, and I cannot help wondering what they are doing here."

"I can tell you that, Mr. Smart," said Hester calmly. "They are here to heckle. They make a great deal of noise, but carry little substance."

"Let us hope so." He gestured toward a particularly unpleasant-looking personage who closely resembled the stuffed rhinoceros she had once seen in the Egyptian Hall.

"His name is Bill Brickley, or simply 'Billy Bricks' and he is not given to empty threats."

"Well, I trust—"

"Miss Blayne," Sir Gerard, a portly gentleman in his early fifties had placed his hand on her arm, "I think we are ready to begin. If you will mount the podium, I shall introduce you."

A few moments later, after a somewhat inflated encomium by Sir Gerard, Hester was launched on her speech.

Chapter Twenty-two

"Good evening," Hester began, "how many of you are happy with your lives as they are?" When she received no other response beyond a few bursts of derisive laughter, she continued. "How many of you would like to change your lives, if only you were showed a way that seemed possible?"

This time, after a few moments, several hands were raised tentatively. Hester stood silent and looked around the crowd, gazing with sympathy and openness into the faces of each of the women who stood before her. More hands appeared, until almost with a sob of union, every hand in the room waved fiercely.

"Tonight," said Hester, her voice cool and clear, "I am going to show you that way. I am going to show you how you can have something of your very own that no one can ever take away from you. The ability to grab with both hands at that new life and to hang on to it."

As she observed the fire of response lit by her words, Hester was off and running. For some fifteen minutes, she spoke almost without taking a breath. She could sense the flame building within her audience, but as she swung into the segment on the possibilities through education for women who wished to better themselves, she noticed a stirring in the back of the room. More men seemed to be entering, each one larger and uglier than the one before. They ranged about the man referred to by Mr. Smart as Billy Bricks, shuffling in a menacing fashion and shifting from one foot to the other.

Unseen by Hester, another figure stood at the back of the

room. Thorne listened to Hester, his own breath bated with awe. He had struggled with himself all day before deciding to attend tonight's forum, but in the end he could not stay away. He was glad he had come, he admitted. Hester was magnificent. It was obvious she spoke to the women's very souls, without talking down to them or making inflated promises.

Before entering the Blue Boar this night, he had known he wanted Hester at his side for the rest of his life; now he knew he could not ask her to abandon her mission in order to be a wife and mother. Was it possible, he wondered, for her to accomplish both? With the help and support of her husband could she manage to inflame the world—or, at least one small corner of it—with her call to arms while reserving a small portion of her passion for him? She cared for the multitudes. Could she care for him and maybe two or three children born of their love for each other?

A strange excitement swelled within him like an inflating balloon, not only at the prospect of winning Hester, but of actually doing something useful with his life. It was a new concept, but one, he thought, that would bring him great pleasure and challenge.

The balloon suddenly turned to lead. There was one thing he had forgotten in his grandiose plans. Hester did not like him—as a human being or as a man. If he could only persuade her to remain in London, perhaps he—

His thoughts were interrupted as he was jostled by three newcomers to the lecture. They were men, burly and sullen-looking, and they smelled of the stews. As Thorne watched, several more sidled in. Pausing for a brief whispered conference with a burly fellow in a greasy cap, they ranged themselves along the back wall with a dozen or so others who had preceded them. They moved awkwardly, and as one of the men pushed past him, Thorne caught sight of a stout cudgel concealed beneath his coat.

Thorne edged slowly to a position along the side wall, where he could get a view of the entire contingent ranked along the back. Yes, they were definitely receiving instructions from the man in the cap.

A glance around the chamber revealed that the only other males present were those who had accompanied Hester from Bythorne House, plus Sir Gerard and a tall thinnish chap who might or might not be able to hold his own in a fight.

Lord, had no one thought to arrange for a real force of men to act as bodyguards? He began to edge his way toward the front of the room and Robert Carver, whom he judged to be the most able of all those present. Before he could make any progress, however, his attention was caught by the sound of a rough voice.

"Oy, mort! 'Oo's goin' t'be takin' care of the bebbies whilst the wimminfolk are out prancy-fancyin' with mathy-matiks and the like?"

It was, of course, Billy Bricks who spoke, and he was joined by a chorus of his supporters.

"Nell! I see ye there. You'd better come away, else I'll give ye what fer!"

"Wot the bloody 'ell d'ye think ye're doin', Flossie Twigg? Ye ain't got the brains of a dishmop!"

At Billy Bricks' first words, the audience of women had swung about as one, and now the hope that had glowed on their features turned to expressions of fear and despair.

"Sir!" Hester's clear voice rang out over the room. "If you have concerns about our programs, we shall be more than happy—"

"We don't have no concern!" shouted Billy Bricks. "We jist want you t' shut yer gob and go back to yer rich house and yer rich life and take yer rich gentlemen friends with ye! And don't come back no more puttin' ideas inta our female's heads."

The mob of men roared their approval of this philosophy and surged forward. Thorne found himself flung against the wall as he made a vain attempt to reach Hester. Elbowing his way forward, he at last reached the podium, where he swung about to face the men, who had by now drawn their cudgels from beneath their coats and were beginning to use them on the women. Screams of panic filled the air.

The footmen from Bythorne House were giving a good

account of themselves, as were Carver, John Wery, and Lord Bracken. Of Trevor Bentham, nothing could be seen. Thorne turned to add his bit to the fray, but was soon beaten back by the sheer weight of the opposition. Hester still stood at her lectern, exhorting the men to leave or face probable disciplinary action by the forces of law, sure to arrive at any moment, drawn by the sounds of the fracas.

Thorne thought she was probably right in her estimation, but there was no telling how soon help would arrive. Struggling to the nearest window, he saw that it looked out over an alley, in which there was parked a large, straw-filled wagon. He beat his way to Carver, who was trying to protect the person of Lady Barbara, while inflicting serious damage to a small-eyed giant who was apparently trying to dismember him.

"The window!" gasped Thorne, removing an impediment in the form of a club-wielding behemoth. He explained in a few words what he fondly termed his "plan of action," and Carver turned away to signal Wery and Lord Bracken. In a few minutes, the gentlemen had corralled their frightened ladies and began unobtrusively to help them from the window into the wagon below.

Meanwhile, Thorne continued his progress toward Hester. She had left the podium and he knew a moment of sheer panic when he could not locate her. A few minutes later, he found her some distance away. He swore fervently. Wouldn't you know it? The little twit had plunged into the fray and was now belaboring a thug four times her size. As Thorne watched, she attacked the man, taking him so much by surprise that she was able to wrench away from him the stick with which he had been beating a terrified young woman. Taking up the cudgel, she began beating him about the head and ears. At the moment, he was cowering before her, his hands covering a bald head and a pair of very large ears. However, Thorne knew this state of affairs would continue only until the fellow had recovered from his surprise.

Yes, he had glanced up at her from under his protective covering and his mean little eyes were red with rage. Dropping his arms, he retrieved his club by the simple expedient of swinging his hand cross Hester's face, knocking her to the ground.

With an inarticulate growl, Thorne sprang past the bodies in his path. He had almost reached Hester's assailant when a scream from one end of the room drew his attention. He noted, to his horror, that someone had knocked over a branch of candles from the buffet table. The floor had been strewn with straw, which immediately flickered into a greedy blaze, and within seconds a small fire began to fed on the room's furnishings.

Thorne turned again to the man who had attacked Hester. He had swung back to his original prey, and Thorne grabbed him, swinging him about and flooring him with one blow to the center of his face.

"Hester!" Thorne cried, horrified, as he bent to cradle her in his arms. "My God, Hester, are you all right?"

A low moan was his only answer, but after a moment, she struggled to a sitting position. He began to lift her, but at that point yet another agitator caught sight of them and with a call to his cohorts surged to where they stood. By now, voices were rising in panic around the room, which was beginning to fill with smoke. Unheeding, the men advanced on Thorne and Hester. Thorne, wholly concerned with shielding Hester from further assault, contented himself with swinging out when the opportunity presented itself, thus accounting for several of the bruisers. By dint of sheer strength and determination on Thorne's part, and with some fierce but admittedly ineffectual assistance from Hester, they at last reached the relative sanctuary of the area just behind the podium.

"Come on," he snapped. "Let's get out of here."

Elsewhere, the combatants were beginning to abandon any notion of mayhem in favor of escaping the flames that were now rising along the walls of the room, consuming the window hangings.

Unfortunately, the path to the chamber's only exit was blocked by a mass of struggling bodies and a fairly substantial wall of fire. The panic level was rising perceptibly, and

Thorne turned Hester back toward the window from which the party from Bythorne House had made their escape. He looked down to see that the group was still in the alley, staring anxiously upward. Sounds of running feet and calling voices sounded from the street in front of the Blue Boar, and an armed contingent of constabulary could be heard inside the building, approaching the stairway. It was obvious that for the moment their presence only added to the general atmosphere of chaos at the doorway.

"Come on," said Thorne again. "I see no reason why we should be here when the rescue squad comes rushing in. They will do doubt scoop up everyone present, and I don't think you would enjoy an evening in the constable's office."

Hester shuddered. "No, indeed. But, the fire . . . Thorne, the others will be trapped!" Unceremoniously, Thorne dropped Hester from the window into the waiting arms of Gussie and Lord Bracken.

He turned to survey the shambles about him. So far, few of the crowd surging about the room had thought to avail themselves of the two windows that overlooked the alley, but persisted in flinging themselves against those who were trying to exit the doorway. These persons were hampered by those attempting to enter the room.

By now, the flames had risen inside the room, and the smoke was making it difficult to breathe. Visibility was reduced to a few feet on either side of him, but ahead he could hear the screams of those trying to escape. Blindly, he groped before him, grasping at the clothing of a woman who turned a terrified face toward him. At another time, he thought fleetingly, he would have passed her by, unseeing, but now she became the immediate center of his universe.

"Come!" he grated. "This way!" He lurched with her toward the window and assisted her through the opening. Returning, he repeated the procedure, this time with a mother and child. After the third or fourth person had been thrust to safety, the crowd began to perceive his efforts, and many swung away from the door.

Some of the men, who moments before had been beating the women unmercifully, now, either in shamed repentance or an urgent desire to escape the attention of the police, began to help the frightened females. The crowd surged toward the windows and in a few moments both men and women were dropping from them like rain to the ground below.

At last, a quick glance around indicated to Thorne that the room was empty. Breathing a choked sigh of relief, he swung a leg over the windowsill and was just about to plunge to the street when he heard the sound of frightened sobbing at the far end of the room.

The room was almost unbearably hot now, and the smoke seemed a living entity—a monster that clawed at his eyes and burned his throat. Making his way toward the sound, he discerned a ragged figure lying prone on the floor, trapped beneath one of the heavy tables, which had collapsed on him. He could not have been more than ten years old, and it was obvious that he could not move.

Thorne was aware that the chamber had become a death trap, but it did not occur to him to do anything other than wrestle with the table. He looked about, but there was no help.

"I'm stuck, mister," whimpered the boy. "I can't move my legs! Please help me! Noo-ooo!" he screeched. "Don't go away!"

"I shan't leave you," Thorne assured him. "I'm just going to find something I can use for leverage. I have to lift this table."

Lifting a nearby chair above his head, he brought it crashing to the floor. He picked up one of the resulting shards of wood and began prying the table away from the boy's legs. He was forced to stop for a moment to beat at the flames that nibbled at his trouser legs. Damn! He *must* get out of here!

"Now," he said at last, "when I tell you, try to pull your legs away. Can you do that?"

"Yessir!" gasped the boy, flailing at the nearing fire.

"Right." Thorne strained at the table with the chair leg. "Now!"

With a supreme effort, Thorne heaved the table up, and

in the next instant the boy had swung his slender body out from under its weight. Scooping him up, Thorne ran for the window, marveling at the fragility of the slight frame in his arms. A violent crash behind him told him that the ceiling was giving way, and with a single, fluid motion, he swung the boy and himself through the window.

Below, Hester scanned the window with anxious eyes. Where *was* he? She had watched with her heart in her throat as he helped one after the other of the women to safety, only to dart back into what seemed like certain death. What could he—oh! There he was! On trembling legs she ran to the wagon where Thorne was even now standing upright and brushing himself off.

With some gratification, Thorne watched the boy scamper away into the throng before jumping to the ground. He turned to Hester and the others who waited in the alley. He cast a sidelong glance at her. Aside from a burgeoning bruise along her cheek she seemed none the worse for wear, and her eyes seemed to catch the glow from the burning building.

"Thorne! Are you—?"

"Yes," he replied hastily. "All's well that ends well, and all that. In the meantime, let us get out of here—now."

It was many minutes, however, filled with exclamations of outrage, condemnation, and gratitude for their escape, before the party from Bythorne House set off for the sedate environs of Mayfair. Thorne, who had traveled in his curricle, insisted on conveying Hester, over her protest, while the others mounted their various vehicles.

"What will happen to those women, now?" she asked brokenly. "Oh, Thorne, I was just beginning to reach them! I saw hope in their faces—and now—" She caught herself. "I do thank you for appearing when you did, however."

Thorne was silent for a moment, and at length brought the curricle to a halt in the shadow of a grove of trees that formed a bit of parkland in the area of Mayfair they had just entered. He turned to her and took her hand in his.

"Hester," he said in a voice harshened by smoke and an emotion Hester dared not name, "you seem to believe that there is help for these young women. That they possess within themselves the means to gain their own salvation."

"Yes, I do," replied Hester stoutly, making an urgent but wholly unsuccessful effort to free her hand.

"Then," he said softly, "do you not think it is possible for yet another worthless scrap of humanity—one who has squandered the blessings of a lifetime, to find a like reclamation?"

For an instant, Hester simply stared at him, openmouthed.

"Dear God, Hester, do you think a man could not remain in your presence for all these weeks without undergoing some sort of—metamorphosis?"

"I thought you had succeeded remarkably well in retaining your individuality—my lord."

"Hester, confound it, I'm trying to propose here. Could you not at least listen to me?"

Across from him, in the confines of the curricle, Hester stared at him, blank-faced. Propose? Now, what maggot had entered his brain? Was he so bent on seduction that he would use the time-honored means of the oily-tongued roué to gain his ends? Yet, he had nothing of the rake about him right now. His clothes were in tatters, and his hair was a sweat-soaked mop, greasy with smoke. He looked, in fact, thoroughly discommoded—rather as though he were ready to explode.

"P-propose?" she whispered, cursing herself for the inanity of her response, as well as for the wild shaft of hope that surged through her.

"Oh God, Hester. I know I am making the most fearful mull of this, but I love you. I'm not sure I even understand what that means, but I know that I want you—only you—forever—and I want you to want me. I want to marry you in a church full of candles and well-wishers, and then I want to take you home and make babies with you.

"Hester," he continued softly, as she continued to gape at him, "I want to be with you as you strive toward your goals. I am in awe of your dedication, and I will not be an impediment to you. I believe, I can even be of some help. I—I want you to be happy."

By now, the hands that were so firmly grasped in Thorne's were trembling so badly that Hester thought he must feel her heart beating in their rhythm.

Talk was easy, she told herself. Thorne appeared to be sincere, but then, was not the appearance of sincerity one of the chief tools of a rake? No. Gazing into his eyes, she could not doubt the genuineness of his declaration.

Thorne had been tested tonight—literally in a crucible of fire—and he had risen magnificently to the crisis. Incredible as it seemed, the Earl of Bythorne had developed a social conscience.

But did he truly love her? How could she believe that he was ready to abandon his beautiful bits of muslin to settle down to hearth and home with the plain Miss Hester Blayne?

As though sensing her doubt, Thorne leaned toward her. "It is my understanding," he murmured, "although I have little experience in the matter, that when a man tells a woman he loves her, there is a hidden clause in there somewhere about 'forsaking all others.' My darling, you caused me to start my forsaking some time ago. You have taken over my heart to such an extent that there is no longer room for anyone else, nor even the desire to explore the possibilities of same. I fear I shall become one of those most tedious of fellows, a faithful husband—and it's all your fault."

His hands cupped her face and very gently, he kissed her, first on one cheek and then the other, and then, at last on her lips.

As before, his touch sent swirls of shocked pleasure shooting through her, and she leaned into him. His only response was yet another tender, gentle kiss on her mouth. Dear Lord, he was actually restraining himself! He was trying to prove his honorable intentions.

Suddenly, her doubts fled, and her veins fairly sizzled with the happiness that surged through her. He loved her! He loved plain Hester Blayne and no other.

She chuckled breathlessly. "My lord earl, has no one ever taught you how to make love to a woman?"

Reaching up, she placed her hands on either side of his

face and pulled him to her. Pressing her lips to his, she kissed him long and passionately. After several moments, Thorne drew back. He gazed at her in momentary surprise before his eyes lit with an incredulous joy. Pulling her toward him, he brought his mouth down ruthlessly on hers. A shudder of response swept through her and she opened herself to him. An overwhelming gladness swept over her in great, pulsing waves.

"Oh, my darling," she gasped, some moments later. "I am not sure I know what love is either, but surely this must be a good start."

It was some minutes later before the curricle was put into motion again. When Hester and Thorne reached Bythorne House, they found the others waiting to greet them. Among them, in the entry hall, stood the gentleman who had made himself so conspicuous by his absence earlier at the Blue Boar.

"Why, Trevor!" said Hester in some surprise. "Whatever happened to you?"

"As I have been explaining," began Mr. Bentham, "I thought it expedient to leave the tavern when those thugs began their agitating. It was necessary for someone to go for help, after all. No, no—it is not necessary to thank me," he concluded, holding up a hand. "I was happy to do my duty. I have since discovered that the police arrived in good time."

John Wery snorted. "Yes, we're all safe and sound—no thanks to you."

"I, of course," continued Trevor as though he had not heard, "made all speed here to Bythorne House to assure myself that you had escaped any harm."

"How very thoughtful of you, Trevor," said Hester dryly.

"Yes, indeed, Bentham." Thorne stepped forward, placing his arm about Hester's shoulders. "And now that you have done so, you will no doubt wish to be on your way. Your mother will be worried."

Trevor stiffened. His face darkened as Hester turned to smile up into the earl's face, and when Thorne dropped a kiss on Hester's cheek, his eyes glittered with rage.

"Now, see here—"

He was interrupted by a delighted trill from Gussie.

"Hester! Thorne! Oh, my dears, it is true? Have you—?"

"Yes, Gussie," replied Thorne. "You may wish us happy—at last."

At this, everyone clustered about the pair, vociferous in their congratulations. Trevor stood apart in an appalled silence, his face pale, his demeanor shaken.

Hester, noticing him at last, experienced a pang of compunction and put out a hand to him.

"I trust you will wish me happy, as well, Trevor?" she asked, smiling.

Trevor, however, did not return the smile.

"I see how it is," he said portentously. "You have chosen to abandon the path you and I chose for you so many years ago. You have decided to place worldly considerations above—"

"The path you and I chose?" gasped Hester incredulously. "Trevor, you do not seriously believe you influenced me in my—"

"What I believe," interposed Thorne smoothly, "is that it is time for Mr. Bentham to make his departure."

Trevor's fists clenched, but, though Thorne gazed mildly at him, there was that in his expression that evidently gave Trevor pause. Reaching for his hat and walking stick, he inclined his head.

"I agree, my lord." He bowed over Hester's hand. "I do wish you happy, my dear, although—" He sucked in a breath and clamped his lips shut, prudence overcoming his desire to have the last word. Whirling, he stalked from the house, his heels clicking on the polished marquetry floor of the entry hall.

"Well!" breathed Chloe before breaking into a giggle.

"Well, indeed," murmured Thorne.

The hour being late, it was not long before the party broke up, Lord and Lady Bracken being the first to depart. Gussie bustled from the house, arm in arm with her husband, her tongue busy with plans for yet another wedding. John, with some difficulty was pried from Chloe's side, and the young miss drifted up the stairs in dreamy contemplation of her future, Aunt Lavinia by her side.

"I think we should seek our beds, as well," said Hester as she and Thorne stood alone at the foot of the stairway."

"What a splendid idea," replied Thorne, grinning. "Ah, but you did say 'beds,' as in the plural, didn't you?" He sighed. "Very well, I am willing to abide by the proprieties, for the time being."

He caught her in his arms. "My dear Miss Blayne," he whispered, "you are my abiding treasure, and you have made me very happy." He held her away from him in his arms for a moment, scrutinizing her face. "You are sure now, are you not, my love—my dearest love?"

Hester smiled mistily, happiness once more welling within her. "Oh yes, Thorne. Neither of us is without flaws, but oh, what a good time we are going to have reforming each other!"

"You," murmured her beloved, "have a one-track mind. Perhaps, just for the moment, we could shelve the topic of Reform."

"Yes, my love," said Miss Blayne meekly, lifting her face to his.